Philip José Farmer's revolutionary impact on the science fiction scene was felt with the appearance of his early novella *The Lovers.* Since then Mr Farmer's work has been noted for its open-minded thought, its humane compassion and its superb craftsmanship. With such stories as the *Carmody* and *Riverworld* series, with such extraordinary novels as *Flesh*, with his Hugo Award-winning short novel *Riders of the Purple Wage*, and with this series *The World of the Tiers* – which includes *Behind the Walls of Terra*, *The Lavalite World*, *The Gates of Creation* and *A Private Cosmos* – Philip José Farmer has shown a talent of the very first rank in science fiction and fantasy. Mr Farmer was born in Peoria, Illinois, lived for many years in Los Angeles, and has now returned with his wife to Illinois.

Also by Philip José Farmer and available from Sphere Books

THE GATES OF CREATION
A PRIVATE COSMOS
THE LAVALITE WORLD
FLESH
LORD OF THE TREES
KEEPERS OF THE SECRETS
BEHIND THE WALLS OF TERRA
THE GREEN ODYSSEY

THE MAKER OF UNIVERSES

The Maker of Universes

PHILIP JOSÉ FARMER

SPHERE SCIENCE FICTION AND
FANTASY LIBRARY

SPHERE BOOKS LIMITED
London and Sydney

First published in Great Britain by Sphere Books Ltd 1970
30–32 Gray's Inn Road, London WC1X 8JL
Reprinted 1973, 1975, 1978, 1985

TRADE
MARK

Set in Linotype Times

Printed in Great Britain by
Hazell Watson & Viney Ltd
Aylesbury, Bucks

CHAPTER ONE

The ghost of a trumpet call wailed from the other side of the doors. The seven notes were faint and far off, ectoplasmic issue of a phantom of silver, if sound could be the stuff from which shades are formed.

Robert Wolff knew that there could be no horn or man blowing upon it behind the sliding doors. A minute ago, he had looked inside the closet. Nothing except the cement floor, the white plasterboard walls, the clothes rod and hooks, a shelf and a lightbulb was there.

Yet he had heard the trumpet notes, feeble as if singing from the other wall of the world itself. He was alone, so that he had no one with whom to check the reality of what he knew could not be real. The room in which he stood entranced was an unlikely place in which to have such an experience. But he might not be an unlikely person to have it. Lately, weird dreams had been troubling his sleep. During the day, strange thoughts and flashes of images passed through his mind, fleeting but vivid and even startling. They were unwanted, unexpected, and unresistable.

He was worried. To be ready to retire and then to suffer a mental breakdown seemed unfair. However, it could happen to him as it had to others, so the thing to do was to be examined by a doctor. But he could not bring himself to act as reason demanded. He kept waiting, and he did not say anything to anybody, least of all to his wife.

Now he stood in the recreation room of a new house in the Hohokam Homes development and stared at the closet doors. If the horn bugled again, he would slide a door back and see for himself that nothing was there. Then, knowing that his own diseased mind was generating the notes, he would forget about buying this house. He would ignore his wife's hysterical protests, and he would see a medical doctor first and then a psychotherapist.

His wife called: "Robert! Haven't you been down there long enough? Come up here. I want to talk to you and Mr. Bresson!"

"Just a minute, dear," he said.

She called again, so close this time that he turned around. Brenda Wolff stood at the top of the steps that led down to the recreation room. She was his age, sixty-six. What beauty she had once had was now buried under fat, under heavily rouged and powdered wrinkles, thick spectacles, and steel-blue hair. He winced on seeing her, as he winced every time he looked into the mirror and saw his own bald head, deep lines from nose to mouth, and stars of grooved skin radiating from the reddened eyes. Was this his trouble? Was he unable to adjust to that which came to all men, like it or not? Or was what he disliked in his wife and himself not the physical deterioration but the knowledge that neither he nor Brenda had realized their youthful dreams? There was no way to avoid the rasps and files of time on the flesh, but time had been gracious to him in allowing him to live this long. He could not plead short duration as an excuse for not shaping his psyche into beauty. The world could not be blamed for what he was. He and he alone was responsible; at least he was strong enough to face that. He did not reproach the universe or that part of it that was his wife. He did not scream, snarl, and whine as Brenda did.

There had been times when it would have been easy to whine or weep. How many men could remember nothing before the age of twenty? He thought it was twenty, for the Wolffs, who had adopted him, had said that he'd looked that age. He had been discovered wandering in the hills of Kentucky, near the Indiana border, by old man Wolff. He had not known who he was or how he had come there. Kentucky or even the United States of America had been meaningless to him, as had all the English tongue.

The Wolffs had taken him in and notified the sheriff. An investigation by the authorities had failed to identify him. At another time, his story might have attracted nationwide attention; however, the nation had been at war with the Kaiser and had had more important things to think about. Robert, named after the Wolff's dead son, had helped work on the farm. He had also gone to school, for he had lost all memory of his education.

Worse than his lack of formal knowledge had been his ignorance of how to behave. Time and again he had embarrassed or offended others. He had suffered from the scornful or sometimes savage reaction of the hill-folk, but had learned swiftly – and his willingness to work hard, plus his great strength in defending himself, had gained respect.

In an amazingly quick time, as if he had been relearning, he had studied and passed through grade and high school. Although he had lacked by many years the full time of attendance required, he had taken and passed the entrance examinations to the university with no trouble. There he'd begun his lifelong love affair with the classical languages. Most of all he loved Greek, for it struck a chord within him; he felt at home with it.

After getting his Ph.D. at the University of Chicago, he had taught at various Eastern and Midwestern universities. He had married Brenda, a beautiful girl with a lovely soul. Or so he had thought at first. Later, he had been disillusioned, but still he was fairly happy.

Always, however, the mystery of his amnesia and his origin had troubled him. For a long time it had not disturbed him, but then, on retiring . . .

"Robert," Brenda said loudly, "come up here right now! Mr. Bresson is a busy man."

"I'm certain that Mr. Bresson has had plenty of clients who like to make a leisurely surveillance," he replied mildly. "Or perhaps you've made up your mind you don't want the house?"

Brenda glared at him, then waddled indignantly off. He sighed because he knew that, later, she would accuse him of deliberately making her look foolish before the real estate agent.

He turned to the closet doors again. Did he dare open them? It was absurd to freeze there, like someone in shock or in a psychotic state of indecision. But he could not move, except to give a start as the bugle again vented the seven notes, crying from behind a thick barricade but stronger in volume.

His heart thudded like an inward fist against his breast bone. He forced himself to step up to the doors and to place his hand within the brass-covered indentation at waist-level and shove the door to one side. The little rumble of the rollers drowned out the horn as the door moved to one side.

The white plaster boards of the wall had disappeared. They had become an entrance to a scene he could not possibly have imagined, although it must have originated in his mind.

Sunlight flooded in through the opening, which was large enough for him to walk through if he stooped. Vegetation that looked something like trees – but no trees of Earth – blocked part of his view. Through the branches and fronds he could see a bright green sky. He lowered his eyes to take in the scene on the ground beneath the trees. Six or seven nightmare creatures were gathered at the base of a giant boulder. It was of red, quartz-impregnated rock and shaped roughly like a toadstool. Most of the things had their black furry, misshapen bodies turned away from him, but one presented its profile against the green sky. Its head was brutal, subhuman, and its expression was malevolent. There were knobs on its body and on its face and head, clots of flesh which gave it a half-formed appearance, as if its Maker had forgotten to smooth it out. The two short legs were like a dog's hind legs. It was stretching its long arms up toward the young man who stood on the flat top of the boulder.

This man was clothed only in a buckskin breechcloth and

moccasins. He was tall, muscular, and broad-shouldered; his skin was sun-browned; his long thick hair was a reddish bronze; his face was strong and craggy with a long upper lip. He held the instrument which must have made the notes Wolff had heard.

The man kicked one of the misshapen things back down from its hold on the boulder as it crawled up toward him. He lifted the silver horn to his lips to blow again, then saw Wolff standing beyond the opening. He grinned widely, flashing white teeth. He called, "So you finally came!"

Wolff did not move or reply. He could only think, *Now I have gone crazy! Not just auditory hallucinations, but visual! What next? Should I run screaming, or just calmly walk away and tell Brenda that I have to see a doctor now? Now! No waiting, no explanations. Shut up, Brenda, I'm going.*

He stepped back. The opening was beginning to close, the white walls were reasserting their solidity. Or rather, he was beginning to get a fresh hold on reality.

"Here!" the youth on top of the boulder shouted. "Catch!"

He threw the horn. Turning over and over, bouncing sunlight off the silver as the light fell through the leaves, it flew straight toward the opening. Just before the walls closed in on themselves, the horn passed through the opening and struck Wolff on his knees.

He exclaimed in pain, for there was nothing ectoplasmic about the sharp impact. Through the narrow opening he could see the red-haired man holding up one hand, his thumb and index forming an O. The youth grinned and cried out, 'Good luck! Hope I see you soon! I am Kickaha!"

Like an eye slowly closing in sleep, the opening in the wall contracted. The light dimmed, and the objects began to blur. But he could see well enough to get a final glimpse, and it was then that the girl stuck her head around the trunk of a tree.

She had unhumanly large eyes, as big in proportion to her face as those of a cat. Her lips were full and crimson, her skin golden-brown. The thick wavy hair hanging loose along the side of her face was tiger-striped: slightly zigzag bands of black almost touched the ground as she leaned around the tree.

Then the walls became white as the rolled-up eye of a corpse. All was as before except for the pain in his knees and the hardness of the horn lying against his ankle.

He picked it up and turned to look at it in the light from the recreation room. Although stunned, he no longer believed that he was insane. He had seen through into another universe and something from it had been delivered to him—why or how, he did not know.

The horn was a little less than two and a half feet long and weighed less than a quarter of a pound. It was shaped like an African buffalo's horn except at the mouth, where it flared out broadly. The tip was fitted with a mouthpiece of some soft golden material; the horn itself was of silver or silver-plated metal. There were no valves, but on turning it over he saw seven little buttons in a row. A half-inch inside the mouth was a web of silvery threads. When the horn was held at an angle to the light from the bulbs overhead, the web looked as if it went deep into the horn.

It was then the light also struck the body of the horn so that he saw what he had missed during his first examination: a hieroglyph was lightly inscribed halfway down the length. It looked like nothing he had seen before, and he was an expert on all types of alphabetic writing, ideographs, and pictographs.

"Robert!" his wife said.

"Be right up, dear!" He placed the horn in the right-hand front corner of the closet and closed the door. There was nothing else he could do except to run out of the house with the horn. If he appeared with it, he would be questioned by both his wife and Bresson. Since he had not come into the house with the horn, he could not claim it was his. Bresson would want to take the instrument into his custody, since it would have been discovered on property of his agency.

Wolff was in an agony of uncertainty. How could he get the horn out of the house? What was to prevent Bresson from bringing around other clients, perhaps today, who would see the horn as soon as they opened the closet door? A client might call it to Bresson's attention.

He walked up the steps and into the large living room. Brenda was still glaring. Bresson, a chubby, spectacled man of about thirty-five, looked uncomfortable, although he was smiling.

"Well, how do you like it?" he asked.

"Great," Wolff replied. "It reminds me of the type of house we have back home."

"I like it," Bresson said. "I'm from the Midwest myself. I can appreciate that you might not want to live in a ranch-type home. Not that I'm knocking them. I live in one myself."

Wolff walked to the window and looked out. The midafternoon May sun shone brightly from the blue Arizona skies. The lawn was covered with the fresh Bermuda grass, planted three weeks before, new as the houses in this just-built development of Hohokam Homes.

"Almost all the houses are ground level," Bresson was saying. "Excavating in this hard caliche costs a great deal, but these houses aren't expensive. Not for what you get."

Wolff thought, *If the caliche hadn't been dug away to make room for the recreation room, what would the man on the other side have seen when the opening appeared? Would he have seen only earth and thus been denied the chance to get rid of that horn? Undoubtedly.*

"You may have read why we had to delay opening this development," Bresson said. "While we were digging, we uncovered a former town of the Hohokam."

"Hohokam?" Mrs. Wolff said. "Who were they?"

"Lots of people who come into Arizona have never heard of them," Bresson replied. "But you can't live long in the Phoenix area without running across references to them. They were the Indians who lived a long time ago in the Valley of the Sun; they may have come here at least 1200 years ago. They dug irrigation canals, built towns here, had a swinging civilization. But something happened to them, no one knows what. They just up and disappeared several hundred years ago. Some archeologists claim the Papago and Pima Indians are their descendants."

Mrs. Wolff sniffed and said, "I've seen them. They don't look like they could build anything except those rundown adobe shacks on the reservation."

Wolff turned and said, almost savagely, "The modern Maya don't look as if they could ever have built their temples or invented the concept of zero, either. But they did."

Brenda gasped. Mr. Bresson smiled even more mechanically. "Anyway, we had to suspend digging until the archeologists were through. Held up operations about three months, but we couldn't do a thing because the state tied our hands.

"However, this may be a lucky thing for you. If we hadn't been held up, these homes might all be sold now. So everything turns out for the best, eh?"

He smiled brightly and looked from one to the other.

Wolff paused, took a deep breath, knowing what was coming from Brenda, and said, "We'll take it. We'll sign the papers right now."

"Robert!" Mrs. Wolff shrilled. "You didn't even ask me!"

"I'm sorry, my dear, but I've made up my mind."

"Well, I haven't!"

"Now, now, folks, no need to rush things," Bresson said. His smile was desperate. "Take your time, talk it over. Even if somebody should come along and buy this particular house—and it might happen before the day's over; they're selling like hotcakes—well, there're plenty more just like this."

"I want *this* house."

"Robert, are you out of your mind?" Brenda wailed. "I've never seen you act like this before."

"I've given in to you on almost everything," he said. "I

wanted you to be happy. So, now, give in to me on this. It's not much to ask. Besides, you said this morning that you wanted this type of house, and Hohokam Homes are the only ones like this that we can afford.

"Let's sign the preliminary papers now. I can make out a check as an earnest."

"I won't sign, Robert."

"Why don't you two go home and discuss this?" Bresson said. "I'll be available when you've reached a decision."

"Isn't my signature good enough?" Wolff replied.

Still holding his strained smile, Bresson said, "I'm sorry, Mrs. Wolff will have to sign, too."

Brenda smiled triumphantly.

"Promise me you won't show it to anybody else," Wolff said. "Not until tomorrow, anyway. If you're afraid of losing a sale, I'll make out an earnest."

"Oh, that won't be necessary." Bresson started toward the door with a haste that betrayed his wish to get out of an embarrassing situation. "I won't show it to anyone until I hear from you in the morning."

On the way back to their rooms in the Sands Motel in Tempe, neither spoke. Brenda sat rigidly and stared straight ahead through the windshield. Wolff glanced over at her now and then, noting that her nose seemed to be getting sharper and her lips thinner; if she continued, she would look exactly like a fat parrot.

And when she finally did burst loose, talking, she would sound like a fat parrot. The same old tired yet energetic torrent of reproaches and threats would issue. She would upbraid him because of his neglect of her all these years, remind him for the latest in God-knew-how-many-times that he kept his nose buried in his books or else was practicing archery or fencing, or climbing mountains, sports she could not share with him because of her arthritis. She would unreel the years of unhappiness, or claimed unhappiness, and end by weeping violently and bitterly.

Why had he stuck with her? He did not know except that he had loved her very much when they were young and also because her accusations were not entirely untrue. Moreover, he found the thought of separation painful, even more painful than the thought of staying with her.

Yet he was entitled to reap the harvests of his labors as a professor of English and classical languages. Now that he had enough money and leisure time, he could pursue studies that his duties had denied him. With this Arizona home as a base, he could even travel. Or could he? Brenda would not refuse to go with him—in fact, she would insist on accompanying him.

But she would be so bored that his own life would be miserable. He could not blame her for that, for she did not have the same interests as he. But should he give up the things that made life rich for him just to make her happy? Especially since she was not going to be happy anyway?

As he expected, her silent tongue became quite active after supper. He listened, tried to remonstrate quietly with her and point out her lack of logic and the injustice and baselessness of her recriminations. It was no use. She ended as always, weeping and threatening to leave him or to kill herself.

This time, he did not give in.

"I want that house, and I want to enjoy life as I've planned to," he said firmly. "That's that."

He put on his coat and strode to the door. "I'll be back later. Maybe."

She screamed and threw an ashtray at him. He ducked; the tray bounced off the door, gouging out a piece of the wood. Fortunately, she did not follow him and make a scene outside, as she had on previous occasions.

It was night now, the moon was not yet up, and the only lights came from the windows of the motel, the lamps along the streets, and numerous headlights of the cars along Apache Boulevard. He drove his car out onto the boulevard and went east, then turned south. Within a few minutes he was on the road to the Hohokam Homes. The thought of what he meant to do made his heart beat fast and turned his skin cold. This was the first time in his life that he had seriously considered committing a criminal act.

The Hohokam Homes were ablaze with lights and noisy with music over a PA system and the voices of children playing out in the street while their parents looked at the houses.

He drove on, went through Mesa, turned around and came back through Tempe and down Van Buren and into the heart of Phoenix. He cut north, then east, until he was in the town of Scottsdale. Here he stopped off for an hour and a half at a small tavern. After the luxury of four shots of *Vat 69*, he quit. He wanted no more—rather, feared to take more, because he did not care to be fuddled when he began his project.

When he returned to Hohokam Homes, the lights were out and silence had returned to the desert. He parked his car behind the house in which he had been that afternoon. With his gloved right fist, he smashed the window which gave him access to the recreation room.

By the time he was within the room, he was panting and his heart beat as if he had run several blocks. Though frightened, he had to smile at himself. A man who lived much in his imagination, he had often conceived of himself as a burglar—

not the ordinary kind, of course, but a Raffles. Now he knew that his respect for law was too much for him ever to become a great criminal or even a minor one. His conscience was hurting him because of this small act, one that he had thought he was fully justified in carrying out. Moreover, the idea of being caught almost made him give up the horn. After living a quiet, decent and respectable life, he would be ruined if he were to be detected. Was it worth it?

He decided it was. Should he retreat now, he would wonder the rest of his life what he had missed. The greatest of all adventures waited for him, one such as no other man had experienced. If he became a coward now, he might as well shoot himself, for he would not be able to endure the loss of the horn or the self-recriminations for his lack of courage.

It was so dark in the recreation room that he had to feel his way to the closet with his fingertips. Locating the sliding doors, he moved the left-hand one, which he had pushed aside that afternoon. He nudged it slowly to avoid noise, and he stopped to listen for sounds outside the house.

Once the door was fully opened, he retreated a few steps. He placed the mouthpiece of the horn to his lips and blew softly. The blast that issued from it startled him so much that he dropped it. Groping, he finally located it in the corner of the room.

The second time, he blew hard. There was another loud note, no louder than the first. Some device in the horn, perhaps the slivery web inside its mouth, regulated the decible level. For several minutes he stood poised with the horn raised and almost to his mouth. He was trying to reconstruct in his mind the exact sequence of the seven notes he had heard. Obviously the seven little buttons on the underside determined the various harmonics. But he could not find out which was which without experimenting and drawing attention.

He shrugged and murmured, "What the hell."

Again he blew, but now he pressed the buttons, operating the one closest to him first. Seven loud notes soared forth. Their values were as he remembered them, but not in the sequence he recalled.

As the final blast died out, a shout came from a distance. Wolff almost panicked. He swore, lifted the horn back to his lips, and pressed the buttons in an order which he hoped would reproduce the open sesame, the musical key, to the other world.

At the same time, a flashlight beam played across the broken window of the room, then passed by. Wolff blew again. The light returned to the window. More shouts arose. Desperate, Wolff tried different combinations of buttons. The third attempt seemed to be the duplicate of that which the youth on top of the toadstool-shaped boulder had produced.

The flashlight was thrust through the broken window. A deep voice growled, "Come on out, you in there! Come out, or I'll start shooting!"

Simultaneously, a greenish light appeared on the wall, broke through, and melted a hole. Moonlight shone through. The trees and the boulder were visible only as silhouettes against a green-silver radiating from a great globe of which the rim alone was visible.

He did not delay. He might have hesitated if he had been unnoticed, but now he knew he had to run. The other world offered uncertainty and danger, but this one had a definite, inescapable ignominy and shame. Even as the watchman repeated his demands, Wolff left him and his world behind. He had to stoop and to step high to get through the shrinking hole. When he had turned around on the other side to get a final glimpse, he saw through an opening no larger than a ship's porthole. In a few seconds, it was gone.

CHAPTER TWO

Wolff sat down on the grass to rest until he quit breathing so hard. He thought of how ironic it would be if the excitement were to be too much for his sixty-six year old heart. Dead on arrival, DOA. They—whoever "they" were—would have to bury him and put above his grave: THE UNKNOWN EARTHMAN.

He felt better then. He even chuckled while rising to his feet. With some courage and confidence, he looked around. The air was comfortable enough, about seventy degrees, he estimated. It bore strange and very pleasant, almost fruity, perfumes. Bird calls—he hoped they were only those—came from all around him. Somewhere far off, a low growl sounded, but he was not frightened. He was certain, with no rational ground for certainty, that it was the distance-muted crash of surf. The moon was full and enormous, two and a half times as large as Earth's.

The sky had lost the bright green it had had during the day and had become except for the moon's radiance, as black as the night-time sky of the world he had left. A multitude of large stars moved with a speed and in directions that made him dizzy with fright and confusion. One of the stars fell toward him, became bigger and bigger, brighter and brighter, until it swooped a few feet overhead. By the orange-yellow glow from its rear, he could see four great elliptoid wings and dangling skinny legs and, briefly, the silhouette of an antennaed head.

It was a firefly of some sort with a wingspread of at least ten feet.

Wolff watched the shifting and expanding and contracting of the living constellations until he became used to them. He wondered which direction to take, and the sound of the surf finally decided him. A shoreline would give a definite point of departure, wherever he went after that. His progress was slow and cautious, with frequent stops to listen and to examine the shadows.

Something with a deep chest grunted nearby. He flattened himself on the grass under the shadow of a thick bush and tried to breathe slowly. There was a rustling noise. A twig crackled. Wolff lifted his head high enough to look out into the moonlit clearing before him. A great bulk, erect, biped, dark and hairy, shambled by only a few yards from him.

It stopped suddenly, and Wolff's heart skipped a beat. Its head moved back and forth, permitting Wolff to get a full view of a gorrilloid profile. However, it was not a gorilla – not a Terrestrial one, anyway. Its fur was not a solid black. Alternate stripes of broad black and narrow white zigzagged across its body and legs. Its arms were much shorter than those of its counterpart on Earth, and its legs were not only longer but straighter. Moreover, the forehead, although shelved with bone above the eyes, was high.

It muttered something, not an animal cry or moan but a sequence of clearly modulated syllables. The gorilla was not alone. The greenish moon exposed a patch of bare skin on the side away from Wolff. It belonged to a woman who walked by the beast's side and whose shoulders were hidden by his huge right arm.

Wolff could not see her face, but he caught enough of long slim legs, curving buttocks, a shapely arm, and long black hair to wonder if she were as beautiful from the front.

She spoke to the gorilla in a voice like the sound of silver bells. The gorilla answered her. Then the two had walked out of the green moon and into the darkness of the jungle.

Wolff did not get up at once, for he was too shaken.

Finally, he rose to his feet and pushed on through the undergrowth, which was not as thick as that of an Earth jungle. Indeed, the bushes were widely separated. If the environment had not been so exotic, he would not have thought of the flora as a jungle. It was more like a park, including the soft grass, which was so short it could have been freshly mown.

Only a few paces further on, he was startled when an animal snorted and then ran in front of him. He got a glimpse of reddish antlers, a whitish nose, huge pale eyes, and a polka-dot body. It crashed by him and disappeared, but a few seconds later he heard steps behind him. He turned to see the same cervine several feet away. When it saw that it was detected, it stepped forward slowly and thrust a wet nose into his outstretched hand. Thereafter, it purred and tried to rub its flank against him. Since it weighed perhaps a quarter of a ton, it tended to push him away from it.

He leaned into it, rubbed it behind its large cup-shaped ears, scratched its nose, and lightly slapped its ribs. The cervine licked him several times with a long wet tongue that rasped as roughly as that of a lion. His hopes that it would tire of its affections were soon realized. It left him with a bound as sudden as that which had brought it within his ken.

After it was gone, he felt less endangered. Would an animal be so friendly to a complete stranger if it had carnivores or hunters to fear?

The roar of the surf became louder. Within ten minutes he was at the edge of the beach. There he crouched beneath a broad and towering frond and examined the moon-brushed scene. The beach itself was white and, as his outstretched hand verified, made of very fine sand. It ran on both sides for as far as he could see, and the breadth of it, between forest and sea, was about two hundred yards. On both sides, at a distance, were fires around which capered the silhouettes of men and women. Their shouts and laughter, though muted by the distance, reinforced his impression that they must be human.

Then his gaze swept back to the beach near him. At an angle, about three hundred yards away and almost in the water, were two beings. The sight of them snatched his breath away.

It was not what they were doing that shocked him but the construction of their bodies. From the waist up the man and woman were as human as he, but at the point where their legs should have begun the body of each tapered into fins.

He was unable to restrain his curiosity. After caching the horn in a bed of feathery grasses, he crept along the edge of the jungle; when he was opposite the two, he stopped to watch. Since the male and female were now lying side by side and talking, their position allowed him to study them in more detail. He became convinced they could not pursue him with any speed on land and had no weapons. He would approach them. They might even be friendly.

When he was about twenty yards from them, he stopped to examine them again. If they were mermen, they certainly were not half-piscine. The fins at the end of their long tails were on a horizontal plane, unlike those of fish, which are vertical. And the tail did not seem to have scales. Smooth brown skin covered their hybrid bodies from top to bottom.

He coughed. They looked up, and the male shouted and the female screamed. In a motion so swift he could not comprehend the particulars but saw it as a blur, they had risen on the ends of their tails and flipped themselves upward and out into the waves. The moon flashed on a dark head rising briefly from the waves and a tail darting upward.

The surf rolled and crashed upon the white sands. The moon shone hugely and greenly. A breeze from the sea patted his sweating face and passed on to cool the jungle. A few weird cries issued from the darkness behind him, and from down the beach came the sound of human revelry.

For awhile he was webbed in thought. The speech of the two merpeople had had something familiar about it, as had that of the zebrilla (his coinage for the gorilla) and the woman. He had not recognized any individual words, but the sounds and the asssociated pitches had stirred something in his memory. But what? They certainly spoke no language he had ever heard before. Was it similar to one of the living languages of Earth and had he heard it on a recording or perhaps in a movie?

A hand closed on his shoulder, lifted him and whirled him around. The Gothic snout and caverned eyes of a zebrilla were thrust in his face, and an alcoholic breath struck his own nostrils. It spoke, and the woman stepped out from the bushes. She walked slowly toward him, and at any other time he would have caught his breath at the magnificent body and beautiful face. Unfortunately, he was having a hard time breathing now for a different cause. The giant ape could hurl him into the sea with even more ease and speed than that which the merpeople had shown when they had dived away. Or the huge hand could close on him and meet on crushed flesh and shattered bone.

The woman said something, and the zebrilla replied. It was then that Wolff understood several words. Their language was akin to pre-Homeric Greek, to Mycenaean.

He did not immediately burst into speech to reassure them that he was harmless and his intentions good. For one thing, he was too stunned to think clearly enough. Also, his knowledge of the Greek of that period was necessarily limited, even if it was close to the Aeolic-Ionic of the blind bard.

Finally, he managed to utter a few inappropriate phrases, but he was not so concerned with the sense as to let them know he meant no harm. Hearing him, the zebrilla grunted, said something to the girl, and lowered Wolff to the sand. He sighed with relief, but he grimaced at the pain in his shoulder. The huge hand of the monster was enormously powerful. Aside from the magnitude and hairiness, the hand was quite human.

The woman tugged at his shirt. She had a mild distaste on her face; only later was he to discover that he repulsed her. She had never seen a fat old man before. Moreover, the clothes puzzled her. She continued pulling at his shirt. Rather than have her request the zebrilla to remove it from him, he pulled it off himself. She looked at it curiously, smelled it, said, "Ugh!" and then made some gesture.

Although he would have preferred not to understand her and was even less reluctant to obey, he decided he might as well. There was no reason to frustrate her and perhaps anger the zebrilla. He shed his clothes and waited for more orders. The woman laughed shrilly; the zebrilla barked and pounded his thigh with his huge hand so that it sounded as if an axe were chopping wood. He and the woman put their arms around each other and, laughing hysterically, staggered off down the beach.

Infuriated, humiliated, ashamed, but also thankful that he had escaped without injury, Wolff put his pants back on. Picking up his underwear, socks, and shoes, he trudged through the sand and back into the jungle. After taking the horn from its hiding place, he sat for a long while, wondering what to do. Finally, he fell asleep.

He awoke in the morning, muscle-sore, hungry, and thirsty.

The beach was alive. In addition to the mermen and merwomen he had seen the night before, several large seals with bright orange coats flopped back and forth over the sand in pursuit of amber balls flung by the merpeople and a man with ram's horns projecting from his forehead, furry legs and a short goatish tail chased a woman who looked much like the one who had been with the zebrilla. She, however, had yellow hair. She ran until the horned man leaped upon her and bore her, laughing, to the sand. What happened thereafter showed him that these beings were as innocent of a sense of sin, and of inhibitions, as Adam and Eve must have been.

This was more than interesting, but the sight of a mermaid eating aroused him in other and more demanding directions. She held a large oval yellow fruit in one hand and a hemisphere that looked like a coconut shell in the other. The female counterpart of the man with ram's horns squatted by a fire only a few yards from him and fried a fish on the end of a stick. The odor made his mouth water and his belly rumble.

First he had to have a drink. Since the only water in sight

was the ocean, he strode out upon the beach and toward the surf.

His reception was what he had expected: surprise, withdrawal, apprehension to some degree. All stopped their activities, no matter how absorbing, to stare at him. When he approached some of them he was greeted with wide eyes, open mouths, and retreat. Some of the males stood their ground, but they looked as if they were ready to run if he said boo. Not that he felt like challenging them, since the smallest had muscles that could easily overpower his tired old body.

He walked into the surf up to his waist and tasted the water. He had seen others drink from it, so he hoped that he would find it acceptable. It was pure and fresh and had a tang that he had never experienced before. After drinking his fill, he felt as if he had had a transfusion of young blood. He walked out of the ocean and back across the beach and into the jungle. The others had resumed their eating and recreations, and though they watched him with a bold direct stare they said nothing to him. He gave them a smile, but quit when it seemed to startle them. In the jungle, he searched for and found fruit and nuts such as the merwoman had been eating. The yellow fruit had a peach pie taste, and the meat inside the pseudococonut tasted like very tender beef mixed with small pieces of walnut.

Afterward he felt very satisfied, except for one thing: he craved his pipe. But tobacco was one thing that seemed to be missing in this paradise.

The next few days he haunted the jungle or else spent some time in or near the ocean. By then, the beach crowd had grown used to him and even began to laugh when he made his morning appearances. One day, some of the men and women jumped him and, laughing uproariously, removed his clothes. He ran after the woman with the pants, but she sped away into the jungle. When she reappeared she was emptyhanded. By now he could speak well enough to be understood if he uttered the phrases slowly. His years of teaching and study had given him a very large Greek vocabulary, and he had only to master the tones and a number of words that were not in his Autenreith.

"Why did you do that?" he asked the beautiful black-eyed nymph.

"I wanted to see what you were hiding beneath those ugly rags. Naked, you are ugly, but those things on you made you look even uglier."

"Obscene?" he said, but she did not understand the word.

He shrugged and thought, *When in Rome* . . . Only this was more like the Garden of Eden. The temperature by day or night was comfortable and varied about seven degrees. There was no problem getting a variety of food, no work demanded, no rent, no politics, no tension except an easily relieved sexual tension, no national or racial animosities. There were no bills to pay. Or were there? That you did not get something for nothing was the basic principle of the universe of Earth. Was it the same here? Somebody should have to foot the bill.

At night he slept on a pile of grass in a large hollow in a tree. This was only one of thousands of such hollows, for a particular type of tree offered this natural accommodation. Wolff did not stay in bed in the mornings, however. For some days he got up just before dawn and watched the sun arrive. Arrive was a better word than rise, for the sun certainly did not rise. On the other side of the sea was an enormous mountain range, so extensive that he could see neither end. The sun always came around the mountain and was high when it came. It proceeded straight across the green sky and did not sink but disappeared only when it went around the other end of the mountain range.

An hour later, the moon appeared. It, too, came around the mountain, sailed at the same level across the skies, and slipped around the other side of the mountain. Every other night it rained hard for an hour. Wolff usually awoke then, for the air did get a little chillier. He would snuggle down in the leaves and shiver and try to get back to sleep.

He was finding it increasingly more difficult to do so with each succeeding night. He would think of his own world, the friends and the work and the fun he had there—and of his wife. What was Brenda doing now? Doubtlessly she was grieving for him. Bitter and nasty and whining though she had been too many times, she loved him. His disappearance would be a shock and a loss. However, she would be well taken care of. She had always insisted on his carrying more insurance than he could afford; this had been a quarrel between them more than once. Then it occurred to him that she would not get a cent of insurance for a long time, for proof of his death would have to be forthcoming. Still, if she had to wait until he was legally declared dead, she could survive on social security. It would mean a drastic lowering of her living standards, but it would be enough to support her.

Certainly he had no intention of going back. He was regaining his youth. Though he ate well, he was losing weight, and his muscles were getting stronger and harder. He had a spring in his legs and a sense of joy lost sometime during his early twenties. The seventh morning, he had rubbed his scalp and discovered that it was covered with little bristles. The tenth morning, he woke up with pain in his gums. He rubbed the swollen flesh and wondered if he were going to be sick. He had forgotten that there was such a thing as disease, for he had been extremely well and none of the beach crowd, as he called them, ever seemed ill.

His gums continued to hurt him for a week, after which he took to drinking the naturally fermented liquor in the "punch-nut". This grew in great clusters high at the top of a slender tree with short, fragile, mauve branches and tobacco-pipe-shaped yellow leaves. When its leathery rind was cut open with a sharp stone, it exuded an odor as of fruity punch. It tasted like a gin tonic with a dash of cherry bitters and had a kick like a slug of tequila. It worked well in killing both the pain in his gums and the irritation the pain had generated in him.

Nine days after he first experienced the trouble with his gums, ten tiny, white, hard teeth began to shove through the flesh. Moveover, the gold fillings in the others were being pushed out by the return of the natural material. And a thick black growth covered his formerly bald pate.

This was not all. The swimming, running, and climbing had melted off the fat. The prominent veins of old age had sunk back into smooth firm flesh. He could run for long stretches without being winded or feel as if his heart would burst. All this he delighted in, but not without wondering why and how it had come about.

He asked several among the beach-crowd about their seemingly universal youth. They had one reply: "It's the Lord's will."

At first he thought they were speaking of the Creator, which seemed strange to him. As far as he could tell, they had no religion. Certainly they did not have one with any organized approach, rituals, or sacraments.

"Who is the Lord?" he asked. He thought that perhaps he had mistranslated their word *wanaks*, that it might have a slightly different meaning than that found in Homer.

Ipsewas, the zebrilla, the most intelligent of all he had so far met, answered, "He lives on top of the world, beyond Okeanos." Ipsewas pointed up and over the sea, toward the mountain range at its other side. "The Lord lives in a beautiful and impregnable palace on top of the world. He it was who made this world and who made us. He used to come down often to make merry with us. We do as the Lord says and play with him. But we are always frightened. If he becomes angry or is displeased, he is likely to kill us. Or worse."

Wolff smiled and nodded his head. So Ipsewas and the others had no more rational explanation of the origins or workings of their world than the people of his. But the beach-crowd did have one thing lacking on Earth. They had uniformity of opinion. Everyone he asked gave him the same answer as the zebrilla.

"It is the will of the Lord. He made the world, he made us."

"How do you know?" Wolff asked. He did not expect any more than he had gotten on Earth when he asked that question. But he was surprised.

"Oh," replied a mermaid, Paiawa, "the Lord told us so. Besides, my mother told me, too. She ought to know. The Lord made her body; she remembers when he did it, although that was so long, long ago."

"Indeed?" Wolff said, wondering whether or not she were pulling his leg, and thinking also that it would be difficult to retaliate by doing the same to her. "And where is your mother? I'd like to talk to her."

Paiawa waved a hand toward the west. "Somewhere along there."

"Somewhere" could be thousands of miles away, for he had no idea how far the beach extended.

"I haven't seen her for a long time," Paiawa added.

"How long?" Wolff said.

Paiawa wrinkled her lovely brow and pursed her lips. Very kissable, Wolff thought. And that body! The return of his youth was bringing back a strong awareness of sex.

Paiawa smiled at him and said, "You *are* showing some interest in me, aren't you?"

He flushed and would have walked away, but he wanted an answer to his question. "How many years since you saw your mother?" he asked again.

Paiawa could not answer. The word for "year" was not in her vocabulary.

He shrugged and walked swiftly away, to disappear behind the savagely colored foliage by the beach. She called after him, archly at first, then angrily when it became evident he was not going to turn back. She made a few disparaging remarks about him as compared to the other males. He did not argue with her—it would have been beneath his dignity, and besides, what she said was true. Even though his body was rapidly regaining its youth and strength, it still suffered in comparison with the near-perfect specimens all around him.

He dropped this line of thought, and considered Paiawa's story. If he could locate her mother or one of her mother's contemporaries in age, he might be able to find out more about the Lord. He did not discredit Paiawa's story, which would have been incredible on Earth. These people just did not lie. Fiction was a stranger to them. Such truthfulness had its advantages, but it also meant that they were decidedly limited in imagination and had little humor or wit. They laughed often enough, but it was over rather obvious and petty things. Slapstick was as high as their comedy went—and crude practical jokes.

He cursed because he was having difficulty in staying on his intended track of thought. His trouble with concentration seemed to get stronger every day. Now, what had he been thinking about when he'd strayed off to his unhappiness over his maladjustment with the local society? Oh, yes, Paiawa's mother! Some of the oldsters might be able to enlighten him—if he could locate any. How could he identify any when all adults looked the same age? There were only a very few youngsters, perhaps three in the several hundred beings he had encountered so far. Moreover, among the many animals and birds here (some rather weird ones, too), only a half-dozen had not been adults.

If there were few births, the scale was balanced by the absence of death. He had seen three dead animals, two killed by accident and the third during a battle with another over a female. Even that had been an accident, for the defeated male, a lemon-colored antelope with four horns curved into figure-eights, had turned to run away and broken his neck while jumping over a log.

The flesh of the dead animal had not had a chance to rot and stink. Several omnipresent creatures that looked like small bipedal foxes with white noses, floppy basset-hound ears, and monkey paws had eaten the corpse within a matter of an hour. The foxes scoured the jungle and scavenged everything—fruit, nuts, berries, corpses. They had a taste for the rotten; they would ignore fresh fruits for bruised. But they were not sour notes in the symphony of beauty and life. Even in the Garden of Eden, garbage collectors were necessary.

At times Wolff would look across the blue, white-capped Okeanos at the mountain range, called Thayaphayawoed. Perhaps the Lord did live up there. It might be worthwhile to cross the sea and climb up the formidable steeps on the chance that some of the mystery of this universe would be revealed. But the more he tried to estimate the height of Thayaphayawoed, the less he thought of the idea. The black cliffs soared up and up and up until the eye wearied and the mind staggered. No man could live on its top, because there would be no air to breathe.

CHAPTER THREE

One day Robert Wolff removed the silver horn from its hiding place in the hollow of a tree. Setting off through the forest, he walked toward the boulder from which the man who called himself Kickaha had thrown the horn. Kickaha and the bumpy creatures had dropped out of sight as if they never existed and no one to whom he had talked had ever seen or heard of them. He would re-enter his native world and give it another chance. If he thought its advantages outweighed those of the Garden planet, he would remain there. Or, perhaps, he could travel back and forth and so get the best of both. When tired of one, he would vacation in the other.

On the way, he stopped for a moment at an invitation from Elikopis to have a drink and to talk. Elikopis, whose name meant "Bright-eyed," was a beautiful, magnificently rounded dryad. She was closer to being "normal" than anyone he had so far met. If her hair had not been a deep purple, she would, properly clothed, have attracted no more attention on Earth than was usually bestowed on a woman of surpassing fairness.

In addition, she was one of the very few who could carry on a worthwhile conversation. She did not think that conversation consisted of chattering away or laughing loudly without cause and ignoring the words of those who were supposed to be communicating with her. Wolff had been disgusted and depressed to find that most of the beach-crowd or the forest-crowd were monologists, however intensely they seemed to be speaking or however gregarious they were.

Elikopis was different, perhaps because she was not a member of any "crowd," although it was more likely that the reverse was the cause. In this world along the sea, the natives, lacking even the technology of the Australian aborigine (and not needing even that) had developed an extremely complex social relationship. Each group had definite beach and forest territories with internal prestige levels. Each was able to recite in detail (and loved to) his/her horizontal/vertical position in comparison with each person of the group, which usually numbered about thirty. They could and would recite the arguments, reconciliations, character faults and virtues, athletic prowess or lack thereof, skill in their many childish games, and evaluate the sexual ability of each.

Elikopis had a sense of humor as bright as her eyes, but she also had some sensitivity. Today, she had an extra attraction, a mirror of glass set in a golden circle encrusted with diamonds. It was one of the few artifacts he had seen.

"Where did you get that?" he asked.

"Oh, the Lord gave it to me," Elikopis replied. "Once, a longtime ago, I was one of his favorites. Whenever he came down from the top of the world to visit here, he would spend much time with me. Chryseis and I were the ones he loved the most. Would you believe it, the others still hate us for that? That's why I'm so lonely—not that being with the others is much help.'

"And what did the Lord look like?"

She laughed and said, "From the neck down, he looked much like any tall, well-built man such as you."

She put her arm around his neck and began kissing him on his cheek, her lips slowly traveling toward his ear.

"His face?" Wolff said.

"I do not know. I could feel it, but I could not see it. A radiance from it blinded me. When he got close to me, I had to close my eyes, it was so bright."

She shut his mouth with her kisses, and presently he forgot his questions. But when she was lying half-asleep on the soft grass by his side, he picked up the mirror and looked into it. His heart opened with delight. He looked like he had when he had been twenty-five. This he had known but had not been able to fully realize until now.

"And if I return to Earth, will I age as swiftly as I have regained my youth?"

He rose and stood for awhile in thought. Then he said, "Who do I think I'm kidding? I'm not going back."

"If you're leaving me now," Elikopis said drowsily, "look for Chryseis. Something has happened to her; she runs away every time anybody gets close. Even I, her only friend, can't approach her. Something dreadful has occurred, something she won't talk about. You'll love her. She's not like the others; she's like me."

"All right," Wolff replied absently. "I will."

He walked until he was alone. Even if he did not intend to use the gate through which he had come, he did want to experiment with the horn. Perhaps there were other gates. It was possible that at any place where the horn was blown, a gate would open.

The tree under which he had stopped was one of the numerous cornucopias. It was two hundred feet tall, thirty feet thick, had a smooth, almost oily, azure bark, and branches as thick as his thigh and about sixty feet long. The branches were twigless and leafless. At the end of each was a hard-shelled flower, eight feet long and shaped exactly like a cornucopia.

Out of the cornucopias intermittent trickles of chocolatey stuff fell to the ground. The product tasted like honey with a very slight flavor of tobacco—a curious mixture, yet one he liked. Every creature of the forest ate it.

Under the cornucopia tree, he blew the horn. No "gate" appeared. He tried again a hundred yards away but without success. So, he decided, the horn worked only in certain areas, perhaps only in that place by the toadstool-shaped boulder.

Then he glimpsed the head of the girl who had come from around the tree that first time the gate had opened. She had the same heart-shaped face, enormous eyes, full crimson lips, and long tiger-stripes of black and auburn hair.

He greeted her, but she fled. Her body was beautiful; her legs were the longest, in proportion to her body, that he had ever seen in a woman. Moreover, she was slimmer than the other too-curved and great-busted females of this world.

Wolff ran after her. The girl cast a look over her shoulder, gave a cry of despair, and continued to run. He almost stopped then, for he had not gotten such a reaction from any of the natives. An initial withdrawal, yes, but not sheer panic and utter fright.

The girl ran until she could go no more. Sobbing for breath, she leaned against a moss-covered boulder near a small cataract. Ankle-high yellow flowers in the form of question-marks surrounded her. An owl-eyed bird with corkscrew feathers and long forward-bending legs stood on top of the boulder and blinked down at them. It uttered soft *wee-wee-wee!* cries.

Approaching slowly and smiling, Wolff said, "Don't be afraid of me. I won't harm you. I just want to talk to you."

The girl pointed a shaking finger at the horn. In a quavery voice she said, "Where did you get that?"

"I got it from a man who called himself Kickaha. You saw him. Do you know him?"

The girl's huge eyes were dark green; he thought them the most beautiful he had ever seen. This despite, or maybe because of, the catlike pupils.

She shook her head. "No. I did not know him. I first saw him when those"—she swallowed and turned pale and looked as if she were going to vomit—"things chased him to the boulder. And I saw them drag him off the boulder and take him away."

"Then he wasn't ended?" Wolff asked. He did not say *killed* or *slain* or *dead*, for these were taboo words.

"No. Perhaps those things meant to do something even worse than . . . ending him?"

"Why run from me?" Wolff said. "I am not one of those things."

"I . . . I can't talk about it."

Wolff considered her reluctance to speak of unpleasantness. These people had so few repulsive or dangerous phenomena in their lives, yet they could not face even these. They were overly conditioned to the easy and the beautiful.

"I don't care whether or not you want to talk about it," he said. "You must. It's very important."

She turned her face away. "I won't."

"Which way did they go?"

"Who?"

"Those monsters. And Kickaha."

"I heard him call them *gworl*," she said. "I never heard that word before. They . . . the gworl . . . must come from somewhere else." She pointed seawards and up. "They must come from the mountain. Up there, somewhere."

Suddenly she turned to him and came close to him. Her huge eyes were raised to his, and even at this moment he could not help thinking how exquisite her features were and how smooth and creamy her skin was.

"Let's get away from here!" she cried. "Far away! Those things are still here. Some of them may have taken Kickaha away, but all of them didn't leave! I saw a couple a few days ago. They were hiding in the hollow of a tree. Their eyes shone like those of animals, and they have a horrible odor, like rotten fungus-covered fruit!"

She put her hand on the horn. "I think they want this!"

Wolff said, "And I blew the horn. If they're anywhere near, they must have heard it!"

He looked around through the trees. Something glittered behind a bush about a hundred yards away.

He kept his eyes on the bush, and presently he saw the bush tremble and the flash of sunlight again. He took the girl's slender hand in his and said, "Let's get going. But walk as if we'd seen nothing. Be nonchalant."

She pulled back on his hand and said, "What's wrong?"

"Don't get hysterical. I think I saw something behind a bush. It might be nothing, then again it could be the gworl. Don't look over there! You'll give us away!"

He spoke too late, for she had jerked her head around. She gasped and moved close to him. "They . . . they!"

He looked in the direction of her pointing finger and saw two dark, squat figures shamble from behind the bush. Each carried a long, wide, curved blade of steel in its hand. They waved the knives and shouted something in a hoarse rasping voice. They wore no clothes over their dark furry bodies, but a broad belt around their waists supported scabbards from which protruded knife-handles.

Wolff said, "Don't panic. I don't think they can run very fast on those short bent legs. Where's a good place to get away from them, someplace they can't follow us?"

"Across the sea," she said in a shaking voice. "I don't think they could find us if we got far enough ahead of them. We can go on a *histoikhthys*."

She was referring to one of the huge molluscs that abounded in the sea. These had bodies covered with paper-thin but tough shells shaped like a racing yacht's hull. A slender but strong rod of cartilage projected vertically from the back of each, and a triangular sail of flesh, so thin it was transparent, grew from the cartilage mast. The angle of the sail was controlled by muscular movement, and the force of the wind on the sail, plus expulsion of a jet of water, enabled the creature to move swiftly in a wind or a calm. The merpeople and the sentients who lived on the beach often hitched rides on these creatures, steering them by pressure on exposed nerve centers.

"You think the gworl will have to use a boat?" he said. "If so, they'll be out of luck unless they make one. I've never seen any kind of sea craft here."

Wolff looked behind him frequently. The gworl were coming at a faster pace, their bodies rolling like those of drunken sailors at every step. Wolff and the girl came to a stream which was about seventy feet broad and, at the deepest, rose to their waists. The water was cool but not chilling, clear, with slivery fish darting back and forth in it. When they reached the other side, they hid behind a large cornucopia tree. The girl urged him to continue, but he said, "They'll be at a disadvantage when they're in the middle of the stream."

"What do you mean?" she asked.

He did not reply. After placing the horn behind the tree, he looked around until he found a stone. It was half the size of his head, round, and rough enough to be held firmly in his hand. He hefted one of the fallen cornucopias. Though huge, it was hollow and weighed no more than twenty pounds. By then, the two gworl were on the bank of the opposite side of the stream. It was then that he discovered a weakness of the hideous creatures. They walked back and forth along the bank, shook their knives in fury, and growled so loudly in their throaty language that he could hear them from his hiding place. Finally, one of them stuck a broad splayed foot in the water. He withdrew it almost immediately, shook it as a cat shakes a wet paw, and said something to the other gworl. That one rasped back, then screamed at him.

The gworl with the wet foot shouted back, but he stepped into the water and reluctantly waded through it. Wolff watched him and also noted that the other was going to hang back until his companion had safely made the trip. Wolff waited until the creature had passed the middle of the stream; then he picked up the cornucopia in one hand, the stone in the other, and ran toward the stream. Behind him, the girl screamed. Wolff cursed because it gave the gworl notice that he was coming.

The gworl paused, the water up to its waist, yelled at Wolff and brandished the knife. Wolff reserved his breath, for he did not want to waste his wind. He sped toward the edge of the water, while the gworl resumed his progress to the same bank.

The gworl on the opposite edge had frozen at Wolff's appearance; now he had plunged into the stream to help the other. This action fell in with Wolff's plans. He only hoped that he could deal with the first before the second reached the middle.

The nearest gworl flipped his knife; Wolff lifted the cornucopia before him. The knife thudded into its thin but tough shell with a force that almost tore it from his grasp. The gworl began to draw another knife from its scabbard. Wolff did not stop to pull the first knife from the cornucopia; he kept on running. Just as the gworl raised the knife to slash at Wolff, Wolff dropped the stone, lifted the great bell-shape high, and slammed it over the gworl.

A muffled squawk came from within the shell. The cornucopia tilted over, the gworl with it, and both began floating downstream. Wolff ran into the water, picked up the stone, and grabbed the gworl by one of its thrashing feet. He took a hurried glance at the other and saw it was raising its knife for a throw. Wolff grabbed the handle of the knife that was sticking in the shell, tore it out, and then threw himself down behind the shelter of the bell-shape. He was forced to release his hold on the gworl's hairy foot, but he escaped the knife. It flew over the rim of the shell and buried itself to the hilt in the mud of the bank.

At the same time, the gworl within the cornucopia slid out, sputtering. Wolff stabbed at its side; the knife slid off one of the cartilaginous bumps. The gworl screamed and turned toward him. Wolff rose and thrust with all his strength at its belly. The knife went in to the hilt. The gworl grabbed at it; Wolff stepped back; the gworl fell into the water. The cornucopia floated away, leaving Wolff exposed, the knife gone, and only the stone in his hand. The remaining gworl was advancing on him, holding its knife across its breast. Evidently it did not intend to try for a second throw. It meant to close in on Wolff.

Wolff forced himself to delay until the thing was only ten feet from him. Meanwhile, he crouched down so that the water came to his chest and hid the stone, which he had shifted from his left to his right hand. Now he could see the gworl's face clearly. It had a very low forehead, a double ridge of bone above the eyes, thick mossy eyebrows, close-set lemon-yellow eyes, a flat, single-nostriled nose, thin black animal lips, a prognathous jaw which curved far out and gave the mouth a froglike appearance, no chin, and the sharp, widely separated teeth of a carnivore. The head, face, and body were covered with long, thick, dark fur. The neck was very thick, and the shoulders were stooped. Its wet fur stank like rotten fungus-diseased fruit.

Wolff was scared at the thing's hideousness, but he held his ground. If he broke and ran, he would go down with a knife in his back.

When the gworl, alternately hissing and rasping in its ugly speech, had come within six feet, Wolff stood up. He raised his stone, and the gworl, seeing his intention, raised his knife to throw it. The stone flew straight and thudded into a bump on the forehead. The creature staggered backward, dropped the knife, and fell on its back in the water. Wolff waded toward it, groped in the water for the stone, found it, and came up from the water in time to face the gworl. Although it had a dazed expression and its eyes were slightly crossed, it was not out of the fight. And it held another knife.

Wolff raised the stone high and brought it down on top of the skull. There was a loud crack. The gworl fell back again, disappeared in the water, and appeared several yards away floating on its face.

Reaction took him. His heart was hammering so hard he thought it would rupture, he was shaking all over, and he was sick. But he remembered the knife stuck in the mud and retrieved it.

The girl was still behind the tree. She looked too horror-struck to speak. Wolff picked up the horn, took the girl's arm with one hand, and shook her roughly.

"Snap out of it! Think how lucky you are! You could be dead instead of them!"

She burst into a long wailing, then began weeping. He waited until she seemed to have no more grief in her before speaking. "I don't even know your name."

Her enormous eyes were reddened, and her face looked older. Even so, he thought, he had not seen an Earthwoman who could compare with her. Her beauty made the terror of the fight thin away.

"I'm Chryseis," she said. As if she were proud of it but at the same time shy of her proudness, she said, "I'm the only woman here who is allowed that name. The Lord forbade others to take it."

He growled, "The Lord again. Always the Lord. Who in hell is the Lord?"

"You really don't know?" she replied as if she could not believe him.

"No, I don't." He was silent for a moment, then said her name as if he were tasting it. "Chryseis, heh? It's not unknown on Earth, although I fear that the university at which I was teaching is full of illiterates who've never heard the name. They know that Homer composed the Iliad, and that's about it.

"Chryseis, the daughter of Chryses, a priest of Apollo. She was captured by the Greeks during the siege of Troy and given to Agamemnon. But Agamemnon was forced to restore her to her father because of the pestilence sent by Apollo."

Chryseis was silent for so long that Wolff became impatient. He decided that they should move away from this area, but he was not certain which direction to take or how far to go.

Chryseis, frowning, said, "That was a long time ago. I can barely remember it. It's all so vague now."

"What are you talking about?"

"Me. My father. Agamemnon. The war."

"Well, what about it?" He was thinking that he would like to go to the base of the mountains. There, he could get some idea of what a climb entailed.

"I am Chryseis," she said. "The one you were talking about. You sound as if you had just come from Earth. Oh, tell me, is it true?"

He sighed. These people did not lie, but there was nothing to keep them from believing that their stories were true. He had heard enough incredible things to know that they were not only badly misinformed but likely to reconstruct the past to suit themselves. They did so in all sincerity, of course.

"I don't want to shatter your little dream-world," he said, "but this Chryseis, if she ever existed, died at least 3000 years ago. Moreover, she was a human being. She did not have tiger-striped hair and eyes with feline pupils."

"Nor did I . . . then. It was the Lord who abducted me, brought me to this universe, and changed my body. Just as it was he who abducted the others, changed them, or else inserted their brains in bodies he created."

She gestured seaward and upward. "He lives up there now, and we don't see him very often. Some say that he disappeared a long time ago, and a new Lord has taken his place."

"Let's get away from here," he said. "We can talk about this later."

They had gone only a quarter of a mile when Chryseis gestured at him to hide with her behind a thick purple-branched, gold-leaved bush. He crouched by her and, parting the branches a little, saw what had disturbed her. Several yards away was a hairy-legged man with heavy ram's horns on top of his head. Sitting on a low branch at a level with the man's eyes was a giant raven. It was as large as a golden eagle and had a high forehead. The skull looked as if it could house a brain the size of a fox terrier's.

Wolff was not surprised at the bulk of the raven, for he had seen some rather enormous creatures. But he was shocked to find the bird and the man carrying on a conversation.

"The Eye of the Lord," Chryseis whispered. She stabbed a finger at the raven in answer to his puzzled look. "That's one of the Lord's spies. They fly over the world and see what's going on and then carry the news back to the Lord."

Wolff thought of Chryseis' apparently sincere remark about the insertion of brains into bodies by the Lord. To his question, she replied, "Yes, but I do not know if he put human brains into the ravens' heads. He may have grown small brains with the larger human brains as models, then educated the ravens. Or he could have used just part of a human brain."

Unfortunately, though they strained their ears, they could only catch a few words here and there. Several minutes passed. The raven, loudly croaking a goodbye in distorted but understandable Greek, launched himself from the branch. He dropped heavily, but his great wings beat fast, and they carried him upward before he touched ground. In a minute he was lost behind the heavy foliage of the trees. A little later, Wolff caught a glimpse of him through a break in the vegetation. The giant black bird was gaining altitude slowly, his point of flight the mountain across the sea.

He noticed that Chryseis was trembling. He said, "What could the raven tell the Lord that would scare you so?"

"I am not frightened so much for myself as I am for you. If the Lord discovers you are here, he will want to kill you. He does not like uninvited guests in his world."

She placed her hand on the horn and shivered again. "I know that it was Kickaha who gave you this, and that you can't help it that you have it. But the Lord might not know it isn't your fault. Or, even if he did, he might not care. He would be terribly angry if he thought you'd had anything to do with stealing it. He would do awful things to you; you would be better off if you ended yourself now rather than have the Lord get his hands on you."

"Kickaha stole the horn? How do you know?"

"Oh, believe me, I know. It is the Lord's. And Kickaha must have stolen it, for the Lord would never give it to anyone."

"I'm confused," Wolff said. "But maybe we can straighten it all out someday. The thing that bothers me right now is, where's Kickaha?"

Chryseis pointed toward the mountain and said, "The gworl took him there. But before they did . . ."

She covered her face with her hands; tears seeped through the fingers.

"They did something to him?" Wolff said.

She shook her head. "No. They did something to . . . to . . ."

Wolff took her hands from her face. "If you can't talk about it, would you show it to me?"

"I can't. It's . . . too horrible. I get sick."

"Show me anyway."

"I'll take you near there. But don't ask me to look at . . . her . . . again."

She began walking, and he followed her. Every now and then she would stop, but he would gently urge her on. After a zig-zag course of over half a mile, she stopped. Ahead of them was a small forest of bushes twice as high as Wolff's head. The leaves of the branches of one bush interlaced with those of its neighbors. The leaves were broad and elephant-ear-shaped, light green with broad red veins, and tipped with a rusty fleur-de-lys.

"She's in there," Chryseis said. "I saw the gworl . . . catch her and drag her into the bushes. I followed . . . I . . ." She could talk no more.

Wolff, knife in one hand, pushed the branches of the bushes aside. He found himself in a natural clearing. In the middle, on the short green grass, lay the scattered bones of a human female. The bones were gray and devoid of flesh, and bore little toothmarks, by which he knew that the bipedal vulpine scavengers had gotten to her.

He was not horrified, but he could imagine how Chryseis must have felt. She must have seen part of what had taken place, probably a rape, then murder in some gruesome fashion. She would have reacted like the other dwellers in the Garden. Death was something so horrible that the word for it had long ago become taboo and then dropped out of the language. Here, nothing but pleasant thoughts and acts were to be contemplated, and anything else was to be shut out.

He returned to Chryseis, who looked with her enormous eyes at him as if she wanted him to tell her that there was nothing within the clearing. He said, "She's only bones now, and far past any suffering."

"The gworl will pay for this!" she said savagely. "The Lord does not allow his creatures to be hurt! This Garden is his, and any intruders are punished!"

"Good for you," he said. "I was beginning to think that you may have become frozen by the shock. Hate the gworl all you want; they deserve it. And you need to break loose."

She screamed and leaped at him and beat on his chest with her fists. Then she began weeping, and presently he took her in his arms. He raised her face and kissed her. She kissed him back passionately, though the tears were still flowing.

Afterward, she said, "I ran to the beach to tell my people what I'd seen. But they wouldn't listen. They turned their backs on me and pretended they hadn't heard me. I kept trying to make them listen, but Owisandros"—the ram-horned man who had been talking with the raven—"Owisandros hit me with his fist and told me to go away. After that, none of them would have anything to do with me. And I . . . I needed friends and love."

"You don't get friends or love by telling people what they don't want to hear," he said. "Here or on Earth. But you have me, Chryseis, and I have you. I think I'm beginning to fall in love with you, although I may just be reacting to loneliness and to the most strange beauty I've ever seen. And to my new youth."

He sat up and gestured at the mountain. "If the gworl are intruders here, where did they come from? Why were they after the horn? Why did they take Kickaha with them? And who is Kickaha?"

"He comes from up there, too. But I think he's an Earthman."

"What do you mean, Earthman? You say you're from Earth."

"I mean he's a newcomer. I don't know. I just had a feeling he was."

He stood up and lifted her up by hands. "Let's go after him."

Chryseis sucked in her breath and, one hand on her breast, backed away from him. "No!"

"Chryseis, I could stay here with you and be very happy. For awhile. But I'd always be wondering what all this is about the Lord and what happened to Kickaha. I only saw him for a few seconds, but I think I'd like him very much. Besides, he didn't throw the horn to me just because I happened to be there. I have a hunch that he did it for a good reason, and that I should find out why. And I can't rest while he's in the hands of those things, the gworl."

He took her hand from her breast and kissed the hand. "It's about time you left this Paradise that is no Paradise. You can't stay here forever, a child forever."

She shook her head. "I wouldn't be any help to you. I'd just get in your way. And . . . leaving . . . leaving I'd, well, I'd just end."

"You're going to have to learn a new vocabulary," he said. "Death will be just one of the many new words you'll be able to speak without a second thought or a shiver. You will be a better woman for it. Refusing to say it doesn't stop it from happening, you know. Your friend's bones are there whether or not you can talk about them."

"That's horrible!"

"The truth often is."

He turned away from her and started toward the beach. After a hundred yards, he stopped to look back. She had just started running after him. He waited for her, took her in his arms, kissed her, and said, "You may find it hard going, Chryseis, but you won't be bored, won't have to drink yourself into a stupor to endure life."

"I hope so," she said in a low voice. "But I'm scared."

"So am I, but we're going."

CHAPTER FOUR

He took her hand in his as they walked side by side toward the roar of the surf. They had traveled not more than a hundred yards when Wolff saw the first gworl. It stepped out from behind a tree and seemed to be as surprised as they. It shouted, snatched its knife out, then turned to yell at others behind it. In a few seconds, a party of seven had formed, each gworl with a long curved knife.

Wolff and Chryseis had a fifty-yard headstart. Still holding Chryseis' hand, the horn in his other hand, Robert Wolff ran as fast as he could.

"I don't know!" she answered despairingly. "We could hide in a tree hollow, but we'd be trapped if they found us."

They ran on. Now and then he looked back: the brush was thick hereabouts and hid some of the gworl, but there was always one or two in evidence.

"The boulder!" he said. "It's just ahead. We'll take that way out!"

Suddenly he knew how much he did not want to return to his native world. Even if it meant a route of escape and a temporary hiding place, he did not want to go back. The prospect of being trapped there and being unable to return here was so appalling that he almost decided not to blow the horn. But he had to do so. Where else could he go?

The decision was taken away from him a few seconds later. As he and Chryseis sped toward the boulder, he saw several dark figures hunched at its base. These rose and became gworl with flashing knives and long white canines.

Wolff and the girl angled away while the three at the boulder joined the chase. These were nearer than the others, only twenty yards behind the fugitives.

"Don't you know any place?" he panted.

"Over the edge," she said. "That's the only place they might not follow us. I've been down the face of the rim; there're caves there. But it's dangerous."

He did not reply, saving his breath for the run. His legs felt heavy and his lungs and throat burned. Chryseis seemed to be in better shape than he: she ran easily, her long legs pumping, breathing deeply but not agonizingly.

"Another two minutes, we'll be there," she said.

The two minutes seemed much longer, but every time he felt he had to stop, he took another look behind him and renewed his strength. The gworl, although even further behind, were in sight. They rolled along on their short, crooked legs, their bumpy faces set with determination.

"Maybe if you gave them the horn," Chryseis said, "they'd go away. I think they want the horn, not us."

"I'll do it if I have to," he gasped. "But only as a last resort."

Suddenly, they were going up a steep slope. Now his legs did feel burdened, but he had caught his second wind and thought that he could go awhile longer. Then they were on top of the hill and at the edge of a cliff.

Chryseis stopped him from walking on. She advanced ahead of him to the edge, halted, looked over, and beckoned him. When he was by her side, he, too, gazed down. His stomach clenched like a fist.

Composed of hard black shiny rock, the cliff went straight down for several miles. Then, nothing.

Nothing but the green sky.

"So . . . it is the edge . . . of the world!" he said.

Chryseis did not answer him. She trotted ahead of him, looking over the side of the cliff, halting briefly now and then to examine the rim.

"About sixty yards more," she said. "Beyond those trees that grow right up to the edge."

She started running swiftly with him closely behind her. At the same time, a gworl burst out of the bushes growing on the inner edge of the hill. He turned once to yell, obviously notifying his fellows that he had found the quarry. Then he attacked without waiting for them.

Wolff ran toward the gworl. When he saw the creature lift its knife to throw, he hurled the horn at it. This took the gworl by surprise—or perhaps the turning horn reflected sunlight into his eyes. Whatever the cause, his hesitation was enough for Wolff to get the advantage. He sped in as the gworl both ducked and reached a hand out for the horn. The huge hairy fingers curled around the horn, a cry of grating delight came from the creature, and Wolff was on him. He thrust at the protruding belly; the gworl brought his own knife up; the two blades clanged.

Having missed the first stroke, Wolff wanted to run again. This thing was undoubtedly skilled at knife-fighting. Wolff knew fencing quite well and had never given up its practice. But there was a big difference between dueling with the rapier and dirty in-close knivery, and he knew it. Yet he could not leave. In the first place, the gworl would down him with a thrown blade in his back before he could take four steps. Also, there was the horn, clenched in the gnarled left fist of the gworl. Wolff could not leave that.

The gworl, realizing that Wolff was in a very bad situation, grinned. His upper canines shone long and wet and yellow and sharp. With those, thought Wolff, the thing did not need a knife.

Something goldenbrown, trailing long black-and-auburn-striped hair, flashed by Wolff. The gworl's eyes opened, and he started to turn to his left. The butt end of a pole, a long stick stripped of its leaves and part of its bark, drove into the gworl's chest. At the other end was Chryseis. She had run at top speed with the dead branch held like a vaulter's pole, but just before impact she had lowered it and it hit the creature with enough speed and weight behind it to bowl him over backward. The horn dropped from his fist, but the knife remained in the other.

Wolff jumped forward and thrust the end of his blade between two cartilaginous bosses and into the gworl's thick neck. The muscles were thick and tough there, but not enough to stop the blade. Only when the steel severed the windpipe did it halt.

Wolff handed Chryseis the gworl's knife. "Here, take it!"

She accepted it, but she seemed to be in shock. Wolff slapped her savagely until the glaze went from her eyes. "You did fine!" he said. "Which would you rather see dead, me or him?"

He removed the belt from the corpse and fastened it on himself. Now he had three knives. He scabbarded the bloody weapon, took the horn in one hand, Chryseis' hand in the other, and began running again. Behind them, a howl arose as the first of the gworl came over the edge of the hill. However, Wolff and Chryseis had about thirty yards' start, which they maintained until they reached the group of trees growing on the rim. Chryseis took the lead. She let herself face down on the rim and rolled over. Wolff looked over once before blindly following and saw a small ledge about six feet down from the rim. She had already let herself down the ledge and now was hanging by her hands. She dropped again, this time to a much more narrow ledge. But it did not end: it ran at a forty-five degree angle down the face of the cliff. They could use it if they faced inward against the stone cliff-wall and moved sideways, their hands spread to gain friction against the wall.

Wolff used both hands also; he had stuck the horn through the belt.

There was a howl from above. He looked up to see the first of the gworl dropping onto the first ledge. Then he glanced back at Chryseis and almost fell off from shock. She was gone.

Slowly, he turned his head to see over his shoulder and down below. He fully expected to find her falling down the face of the cliff, if not already past it and plunging into the green abyss.

"Wolff!" she said. Her head was sticking out from the cliff itself. "There's a cave here. Hurry."

Trembling, sweating, he inched along the ledge to her and presently was inside an opening. The ceiling of the cave was several feet higher than his head; he could almost touch the walls on both sides when he stretched out his arms; the interior ran into the darkness.

"How far back does it go?"

"Not very far. But there's a natural shaft, a fault in the rock, that leads down. It opens on the bottom of the world; there's nothing below, nothing but air and sky."

"This can't be," he said slowly. "But it is. A universe founded on physical principles completely different than those of my universe. A flat planet with edges. But I don't understand how gravity works here. Where is its center?"

She shrugged and said, "The Lord may have told me a long time ago. But I've forgotten. I'd even forgotten he told me that Earth was round."

Wolff took the leather belt off, slid the scabbards off it, and picked up an oval black rock weighing about ten pounds. He slipped the belt through the buckle and then placed the stone within the loop. After piercing a hole near the buckle with the point of his knife, he tightened the loop. He had only to buckle the belt, and he was armed with a thong at the end of which was a heavy stone.

"You get behind and to one side of me," he said. "If I miss any, if one gets in past me, you push while he's off-balance. But don't go over yourself. Do you think you can do it?"

She nodded her head but evidently did not trust herself to speak.

"This is asking a lot of you. I'd understand if you cracked up completely. But, basically, you're made of sturdy ancient-Hellenic stock. They were a pretty tough lot in those days; you can't have lost your strength, even in this deadening pseudo-Paradise."

"I wasn't Achaean," she said. "I was Sminthean. But you are, in a way, right. I don't feel as badly as I thought I would. Only . . ."

"Only it takes getting used to," he said. He was encouraged, for he had expected a different reaction. If she could keep it up, the two of them might make it through this. But if she fell apart and he had a hysterical woman to control, both might fall under the attack of the gworl.

"Speaking of which," he muttered as he saw black, hairy,

gnarled fingers slide around the corner of the cave. He swung the belt hard so that the stone at its end smashed the hand. There was a bellow of surprise and pain, then a long ululating scream as the gworl fell. Wolff did not wait for the next one to appear. He got as close to the lip of the cave ledge as he dared and swung the stone again. It whipped around the corner and thudded against something soft. Another scream came, and it, too, faded away into the nothingness of the green sky.

"Three down, seven to go! Provided that no more have joined them."

He said to Chryseis, "They may not be able to get in here. But they can starve us out."

"The horn?"

He laughed. "They wouldn't let us go now even if I did hand them the horn. And I don't intend for them to get it. I'll throw the horn into the sky rather than do that."

A figure was silhouetted against the mouth of the cave as it dropped from above. The gworl, swinging in, landed on his feet and teetered for a second. But he threw himself forward, rolled in a hairy ball, and was up on his feet again. Wolff was so surprised that he failed to react immediately. He had not expected them to be able to climb above the cave and let themselves down, for the rock above the cave had looked smooth. Somehow, one had done it, and now he was inside, on his feet, a knife in hand.

Wolff whirled the stone at the belt-end and loosed it at the gworl. The creature flipped its knife at him; Wolff dodged but spoiled his aim of the stone. It flew over the furry bumpy head; the thrown knife brushed him lightly on his shoulder. He jumped for his own knife on the floor of the cave, saw another dark shape drop into the cave from above, and a third come around the corner of the mouth.

Something hit his head. His vision blurred, his senses grew dim, his knees buckled.

When he awoke, a pain in the side of his head, he had a frightening sensation. He seemed to be upside down and floating above a vast polished black disc. A rope was tied around his neck, and his hands were tied behind his back. He was hanging with his feet up in the empty air, yet there was only a slight tension of rope around his neck.

Bending his head back, he could see that the rope led upward into a shaft in the disc and that at the far end of the shaft was a pale light.

He groaned and closed his eyes, but opened them again. The world seemed to spin. Suddenly, he was reoriented. Now he knew that he was not suspended upside down against all the laws of gravity. He was hanging by a rope from the bottom underside of the planet. The green below him was the sky.

He thought, *I should have strangled before now. But there is no gravity pulling me downward.*

He kicked his feet, and the reaction drove him upward. The mouth of the shaft came closer. His head entered it, but something resisted him. His motion slowed, stopped, and, as if there were an invisible and compressed spring against his head, he began to move back down. Not until the rope tightened again did he stop his flight.

The gworl had done this to him. After knocking him out, they had let him down the shaft, or more probably, had carried him down. The shaft was narrow enough for a man to get down it with his back to one wall and his feet braced against the other. The descent would scrape the skin off a man, but the hairy hide of the gworl had looked tough enough to withstand descent and ascent without injury. Then a rope had been lowered, placed around his neck, and he had been dropped through the hole in the bottom of the world.

There was no way of getting himself back up. He would starve to death. His body would dangle in the winds of space until the rope rotted. He would not then fall, but would drift about in the shadow cast by the disc. The gworl he had knocked off the ledge had fallen, but their acceleration had kept them going.

Though despairing because of his situation, he could not help speculating about the gravitational configuration of the flat planet. The center must be at the very bottom; all attraction was upward through the mass of the planet. On this side, there was none.

What had the gworl done to Chryseis? Had they killed her as they had her friend?

He knew then that however they had dealt with her, they had purposely not hung her with him. They had planned that part of his agony would be that of not knowing her fate. As long as he could live at the end of this rope, he would wonder what had happened to her. He would conjure a multitude of possibilities, all horrible.

For a long time he hung suspended at a slight degree from the perpendicular, since the wind held him steady. Here, where there was no gravity, he could not swing like a pendulum.

Although he remained in the shadow of the black disc, he could see the progress of the sun. The sun itself was invisible, hidden by the disc, but the light from it fell on the rim of the great curve and slowly marched along it. The green sky beneath the sun glowed brightly, while the unlit portions before and after became dark. Then a paler lighting along the edge of the disc came into his sight, and he knew that the moon was following the sun.

It must be midnight, he thought. *If the gworl are taking her someplace, they could be some distance out on the sea. If they've been torturing her, she could be dead. If they've hurt her, I hope she's dead.*

Abruptly, while he hung in the gloom beneath the bottom of the world, he felt the rope at his neck jerk. The noose tightened, although not enough to choke him, and he was being drawn upward toward the shaft. He craned his neck to see who was hauling him up, but he could not penetrate the darkness of the mouth of the shaft. Then his head broke through the web of gravity—like surface tension on water, he thought—and he was hoisted clear of the abyss. Great strong hands and arms came around him to hug him against a hard, warm, furry chest. An alcoholic breath blew into his face. A leathery mouth scraped his cheek as the creature hugged him closer and began inching up the shaft with Wolff in its arms. Fur scraped on rock as the thing pushed with its legs. There was a jerk as the legs came up suddenly and took a new hold, followed by another scrape and lunge upward.

"Ipsewas?" Wolff said.

The zebrilla replied, "Ipsewas. Don't talk now. I have to save my wind. This isn't easy."

Wolff obeyed, although he had a difficult time in not asking about Chryseis. When they reached the top of the shaft, Ipsewas removed the rope from his neck and tossed him onto the floor of the cave.

Now at last he dared to speak. "Where is Chryseis?"

Ipsewas landed on the cave floor softly, turned Wolff over, and began to untie the knots around his wrists. He was breathing heavily from the trip up the shaft, but he said, "The gworl took her with them to a big dugout and began to sail across the sea toward the mountain. She shouted at me, begged me to help her. Then a gworl hit her, knocked her unconscious, I suppose. I was sitting there, drunk as the Lord, half-unconscious myself with nut juice, having a good time with Autonoe—you know, the *akowile* with the big mouth.

"Before Chryseis was knocked out, she screamed something about you hanging from the Hole in the Bottom of the World. I didn't know what she was talking about, because it's been a long time since I was here. How long ago I hate to say. Matter of fact, I don't really know. Everything's pretty much of a haze any more, you know."

"No, I don't," Wolff said. He rose and rubbed his wrists.

"But I'm afraid that if I stay here much longer, I might end up in an alcoholic fog, too."

"I was thinking about going after her," Ipsewas said. "But the gworl flashed those long knives at me and said they'd kill me. I watched them drag their boat out of the bushes, and about then I decided, what the hell, if they killed me, so what? I wasn't going to let them get away with threatening me or taking poor little Chryseis off to only the Lord knows what. Chryseis and I were friends in the old days, in the Troad, you know, although we haven't had too much to do with each other here for some time. I think it's been a long time. Anyway, I suddenly craved some real adventure, some genuine excitement—and I loathed those monstrous bumpy creatures.

"I ran after them, but by then they'd launched the boat, with Chryseis in it. I looked around for a *histoikhthys*, thinking I could ram their boat with it. Once I had them in the water, they'd be mine, knives or not. The way they acted in the boat showed me that they felt far from confident on the sea. I doubt they can even swim."

"I doubt it, too," Wolff said.

"But there wasn't a *histoikhthys* in reaching distance. And the wind was taking the boat away; it had a large lateen sail. I went back to Autonoe and took another drink. I might have forgotten about you, just as I was trying to forget about Chryseis. I was sure she was going to get hurt, and I couldn't bear to think about it, so I wanted to drink myself into oblivion. But Autonoe, bless her poor boozed-up brain, reminded me of what Chryseis had said about you.

"I took off fast, and looked around for awhile, because I couldn't remember just where the ledges were that led to the cave. I almost gave up and started drinking again. But something kept me going. Maybe I wanted to do just one good thing in this eternity of doing nothing, good or evil."

"If you hadn't come, I'd have hung there until I died of thirst. Now, Chryseis has a chance, if I can find her. I'm going after her. Do you want to come along?"

Wolff expected Ipsewas to say yes, but he did not think that Ipsewas would stick to his determination once the trip across the sea faced him. He was surprised, however.

The zebrilla swam out, seized a projection of shell as a *histoikhthys* sailed by, and swung himself upon the back of the creature. He guided it back to the beach by pressing upon the great nerve spots, dark purple blotches visible on the exposed skin just back of the cone-shaped shell that formed the prow of the creature.

Wolff, under Ipsewas' guidance, maintained pressure on a spot to hold the sailfish (for that was the literal translation of *histoikhthys*) on the beach. The zebrilla gathered several armloads of fruit and nuts and a large collection of the punchnuts.

"We have to eat and drink, especially drink," Ipsewas muttered. "It may be a long way across Okeanos to the foot of the mountain. I don't remember."

A few minutes after the supplies had been stored in one of the natural receptacles on the sailfish's shell, they left. The wind caught the thin cartilage sail, and the great mollusc gulped in water through its mouth and ejected it through a fleshy valve in its rear.

"The gworl have a headstart," Ipsewas said, "but they can't match our speed. They won't get to the other side long before we do." He broke open a punchnut and offered Wolff a drink. Wolff accepted. He was exhausted but nervestrung. He needed something to knock him out and let him sleep. A curve of the shell afforded a cavelike ledge for him to crawl within. He lay hugged against the bare skin of the sailfish, which was warm. In a short time he was asleep, but his last glimpse was of the shouldering bulk of Ipsewas, his stripes blurred in the moonlight, crouching by the nerve spots. Ipsewas was lifting another punchnut above his head and pouring the liquid contents into his outthrust gorilloid lips.

When Wolff awoke, he found the sun was just coming around the curve of the mountain. The full moon (it was always full, for the shadow of the planet never fell on it) was just slipping around the other side of the mountain.

Refreshed but hungry, he ate some of the fruit and the protein-rich nuts. Ipsewas showed him how he could vary his diet with the "bloodberries". These were shiny maroon balls that grew in clusters at the tips of fleshy stalks that sprouted out of the shell. Each was large as a baseball and had a thin, easily torn skin that exuded a liquid that looked and tasted like blood. The meat within tasted like raw beef with a soupcon of shrimp.

"They fall off when they're ripe, and the fish get most of them," Ipsewas said. "But some float in to the beach. They're best when you get them right off the stalk."

Wolff crouched down by Ipsewas. Between mouthfuls, he said, "The *histoikhthys* is handy. They seem almost too much of a good thing."

"The Lord designed and made them for our pleasure and his," Ipsewas replied.

"The Lord made this universe?" Wolff said, no longer sure that the story was a myth.

"You better believe it," Ipsewas replied, and took another drink. "Because if you don't, the Lord will end you. As it is,

I doubt that he'll let you continue, anyway. He doesn't like uninvited guests."

Ipsewas lifted the nut and said, "Here's to your escaping his notice. And a sudden end and damnation to the Lord."

He dropped the nut and leaped at Wolff. Wolff was so taken by surprise he had no chance to defend himself. He went sprawling into the hollow of shell in which he had slept, with Ipsewas' bulk on him.

"Quiet!" Ipsewas said. "Stay curled up inside here until I tell you it's all right. It's an Eye of the Lord."

Wolff shrank back against the hard shell and tried to make himself one with the shadow of the interior. However, he did look out with one eye and thus he saw the ragged shadow of the raven scud across, followed by the creature itself. The dour bird flashed over once, wheeled, and began to glide in for a landing on the stern of the sailfish.

"Damn him! He can't help seeing me," Wolff muttered to himself.

"Don't panic," Ipsewas called. "Ahhh!"

There was a thud, a splash, and a scream that made Wolff start up and bump his head hard against the shell above him. Through the flashes of light and darkness, he saw the raven hanging limply within two giant claws. If the raven was eagle-sized, the killer that had dropped like a bolt from the green sky seemed, in that first second of shock, to be as huge as a roc. Wolff's vision straightened and cleared, and he saw an eagle with a light-green body, a pale red head, and a pale yellow beak. It was six times the bulk of the raven, and its wings, each at least thirty feet long, were flapping heavily as it strove to lift higher from the sea into which its missile thrust had carried both it and its prey. With each powerful downpush, it rose a few inches higher. Presently it began climbing higher, but before it got too far away, it turned its head and allowed Wolff to see its eyes. They were black shields mirroring the flames of death. Wolff shuddered; he had never seen such naked lust for killing.

"Well may you shudder," Ipsewas said. His grinning head was thrust into the cave of the shell. "That was one of Podarge's pets. Podarge hates the Lord and would attack him herself if she got the chance, even if she knew it would be her end. Which it would. She knows she can't get near the Lord, but she can tell her pets to eat up the Eyes of the Lord. Which they do, as you have seen."

Wolff left the cavern of the shell and stood for awhile, watching the shrinking figure of the eagle and its kill.

"Who is Podarge?"

"She is, like me, one of the Lord's monsters. She, too, once lived on the shores of the Aegean; she was a beautiful young girl. That was when the great king Priamos and the godlike Akhilleus and crafty Odysseus lived. I knew them all; they would spit on the Kretan Ipsewas, the once-brave sailor and spear-fighter, if they could see me now. But I was talking of Podarge. The Lord took her to this world and fashioned a monstrous body and placed her brain within it.

"She lives up there someplace, in a cave on the very face of the mountain. She hates the Lord; she also hates every normal human being and will eat them, if her pets don't get them first. But most of all she hates the Lord."

That seemed to be all that Ipsewas knew about her, except that Podarge had not been her name before the Lord had taken her. Also, he remembered having been well acquainted with her. Wolff questioned him further, for he was interested in what Ipsewas could tell him about Agamemnon and Achilles and Odysseus and the other heroes of Homer's epic. He told the zebrilla that Agamemnon was supposed to be a historical character. But what about Achilles and Odysseus? Had they really existed?

"Of course they did," Ipsewas said. He grunted, then continued, "I suppose you're curious about those days. But there is little I can tell you. It's been too long ago. Too many idle days. Days?—centuries, millenia!—the Lord alone knows. Too much alcohol, too."

During the rest of the day and part of the night, Wolff tried to pump Ipsewas, but he got little for his trouble. Ipsewas, bored, drank half his supply of nuts and finally passed out snoring. Dawn came green and golden around the mountain. Wolff stared down into the waters, so clear that he could see the hundreds of thousands of fish, of fantastic configurations and splendors of colors. A bright-orange seal rose from the depths, a creature like a living diamond in its mouth. A purple-veined octopus, shooting backward, jetted by the seal. Far, far down, something enormous and white appeared for a second, then dived back toward the bottom.

Presently the roar of surf came to him, and a thin white line frothed at the base of Thayaphayawoed. The mountain, so smooth at a distance, was now broken by fissures, by juts and spires, by rearing scarps and frozen fountains of stone. Thayaphayawoed went up and up and up; it seemed to hang over the world.

Wolff shook Ipsewas until, moaning and muttering, the zebrilla rose to his feet. He blinked reddened eyes, scratched, coughed, then reached for another punchnut. Finally, at Wolff's urging, he steered the sailfish so that its course paralleled the base of the mountain.

"I used to be familiar with this area," he said. "Once I thought about climbing the mountain, finding the Lord, and trying to . . ." He paused, scratched his head, winced, and said, "Kill him! There! I knew I could remember the word. But it was no use. I didn't have the guts to try it alone."

"You're with me now," Wolff said.

Ipsewas shook his head and took another drink. "Now isn't then. If you'd been with me then . . . Well, what's the use of talking? You weren't even born then. Your great-great-great-great-grandfather wasn't born then. No, it's too late."

He was silent while he busied himself with guiding the sail-fish through an opening in the mountain. The great creature abruptly swerved; the cartilage sail folded up against the mast of stiff bone-braced cartilage; the body rose on a huge wave. And then they were within the calm waters of a narrow, steep, and dark fjord.

Ipsewas pointed at a series of rough ledges.

"Take that. You can get far. How far I don't know. I got tired and scared and I went back to the Garden. Never to return, I thought."

Wolff pleaded with Ipsewas. He said that he needed Ipsewas' strength very much and that Chryseis needed him. But the zebrilla shook his massive somber head.

"I'll give you my blessing, for what it's worth."

"And I thank you for what you've done," Wolff said. "If you hadn't cared enough to come after me, I'd still be swinging at the end of a rope. Maybe I'll see you again. With Chryseis."

"The Lord is too powerful," Ipsewas replied. "Do you think you have a chance against a being who can create his own private universe?"

"I have a chance," Wolff said. "As long as I fight and use my wits and have some luck, I have a chance."

He jumped off the decklike shell and almost slipped on the wet rock. Ipsewas called, "A bad omen, my friend!"

Wolff turned and smiled at him and shouted, "I don't believe in omens, my superstitious Greek friend! So long!"

CHAPTER FIVE

He began climbing and did not stop to look down until about an hour had passed. The great white body of the *histoikhthys* was a slim, pale thread by then, and Ipsewas was only a black dot on its axis. Although he knew he could not be seen, he waved at Ipsewas and resumed climbing.

Another hour's scrambling and clinging on the rocks brought him out of the fjord and onto a broad ledge on the face of the cliff. Here it was bright sunshine again. The mountain seemed as high as ever, and the way was as hard. On the other hand, it seemed no more difficult, although that was nothing over which to exult. His hands and knees were bleeding, and the ascent had made him tired. At first he was going to spend the night there, but he changed his mind. As long as the light lasted, he should take advantage of it.

Again he wondered if Ipsewas was correct about the gworl probably having taken just this route. Ipsewas claimed that there were other passages along the mountain where the sea rammed against it, but these were far away. He had looked for signs that the gworl had come this way and had found none. This did not mean that they had taken another path—if you could call this ragged verticality a path.

A few minutes later he came to one of the many trees that grew out of the rock itself. Beneath its twisted gray branches and mottled brown and green leaves were broken and empty nutshells and the cores of fruit. They were fresh. Somebody had paused for lunch not too long ago. The sight gave him new strength. Also, there was enough meat left in the nut shells for him to half-satisfy the pangs in his belly. The remnants of the fruits gave him moisture to put in his dry mouth.

Six days he climbed, and six nights rested. There was life on the face of the perpendicular, small trees and large bushes grew on the ledges, from the caves, and from the cracks. Birds of all sorts abounded, and many little animals. These fed off the berries and nuts or on each other. He killed birds with stones and ate their flesh raw. He discovered flint and chipped out a crude but sharp knife. With this, he made a short spear with a wooden shaft and another flint for the tip. He grew lean and hard with thick callouses on his hands and feet and knees. His beard lengthened.

On the morning of the seventh day, he looked out from a ledge and estimated that he must be at least twelve thousand feet above the sea. Yet the air was no thinner or colder than when he had begun climbing. The sea, which must have been at least two hundred miles across, looked like a broad river. Beyond was the rim of the world's edge, the Garden from which he had set out in pursuit of Chryseis and the gworl. It was as narrow as a cat's whisker. Beyond it, only the green sky.

A midnoon on the eighth day, he came across a snake feeding upon a dead gworl. Forty feet long, it was covered with black diamond spots and crimson seals of Solomon. The feet that arrayed both sides grew out of the body without blessing of legs and were distressingly human-shaped. Its jaws were lined with three rows of sharkish teeth.

Wolff attacked it boldly, because he saw that a knife was sticking from its middle part and fresh blood was still oozing out. The snake hissed, uncoiled, and began to back away. Wolff stabbed at it a few times, and it lunged at him. Wolff drove the point of the flint into one of the large dull-green eyes. The snake hissed loudly and reared, its two-score of five-toed feet kicking. Wolff tore the spear loose from the bloodied eye and thrust it into the dead white area just below the snake's jaw. The flint went in deeply; the snake jerked so violently that it tore the shaft loose from Wolff's grip. But the creature fell over on its side, breathing deeply, and after awhile it died.

There was a scream above him, followed by a shadow. Wolff had heard that scream before, when he had been on the sailfish. He dived to one side and rolled across the ledge. Coming to a fissure, he crawled within it and turned to see what had threatened him. It was one of the enormous wide-winged, green-bodied, red-headed, yellow-beaked eagles. It was crouched on the snake and tearing out gobbets with a beak as sharp as the teeth in the snake's jaws. Between gulps it glared at Wolff, who tried to shrink even further within the protection of the fissure.

Wolff had to stay within his crevice until the bird had filled its crop. Since this took all of the rest of the day and the eagle did not leave the two corpses that night, Wolff became hungry, thirsty, and more than uncomfortable. By morning, he was also getting angry. The eagle was sitting by the two corpses, its wings folded around its body and its head drooping. Wolff thought that, if it were asleep, now would be the time to make a break. He stepped out of the crevice, wincing with the pain of stiff muscles. As he did so, the eagle jerked its head up, half-spread its wings, and screamed at him. Wolff retreated to the crevice.

By noon, the eagle still showed no intention of leaving. It ate little and seemed to be fighting drowsiness. Occasionally it belched. The sun beat down upon the bird and the two corpses. All three stank. Wolff began to despair. For all he knew, the eagle would remain until it had picked both reptile and gworl bare to the bone. By that time, he, Wolff, would be half-dead of starvation and thirst.

He left the fissure and picked up the spear. This had fallen out when the bird had ripped out the flesh around it. He jabbed threateningly at the eagle, which glared, hissed, and then screamed at him. Wolff shouted back and slowly backed away from the bird. It advanced with short slow steps, rolling slightly. Wolff stopped, yelled again, and jumped at the eagle. Startled, it leaped back and screamed again.

Wolff resumed his cautious retreat, but this time the eagle did not go after him. Only when the curve of the mountain took the predator out of view did Wolff resume climbing. He made sure that there was always a place to dodge into if the bird should come after him. However, no shadow fell on him. Apparently the eagle had wanted only to protect its food.

The middle of the next morning, he came across another gworl. This one had a smashed leg and was sitting with its back against the trunk of a small tree. It brandished a knife at a dozen red and rangy hoglike beasts with hooves like those of mountain goats. These paced back and forth before the crippled gworl and grunted in their throats. Now and then one made a short charge, but stopped a few feet away from the waving knife.

Wolff climbed a boulder and began throwing rocks at the hooved carnivores. A minute later, he wished he had not drawn attention to himself. The beasts clambered up the steep boulder as if stairs had been built for them. Only by rapid thrusting with the spear did he manage to push them back down on the ledge below. The flint tip dug into their tough hides a little but not enough to seriously hurt them.

Squealing, they landed on the rock below, only to scramble back up toward him. Their boar-tusks slashed close to him; a pair almost snipped one of his feet. He was busy trying to keep them from swarming over him when a moment came when all were on the ledge and none on the boulder. He dropped his spear, lifted a rock twice the size of his head, and hurled it down on the back of a boar. The beast screamed and tried to crawl away on its two undamaged front legs. The pack closed in on his paralyzed rear legs and began eating them. When the wounded beast turned to defend himself, he was seized by the throat. In a moment he was dead and being torn apart.

Wolff picked up his spear, climbed down the other side of the rock, and walked to the gworl. He kept an eye upon the feeders, but they did no more than raise their heads briefly to check on him before resuming their tearing at the carcass.

The gworl snarled at Wolff and held its knife ready. Wolff stopped far enough away so that he could dodge if the knife were thrown. A splinter of bone stuck out from the ravaged leg below the knee. The eyes of the gworl, sunk under the pads of cartilage on its low forehead, looked glassy.

Wolff had an unexpected reaction. He had thought that he would at once and savagely kill any gworl he came across. But now he wanted to talk to him. So lonely had he become during the days and nights of climbing that he was glad to speak even to this loathsome creature.

He said, in Greek, "Is there any way in which I can help you?"

The gworl spoke in the back-of-the-throat syllables of its kind and raised the knife. Wolff started walking toward it, then hurled himself to one side as the knife whished by his head. He retrieved the knife, then walked up to the gworl and spoke to him again. The thing grated back, but in a weaker voice. Wolff, bending over to repeat his question, was struck in the face with a mass of saliva.

That triggered off his hate and fear. He rammed the knife into the thick neck; the gworl kicked violently several times and died. Wolff wiped the knife on the dark fur and looked through the leather bag attached to the gworl's belt. It contained dried meat, dried fruit, some dark, hard bread, and a canteen with a fiery liquor. Wolff was not sure about where the meat came from, but he told himself that he was too hungry to be picky. Biting into the bread was an experience; it was almost as hard as stone but, when softened with saliva, tasted like graham crackers.

Wolff kept on climbing. The days and nights passed with no more signs of the gworl. The air was as thick and warm as at sea level, yet he estimated that he must be at least 30,000 feet up. The sea below was a thin silver girdle around the waist of the world.

That night he awakened to feel dozens of small furry hands on his body. He struggled, only to find that the many hands were too strong. They gripped him fast while others tied his hands and feet together with a rope that had a grassy texture. Presently he was lifted high and carried out onto the stone apron before the small cave in which he had slept. The moonlight showed several score bipeds, each about two and a half feet high. They were covered with sleek gray fur, mouselike, but had a white ruff around their necks. The faces were black and pushed in and resembled a bat's. Their ears were enormous and pointed.

Silently, they rushed him over the apron and into another fissure. This opened to reveal a large chamber about thirty feet wide and twenty high. Moonlight bored through a crack in the ceiling and revealed what his nose had already detected, a pile of bones with some rotting flesh. He was set down near the bones while his captors retreated to one corner of the cave. They began talking, or at least twittering, among themselves. One walked over to Wolff, looked at him a moment, and sank onto his knees by Wolff's throat. A second later, he was gnawing at the throat with tiny but very sharp teeth. Others followed him; teeth began chewing all over his body.

It was all done in a literally deadly silence. Even Wolff made no noise beyond his harsh breathing as he struggled. The sharp little pains of the teeth quickly passed, as if some mild anaesthetic were being released into his blood.

He began to feel drowsy. Despite himself, he quit fighting. A pleasant numbness spread through him. It did not seem worthwhile to battle for his life; why not go out pleasantly? At least his death would not be useless. There was something noble in giving his body so that these little beings could fill their bellies and be well-fed and happy for a few days.

A light burst into the cave. Through the warm haze, he saw the batfaces leap away from him and run to the extreme end of the cave, where they cowered together. The light became stronger and was revealed as a torch of burning pine. An old man's face followed the light and bent over him. He had a long white beard, a sunken mouth, a curved sharp nose, and huge supraorbital ridges with bristling eyebrows. A dirty white robe covered his shrunken body. His big-veined hand held a staff on the end of which was a sapphire, large as Wolff's fist, carved in the image of a harpy.

Wolff tried to speak but could only mutter a tangled speech, as if he were coming up out of ether after an operation. The old man gestured with the staff, and several of the batfaces detached themselves from the mass of fur. They scurried sideways across the floor, their slanted eyes turned fearfully toward the old man. Quickly, they untied Wolff. He managed to rise to his feet, but he was so wobbly that the old man had to support him out of the cave.

The ancient spoke in Mycenaean Greek. "You'll feel better soon. The venom does not last long."

"Who are you? Where are you taking me?"

"Out of this danger," the old man said. Wolff pondered the enigmatic answer. By the time that his mind and body were functioning well again, they had come to another entrance to a cave. They went through a complex of chambers that gradually led them upward. When they had covered about two miles, the old man stopped before a cave with a large iron door. He handed the torch to Wolff, pulled the door open, and waved him on in. Wolff entered into a large cavern bright with torches. The door clanged behind him, succeeded by the thud of a bolt shooting fast.

The first thing that struck him was the choking odor. The next, the two green red-headed eagles that closed in on him. One spoke in a voice like a giant parrot's and ordered him to march on ahead. He did so, noting at the same time that the batfaces must have removed his knife. The weapon would not have done him much good. The cave was thronged with the birds, each of which towered above him.

Against one wall were two cages made of thin iron bars. In one was a group of six gworl. In the other was a tall well-built youth wearing a deerskin breech-cloth. He grinned at Wolff and said, "So you made it! How you've changed!"

Only then did the reddish-bronze hair, long upper lip, and craggy but merry face become familiar. Wolff recognized the man who had thrown the horn from the gworl-besieged boulder and who called himself Kickaha.

CHAPTER SIX

Wolff did not have time to reply, for the cage door was opened by one of the eagles, who used his foot as effectively as a hand. A powerful head and hard beak shoved him into the cage; the door ground shut behind him.

"So, here you are," Kickaha said in a rich baritone voice. "The question is, what do we do now? Our stay here may be short and unpleasant."

Wolff, looking through the bars, saw a throne carved out of rock, and on it a woman. A half-woman, rather, for she had wings instead of arms and the lower part of her body was that of a bird. The legs, however, were much thicker in proportion than those of a normal-sized Earth eagle. They had to support more weight, Wolff thought, and he knew that here was another of the Lord's laboratory-produced monsters. She must be the Podarge of whom Ipsewas had spoken.

From the waist up she was such a woman as few men are privileged to see. Her skin was white as a milky opal, her breasts superb, the throat a column of beauty. The hair was long and black and straight and fell on both sides of a face that was even more beautiful than Chryseis', an admission that he had not thought it possible to evoke from him.

However, there was something horrible in the beauty: a madness. The eyes were fierce as those of a caged falcon teased beyond endurance.

Wolff tore his eyes from hers and looked about the cave. "Where is Chryseis?" he whispered.

"Who?" Kickaha whispered back.

With a few quick sentences, Wolff described her and what had happened to him.

Kickaha shook his head. "I've never seen her."

"But the gworl?"

"There were two bands of them. The other must have Chryseis and the horn. Don't worry about them. If we don't talk our way out of this, we're done for. And in a very hideous way."

Wolff asked about the old man. Kickaha replied that he had once been Podarge's lover. He was an aborigine, one of those who had been brought into this universe shortly after the Lord had fashioned it. The harpy now kept him to do the menial work which required human hands. The old man had come at Podarge's order to rescue Wolff from the batfaces, undoubtedly because she had long ago heard from her pets of Wolff's presence in her domain.

Podarge stirred restlessly on her throne and unfolded her wings. They came together before her with a splitting noise like distant lightning.

"You two there!" she shouted. "Quit your whispering! Kickaha, what more do you have to say for yourself before I loose my pets?"

"I can only repeat, at the risk of seeming tiresome, what I said before!" Kickaha replied loudly. "I am as much the enemy of the Lord as you, and he hates me, he would kill me! He knows I stole his horn and that I'm a danger to him. His Eyes rove the four levels of the world and fly up and down the mountains to find me. And . . ."

"Where is this horn you said you stole from the Lord? Why don't you have it now? I think you are lying to save your worthless carcass!"

"I told you that I opened a gate to the next world and that I threw it to a man who appeared at the gate. He stands before you now."

Podarge turned her head as an eagle swivels hers, and she glared at Wolff. "I see no horn. I see only some tough stringy meat behind a black beard!"

"He says that another band of gworl stole it from him," Kickaha replied. "He was chasing after them to get it back when the batfaces captured him and you so magnanimously rescued him. Release us, gracious and beautiful Podarge, and we will get the horn back. With it, we will be in a position to fight the Lord. He can be beaten! He may be the powerful Lord, but he is not all-powerful! If he were, he would have found us and the horn long ago!"

Podarge stood up, preened her wings, and walked down the steps from the throne and across the floor to the cage. She did not bob as a bird does when walking, but strode stiff-legged.

"I wish that I could believe you," she said in a lower but just as intense voice. "If only I could! I have waited through the years and the centuries and the millenia, oh, so long that my heart aches to think of the time! If I thought that the weapons for striking back at him had finally come within my hands . . ."

She stared at them, held her wings out before her, and said, "See! 'My hands,' I said. But I do not have hands, nor the body that once was mine. That . . ." And she burst into a raging invective that made Wolff shrink. It was not the words but the fury, bordering on divinity or mindlessness, that made him grow cold.

"If the Lord can be overthrown—and I believe he can—you will be given back your human body," Kickaha said when she had finished.

She panted with a clench of her anger and stared at them with the lust of murder. Wolff felt that all was lost, but her next words showed that the passion was not for them.

"The old Lord has been gone for a long time, so the rumor says. I sent one of my pets to investigate, and she came back with a strange tale. She said that there is a new Lord there, but she did not know whether or not it was the same Lord in a new body. I sent her back to the Lord, who refused my pleas to be given my rightful body again. So it does not matter whether or not there is another Lord. He is just as evil and hateful as the old one, if he is indeed not the old one. But I must know!

"First, whoever now is the Lord must die. Then I will find out if he had a new body or not. If the old Lord has left this universe, I will track him through the worlds and find him!"

"You can't do that without the horn," Kickaha said. "It and it alone opens the gate without a counter-device in the other world."

"What have I to lose?" Podarge said. "If you are lying and betray me, I will have you in the end, and the hunt might be fun. If you mean what you say, then we will see what happens."

She spoke to the eagle beside her, and it opened the gate. Kickaha and Wolff followed the harpy across the cave to a great table with chairs around it. Only then did Wolff see that the chamber was a treasure house; the loot of a world was piled up in it. There were large open chests crammed with gleaming jewels, pearl necklaces, and golden and silver cups of exquisite shape. There were small figurines of ivory and of some shining hard-grained black wood. There were magnificent paintings. Armor and weapons of all kinds, except firearms, were piled carelessly at various places.

Podarge commanded them to sit down in ornately wrought chairs with carved lion's feet. She beckoned with a wing, and out of the shadows stepped a young man. He carried a heavy golden tray on which were three finely chiseled cups of crystal-quartz. These were fashioned as leaping fish with wide open mouths; the mouths were filled with a rich dark red wine.

"One of her lovers," Kickaha whispered in answer to Wolff's curious stare at the handsome blond youth. "Carried by her eagles from the level known as Dracheland or Teutonia. Poor fellow! But it's better than being eaten alive by her pets, and he always has the hope of escaping to make his life bearable."

Kickaha drank and breathed out satisfaction at the heavy but blood-brightening taste. Wolff felt the wine writhe as if alive. Podarge gripped the cup between the tips of her two wings and lifted it to her lips.

"To the death and damnation of the Lord. Therefore, to your success!"

The two drank again. Podarge put her cup down and flicked Wolff lightly across the face with the ends of the feathers of one wing. "Tell me your story."

Wolff talked for a long while. He ate from slices of a roast goat-pig, a light brown bread, and fruit, and he drank the wine. His head began reeling, but he talked on and on, stopping only when Podarge questioned him about something. Fresh torches replaced the old and still he talked.

Abruptly, he awoke. Sunshine was coming in from another cave, lighting the empty cup and the table on which his head had lain while he had slept. Kickaha, grinning, stood by him.

"Let's go," he said. "Podarge wants us to get started early. She's eager for revenge. And I want to get out before she changes her mind. You don't know how lucky we are. We're the only prisoners she's ever given freedom."

Wolff sat up and groaned with the ache in his shoulders and neck. His head felt fuzzy and a little heavy, but he had had worse hangovers.

"What did you do after I fell asleep?" he said.

Kickaha smiled broadly. "I paid the final price. But it wasn't bad, not bad at all. Rather peculiar at first, but I'm an adaptable fellow."

They walked out of the cave into the next one and from thence onto the wide lip of stone jutting from the cliff. Wolff turned for one last look and saw several eagles, green monoliths, standing by the entrance to the inner cave. There was a flash of white skin and black wings as Podarge crossed stiff-legged before the giant birds.

"Come on," Kickaha said. "Podarge and her pets are hungry. You didn't see her try to get the gworl to plead for mercy. I'll say one thing for them, they didn't whine or cry. They spat at her."

Wolff jumped as a ripsaw scream came from the cave mouth.

Kickaha took Wolff's arm and urged him into a fast walk. More jagged cries tore from eagle beaks, mingled with the ululations from beings in fear and pain of death.

"That'd be us, too," Kickaha said, "if we hadn't had something to trade for our lives."

They began climbing and by nightfall were three thousand feet higher. Kickaha untied the knapsack of leather from his back and produced various articles. Among these was a box of matches, with one of which he started a fire. Meat and bread and a small bottle of the Rhadamanthean wine followed. The bag and the contents were gifts from Podarge.

"We've got about four days of climbing before we get to the next level," the youth said. "Then, the fabulous world of Amerindia.'

Wolff started to ask questions, but Kickaha said that he ought to explain the physical structure of the planet. Wolff listened patiently, and when he had heard Kickaha out, he did not scoff. Moreover, Kickaha's explanation corresponded with what he had so far seen. Wolff's intentions to ask how Kickaha, obviously a native of Earth, had come here were frustrated. The youth, complaining that he had not slept for a long time and had had an especially exhausting night, fell asleep.

Wolff stared for awhile into the flames of the dying fire. He had seen and experienced much in a short time, but he had much more to go through. That is, he would if he lived. A whooping cry rose from the depths, and a great green eagle screamed somewhere in the air along the mountain-face.

He wondered where Chryseis was tonight. Was she alive, and if so, how was she faring? And where was the horn? Kickaha had said that they had to find the horn if they were to have any success at all. Without it, they would inevitably lose.

So thinking, he too fell asleep.

Four days later, when the sun was in the midpoint of its course around the planet, they pulled themselves over the rim. Before them was a plain that rolled for at least 160 miles before the horizon dropped it out of sight. To both sides, perhaps a hundred miles away, were mountain ranges. These might be large enough to cause comparison with the Himalayas. But they were mice beside the monolith, Abharhploonta, that dominated this section of the multilevel planet. Abharhploonta was, so Kickaha claimed, fifteen hundred miles from the rim, yet it looked no more than fifty miles away. It towered fully as high as the mountain up which they had just climbed.

"Now you get the idea," Kickaha said. "This world is not pear-shaped. It's a planetary Tower of Babylon. A series of staggered columns, each smaller than the one beneath it. On the very apex of this Earth-sized tower is the palace of the Lord. As you can see, we have a long way to go.

"But it's a great life while it lasts! I've had a wild and wonderful time! If the Lord struck me at this moment, I couldn't complain. Although, of course, I would, being human and therefore bitter about being cut off in my prime! And believe me, my friend, I'm prime!"

Wolff could not help smiling at the youth. He looked so gay and buoyant, like a bronze statue suddenly touched into animation and overflowingly joyous because he was alive.

"Okay!" Kickaha cried. "The first thing we have to do is get some fitting clothes for you! Nakedness is chic in the level below, but not on this one. You have to wear at least a breech-cloth and a feather in your hair; otherwise the natives will have contempt for you. And contempt here means slavery or death for the contemptible."

He began walking along the rim, Wolff with him.

"Observe how green and lush the grass is and how it is as high as our knees, Bob. It affords pasture for browsers and grazers. But it is also high enough to conceal the beasts that feed on the grass-eaters. So beware! The plains puma and the dire wolf and the striped hunting dog and the giant weasel prowl through the grasses. Then there is Felis Atrox, whom I call the atrocious lion. He once roamed the plains of the North American Southwest, became extinct there about 10,000 years ago. He's very much alive here, one-third larger than the African lion and twice as nasty.

"Hey, look there! Mammoths!"

Wolff wanted to stop to watch the huge gray beasts, which were about a quarter of a mile away. But Kickaha urged him on. "There're plenty more around, and there'll be times when you wish there weren't. Spend your time watching the grass. If it moves contrary to the wind, tell me."

They walked swiftly for two miles. During this time, they came close to a band of wild horses. The stallions whickered and raced up to investigate them, then stood their ground, pawing and snorting, until the two had passed. They were magnificent animals, tall, sleek, and black or glossy red or spotted white and black.

"Nothing of your Indian pony there," Kickaha said. "I think the Lord imported nothing but the best stock."

Presently, Kickaha stopped by a pile of rocks. "My marker," he said. He walked straight inward across the plain from the cairn. After a mile they came to a tall tree. The youth leaped up, grabbed the lowest branch, and began climbing. Half-way up, he reached a hollow and brought out a large bag. On returning, Kickaha took out of the bag two bows, two quivers of arrows, a deerskin breechcloth, and a belt with a skin scabbard in which was a long steel knife.

Wolff put on the loincloth and belt and took the bow and quiver.

"You know how to use these?" Kickaha said.

"I've practised all my life."

"Good. You'll get more than one chance to put your skill to the test. Let's go. We've many a mile to cover."

They began wolf-trotting: run a hundred steps, walk a hundred steps. Kickaha pointed to the range of mountains to their right.

"There is where my tribe, the Hrowakas, the Bear People, live. Eighty miles away. Once we get there, we can take it easy for awhile, and make preparations for the long journey ahead of us."

"You don't look like an Indian," Wolff said.

"And you, my friend, don't look like a sixty-six-year old man, either. But here we are. Okay. I've put off telling my story because I wanted to hear yours first. Tonight I'll talk."

They did not speak much more that day. Wolff exclaimed now and then at the animals he saw. There were great herds of bison, dark, shaggy, bearded, and far larger than their cousins of Earth. There were other herds of horses and a creature that looked like the prototype of the camel. More mammoths and then a family of steppe mastodons. A pack of six dire wolves raced alongside the two for awhile at a distance of a hundred yards. These stood almost as high as Wolff's shoulder.

Kickaha, seeing Wolff's alarm, laughed and said, "They won't attack us unless they're hungry. That isn't very likely with all the game around here. They're just curious."

Presently, the giant wolves curved away, their speed increasing as they flushed some striped antelopes out of a grove of trees.

"This is North America as it was a long time before the white man," Kickaha said. "Fresh, spacious, with a multitude of animals and a few tribes roaming around."

A flock of a hundred ducks flew overhead, honking. Out of the green sky, a hawk fell, struck with a thud, and the flock was minus one comrade. "The Happy Hunting Ground!" Kickaha cried. "Only it's not so happy sometimes!"

Several hours before the sun went around the mountain, they stopped by a small lake. Kickaha found the tree in which he had built a platform.

"We'll sleep here tonight, taking turns on watch. About the only animal that might attack us in the tree is the giant weasel, but he's enough to worry about. Besides, and worse, there could be war parties."

Kickaha left with his bow in hand and returned in fifteen minutes with a large buck rabbit. Wolff had started a small fire with little smoke; over this they roasted the rabbit. While they ate, Kickaha explained the topography of the country.

"Whatever else you can say about the Lord, you can't deny he did a good job of designing this world. You take this level, Amerindia. It's not really flat. It has a series of slight curves each about 160 miles long. These allow the water to run off, creeks and rivers and lakes to form. There's no snow anywhere on the planet—can't be, with no seasons and a fairly uniform climate. But it rains every day—the clouds come in from space somewhere."

They finished eating the rabbit and covered the fire. Wolff took first watch. Kickaha talked all through Wolff's turn at guard. And Wolff stayed awake through Kickaha's watch to listen.

In the beginning, a long time ago, more than 20,000 years, the Lords had dwelt in a universe parallel to Earth's. They were not known as the Lords then. There were not very many of them at that time, for they were the survivors of a millenia-long struggle with another species. They numbered perhaps ten thousand in all.

"But what they lacked in quantity they more than possessed in quality," Kickaha said. "They had a science and technology that makes ours, Earth's, look like the wisdom of Tasmanian aborigines. They were able to construct these private universes. And they did.

"At first each universe was a sort of playground, a microcosmic country club for small groups. Then, as was inevitable, since these people were human beings no matter how godlike in their powers, they quarreled. The feeling of property was, is, as strong in them as in us. There was a struggle among them. I suppose there were also deaths from accident and suicide. Also, the isolation and loneliness of the Lords made them megalomaniacs, natural when you consider that each played the part of a little god and came to believe in his role.

"To compress an eons-long story into a few words, the Lord who built this particular universe eventually found himself alone. Jadawin, was his name, and he did not even have a mate of his own kind. He did not want one. Why should he share this world with an equal, when he could be a Zeus with a million Europas, with the loveliest of Ledas?

"He had populated this world with beings abducted from

other universes, mainly Earth's, or created in the laboratories in the palace on top of the highest tier. He had created divine beauties and exotic monsters as he wished.

"The only trouble was, the Lords were not content to rule over just one universe. They began to covet the worlds of the others. And so the struggle was continued. They erected nearly impregnable defenses and conceived almost invincible offenses. The battle became a deadly game. This fatal play was inevitable, when you consider that boredom and ennui were enemies the Lords could not keep away. When you are near-omnipotent, and your creatures are too lowly and weak to interest you forever, what thrill is there besides risking your immortality against another immortal?"

"But how did you come into this?" Wolff said.

"I? My name on Earth was Paul Janus Finnegan. My middle name was my mother's family name. As you know, it also happens to be that of the Latin god of gates and of the old and new year, the god with two faces, one looking ahead and one looking behind."

Kickaha grinned and said, "Janus is very appropriate, don't you think? I am a man of two worlds, and I came through the gate between. Not that I have ever returned to Earth or want to. I've had adventures and I've gained a stature here I never could have had on that grimy old globe. Kickaha isn't my only name, and I'm a chief on this tier and a big shot of sorts on other tiers. As you will find out."

Wolff was beginning to wonder about him. He had been so evasive that Wolff suspected Kickaha had another identity about which he did not intend to talk.

"I know what you're thinking, but don't you believe it," Kickaha said. "I'm a trickster, but I'm leveling with you. By the way, did you know how I came by my name among the Bear People? In their language, a *kickaha* is a mythological character, a semidivine trickster. Something like the Old Man Coyote of the Plains Indians or Nanabozho of the Ojibway or Wakdjunkaga of the Winnebago. Some day I'll tell you how I earned that name and how I became a councilor of the Hrowakas. But I've more important things to tell you now."

CHAPTER SEVEN

In 1941, at the age of twenty-three Paul Finnegan had volunteered for the U.S. Cavalry because he loved horses. A short time later, he found himself driving a tank. He was with the Eighth Army and so eventually crossed the Rhine. One day, after having helped take a small town, he discovered an extraordinary object in the ruins of the local museum. It was a crescent of silvery metal, so hard that hammer blows did not dent it nor an acetylene torch melt it.

"I asked some of the citizens about it. All they knew was that it had been in the museum a long time. A professor of chemistry, after making some tests on it, had tried to interest the University of Munich in it but had failed.

"I took it home with me after the war, along with other souvenirs. Then I went back to the University of Indiana. My father had left me enough money to see me through for a few years, so I had a nice little apartment, a sports car, and so on.

"A friend of mine was a newspaper reporter. I told him about the crescent and its peculiar properties and unknown composition. He wrote a story about it which was printed in Bloomington, and the story was picked up by a syndicate. It didn't create much interest among scientists—in fact, they wanted nothing to do with it.

"Three days later, a man calling himself Mr. Vannax appeared at my apartment. I thought he was Dutch because of his name and his foreign accent. He wanted to see the crescent. I obliged. He got very excited, although he tried to appear calm. He said he'd like to buy it from me. I asked how much he'd pay, and he said he'd give ten thousand dollars, but no more.

" 'Sure you can go higher,' I said," Kickaha continued. " 'Because if you don't, you'll get nowhere.'

" 'Twenty thousand?' Vannax said.

" 'Let's pump it up a bit,' I said.

" 'Thirty thousand?' "

Finnegan decided to plunge. He asked Vannax if he would pay $100,000. Vannax became even redder in the face and swelled up "like a hoppy toad", as Finnegan-Kickaha said. But he replied that he would have the sum in twenty-four hours.

"Then I knew I really had something," Kickaha said to Wolff. "The question was, what? Also, why did this Vannax character so desperately want it? And what kind of a nut was he? No one with good sense, no normal human being, would rise so fast to the bait. He'd be cagier."

"What did Vannax look like?" Wolff asked.

"Oh, he was a big guy, a well-preserved sixty-five. He had an eagle beak and eagle eyes. He was dressed in expensive conservative clothes. He had a powerful personality, but he was trying to restrain it, to be real nice. And having a hell of a time doing it. He seemed to be a man who wasn't used to being balked in any thing."

" 'Make it $300,000, and it's yours' I said. I never dreamed he'd say yes. I thought he'd get made and take off. Because I wasn't going to sell the crescent, not if he offered me a million."

Vannax, although furious, said that he would pay $300,000 but Finnegan would have to give him an additional twenty-four hours.

" 'You have to tell me why you want the crescent and what good it is first,' I said.

" 'Nothing doing!' he shouted. 'It is enough for you to rob me, you pig of a merchant, you, you earth . . . worm!'

" 'Get out before I throw you out. Or before I call the police,' I said."

Vannax began shouting in a foreign tongue. Finnegan went into his bedroom and came out with a .45 automatic. Vannax did not know it was not loaded. He left, although he was cursing and talking to himself all the way to his 1940 Rolls-Royce.

That night Finnegan had trouble getting to sleep. It was after 2:00 P.M. before he succeeded, and even then he kept waking up. During one of his rousings he heard a noise in the front room. Quietly, he rolled out of bed and took the .45, now loaded, from under his pillow. On the way to the bedroom door he picked up his flashlight from the bureau.

Its beam caught Vannax stooping over in the middle of the living room. The silvery crescent was in his hand.

"Then I saw the second crescent on the floor. Vannax had brought another with him. I'd caught him in the act of placing the two together to form a complete circle. I didn't know why he was doing it, but I found out a moment later.

"I told him to put his hands up. He did so, but he lifted his foot to step into the circle. I told him not to move even a trifle, or I'd shoot. He put one foot inside the circle, anyway. So I fired. I shot over his head, and the slug went into a corner of the room. I just wanted to scare him, figuring if he got shaken up enough he might start talking. He was scared all right; he jumped back.

"I walked across the room while he backed up toward the door. He was babbling like a maniac, threatening me in one breath and offering me half a million in the next. I thought I'd back him up against the door and jam the .45 in his belly. He'd really talk then, spill his guts out about the crescent.

"But as I followed him across the room I stepped into the circle formed by the two crescents. He saw what I was doing and screamed at me not to. Too late then. He and the apartment disappeared, and I found myself still in the circle—only it wasn't quite the same—and in this world. In the palace of the Lord, on top of the world."

Kickaha said he might have gone into shock then. But he had avidly read fantasy and science-fiction since the fourth grade of grammar school. The idea of parallel universes and devices for transition between them was familiar. He had been conditioned to accept such concepts. In fact, he half-believed in them. Thus he was flexible-minded enough to bend without breaking and then bounce back. Although frightened, he was at the same time excited and curious.

"I figured out why Vannax hadn't followed me through the gate. The two crescents, placed together, formed a 'circuit'. But they weren't activated until a living being stepped within whatever sort of 'field' they radiated. Then one semicircle remained behind on Earth while the other was gated through to this universe, where it latched onto a semicircle waiting for it. In other words, it takes three crescents to make a circuit. One in the world to which you're going, and two in the one you're leaving. You step in; one crescent transfers over to the single one in the next universe, leaving only one crescent in the world you just left.

"Vannax must have come to Earth by means of these crescents. And he would not, could not, do so unless there had been a crescent already on Earth. Somehow, maybe we'll never know, he lost one of them on Earth. Maybe it was stolen by someone who didn't know its true value. Anyway, he must've been searching for it, and when that news story went out about the one I had found in Germany, he knew what it was. After talking to me, he concluded I might not sell it. So he got into my apartment with the crescent he did have. He was just about to complete the circle and pass on over when I stopped him.

"He must be stranded on Earth and unable to get here unless he finds another crescent. For all I know, there may be others on Earth. The one I got in Germany might not even be the one he lost."

Finnegan wandered about the "palace" for a long while. It was immense, staggeringly beautiful and exotic and filled with treasure, jewels and artifacts. There were also laboratories, or perhaps bioprocess chambers was a better title. In these, Finnegan saw strange creatures slowly forming within huge transparent cylinders. There were many consoles with many operating devices, but he had no idea what they did. The symbols beneath the buttons and levers were unfamiliar.

"I was lucky. The palace is filled with traps to snare or kill the uninvited. But they were not set—why, I don't know, any more than I knew then why the place was untenanted. But it was a break for me."

Finnegan left the palace for awhile to go through the exquisite garden that surrounded it. He came to the edge of the monolith on which the palace and garden were.

"You've seen enough to imagine how I felt when I looked over the edge. The monolith must be at least thirty thousand feet high. Below it is the tier that the Lord named Atlantis. I don't know whether the Earth myth of Atlantis was founded on this Atlantis or whether the Lord got the name from the myth.

"Below Atlantis is the tier called Dracheland. Then, Amerindia. One sweep of my eye took it in, just as you can see one side of the Earth from a rocket. No details, of course, just big clouds, large lakes, seas, and outlines of continents. And a good part of each successively lower tier was obscured by the one just above it.

"But I could make out the Tower of Babylon structure of this world, even though I didn't, at that time, understand what I was seeing. It was just too unexpected and alien for me to apprehend any sort of *gestalt*. It didn't mean anything."

Finnegan could, however, understand that he was in a desperate situation. He had no means of leaving the top of this world except by trying to return to Earth through the crescents. Unlike the sides of the other monoliths, the face of this one was smooth as a bearing ball. Nor was he going to use the crescents again, not with Vannax undoubtedly waiting for him.

Although he was in no danger of starving—there was food and water enough to last for years—he could not and did not want to stay there. He dreaded the return of the owner, for he might have a very nasty temper. There were some things in the palace which made Kickaha feel uneasy.

"But the gworl came," Kickaha said. "I suppose—I know—they came from another universe through a gate similar to that which had opened the way for me. At the time, I had no way of knowing how or why they were in the palace. But I was glad I'd gotten there first. If I'd fallen into their hands. . . ! Later, I figured out they were agents for another Lord. He's sent them to steal the horn. Now, I'd seen the horn during my wandering about the palace, and had even blown it. But I didn't know how to press the combinations of buttons on it to make it work. As a matter of fact, I didn't know its real purpose.

"The gworl came into the palace. A hundred or so of them. Fortunately, I saw them first. Right away, they let their lust for murder get them into trouble. They tried to kill some of the Eyes of the Lord, the eagle-sized ravens in the garden. These hadn't bothered me, perhaps because they thought I was a guest or didn't look dangerous.

"The gworl tried to slit a raven's throat, and the ravens attacked them. The gworl retreated into the palace, where the big birds followed them. There were blood and feathers and pieces of bumpy hairy hide and a few corpses of both sides all over that end of the palace. During the battle, I noticed a gworl coming out of a room with the horn. He went through the corridors as if looking for something."

Finnegan followed the gworl into another room, about the size of two dirigible hangars. This held a swimming pool and a number of interesting but enigmatic devices. On a marble pedestal was a large golden model of the planet. On each of its levels were several jewels. As Finnegan was to discover, the diamonds, rubies, and sapphires were arranged to form symbols. These indicated various points of resonance.

"Points of resonance?"

"Yes. The symbols were coded mnemonics of the combination of notes required to open gates at certain places. Some gates open to other universes, but others are simply gates between the tiers on this world. These enabled the Lord to travel instantaneously from one level to the next. Associated with the symbols were tiny models of outstanding characteristics of the resonant points on the various tiers."

The gworl with the horn must have been told by the Lord how to read the symbols. Apparently, he was testing for the Lord to make sure he had the correct horn. He blew seven notes toward the pool, and the waters parted to reveal a piece of dry land with scarlet trees around it and a green sky beyond.

"It was the conceit of the original Lord to enter into the Atlantean tier through the pool itself. I didn't know at that time where the gate led to. But I saw my only chance to escape from the trap of the palace, and I took it. Coming up from behind the gworl, I snatched the horn from his hand and pushed him sideways into the pool—not into the gate, but into the water.

"You never heard such squawks and screams and such thrashings around. All the fear they don't have for other things is packed into a dread of water. This gworl went down, came up sputtering and yelling, and then managed to grab hold of the side of the gate. A gate has definite edges, you know, tangible if changing.

"I heard roars and shouts behind me. A dozen gworl with big and bloody knives were entering the room. I dived into the hole, which had started shrinking. It was so small I scraped the skin off my knees going through. But I got through, and the hole closed. It took off both the arms of the gworl who was trying to get out of the water and follow me. I had the horn in my hand, and I was out of their reach for the time being."

Kickaha grinned as if relishing the memory. Wolff said,

"The Lord who sent the gworl ahead is the present Lord, right? Who is he?"

"Arwoor. The Lord who's missing was known as Jadawin. He must be the man who called himself Vannax. Arwoor moved in, and ever since he's been trying to find me and the horn."

Kickaha outlined what had happened to him since he had found himself on the Atlantean tier. During the twenty years (of Earth time), he had been living on one tier or another, always in disguise. The gworl and the ravens, now serving the new Lord Arwoor, had never stopped looking for him. But there were long periods of time, sometimes two or three years on end, when Kickaha had not been disturbed.

"Wait a minute," Wolff said. "If the gates between the tiers were closed, how did the gworl get down off the monolith to chase you?"

Kickaha had not been able to understand that either. However, when captured by the gworl in the Garden level, he had questioned them. Although surly, they had given him some answers. They had been lowered to the Atlantean tier by cords.

"Thirty thousand feet?" Wolff said.

"Sure, why not? The palace is a fabulous many-chambered storehouse. If I'd had a chance to look long enough, I'd have found the cords myself. Anyway, the gworl told me they were charged by the Lord Arwoor not to kill me. Even if it meant having to let me escape at the time. He wants me to enjoy a series of exquisite tortures. The gworl said that Arwoor had been working on new and subtle techniques, plus refining some of the well established methods. You can imagine how I was sweating it out on the journey back."

After his capture in the Garden, Kickaha was taken across Okeanos to the base of the monolith. While they were climbing up it, a raven Eye stopped them. He had carried the news of Kickaha's capture to the Lord, who sent him back with orders. The gworl were to split into two bands. One was to continue with Kickaha. The other was to return to the Garden rim. If the man who now had the horn were to return through the gate with it, he was to be captured. The horn would be brought back to the Lord.

Kickaha said, "I imagine Arwoor wanted you brought back, too. He probably forgot to relay such an order to the gworl through the raven. Or else he assumed you'd be taken to him, forgetting that the gworl are very literal-minded and unimaginative.

"I don't know why the gworl captured Chryseis. Perhaps they intend to use her as a peace-offering to the Lord. The gworl know he is displeased with them because I've led them such a long and sometimes even merry chase. They may mean to placate him with the former Lord's most beautiful masterpiece."

Wolff said, "Then the present Lord can't travel between tiers via the resonance points?"

"Not without the horn. And I'll bet he's in a hot-and-cold running sweat right now. There's nothing to prevent the gworl from using the horn to go to another universe and present it to another Lord. Nothing except their ignorance of where the resonance points are. If they should find one . . . However, they didn't use it by the boulder, so I imagine they won't try it elsewhere. They're vicious but not bright."

Wolff said, "If the Lords are such masters of super-science, why doesn't Arwoor use aircraft to travel?"

Kickaha laughed for a long time. Then he said, "That's the joker. The Lords are heirs to a science and power far surpassing Earth's. But the scientists and technicians of their people are dead. The ones now living know how to operate their devices, but they are incapable of explaining the principles behind them or of repairing them.

"The millenia-long power struggle killed off all but a few. These few, despite their vast powers, are ignoramuses. They're sybarites, megalomaniacs, paranoiacs, you name it. Anything but scientists.

"It's possible that Arwoor may be a dispossessed Lord. He had to run for his life, and it was only because Jadawin was gone for some reason from this world that Arwoor was able to gain possession of it. He came empty-handed into the palace; he has no access to any powers except those in the palace, many of which he may not know how to control. He's one up in this Lordly game of musical universes, but he's still handicapped."

Kickaha fell asleep. Wolff stared into the night, for he was on first watch. He did not find the story incredible, but he did think that there were holes in it. Kickaha had much more explaining to do. Then there was Chryseis. He thought of an achingly beautiful face with delicate bone structure and great cat-pupiled eyes. Where was Chryseis, how was she faring, and would he ever see her again?

CHAPTER EIGHT

During Wolff's second watch, something black and long and swift slipped through the moonlight between two bushes. Wolff sent an arrow into the predator, which gave a whistling scream and reared up on its hind legs, towering twice as high as a horse. Wolff fitted another arrow to the string and fired it into the white belly. Still the animal did not die, but went whistling and crashing away through the brush.

By then Kickaha, knife in hand, was beside him. "You were lucky," he said. "You don't always see them, and then, pffft! They go for the throat."

"I could have used an elephant gun," Wolff said, "and I'm not sure that would have stopped it. By the way, why don't the gworl—or the Indians, from what you've told me—use firearms?"

"It's strictly forbidden by the Lord. You see, the Lord doesn't like some things. He wants to keep his people at a certain population level, at a certain technological level, and within certain social structures. The Lord runs a tight planet.

"For instance, he likes cleanliness. You may have noticed that the folk of Okeanos are a lazy, happy-go-lucky lot. Yet they always clean up their messes. No litter anywhere. The same goes on this level, on every level. The Amerindians are also personally clean, and so are the Drachelanders and Atlanteans. The Lord wants it that way, and the penalty for disobedience is death."

"How does he enforce his rules?" Wolff asked.

"Mostly by having implanted them in the mores of the inhabitants. Originally, he had a close contact with the priests and medicine men, and by using religion—with himself as the deity—he formed and hardened the ways of the populace. He liked neatness, disliked firearms or any form of advanced technology. Maybe he was a romantic; I don't know. But the various societies on this world are mainly conformist and static."

"So there's no progress?"

"So what? Is progress necessarily desirable or a static society undesirable? Personally, though I detest the Lord's arrogance, his cruelty and lack of humanity, I approve of some of the things he's done. With some exceptions, I like this world, far prefer it to Earth."

"You're a romantic, too!"

"Maybe. This world is real and grim enough, as you already know. But it's free of grit and grime, of diseases of any kind, of flies and mosquitoes and lice. Youth lasts as long as you live. All in all, it's not such a bad place to live in. Not for me, anyway."

Wolff was on the last watch when the sun rounded the corner of the world. The starflies paled, and the sky was green wine. The air passed cool fingers over the two men and washed their lungs with invigorating currents. They stretched and then went down from the platform to hunt for breakfast. Later, full of roast rabbit and juicy berries, they renewed their journey.

The evening of the third day after, while the sun was a hand's breadth from slipping around the monolith, they were out on the plain. Ahead of them was a tall hill beyond which, so Kickaha said, was a small woods. One of the high trees there would give them refuge for the night.

Suddenly a party of about forty men rode around the hill. They were dark-skinned and wore their hair in two long braids. Their faces were painted with white and red streaks and black X's. Their lower arms bore small round shields, and they held lances or bows in their hands. Some wore bear-heads as helmets; others had feathers stuck into caps or wore bonnets with sweeping bird feathers.

Seeing the two men on foot before them, the riders yelled and urged their horses into a gallop. Lances tipped with steel points were leveled. Bows were fitted with arrows, and heavy steel axes or blade-studded clubs were lifted.

"Stand firm!" Kickaha said. He was grinning. "They are the Hrowakas, the Bear People. My people."

He stepped forward and lifted his bow above him with both hands. He shouted at the charging men in their own tongue, a speech with many glottalized stops, nasalized vowels, and a swift-rising but slow-descending intonation.

Recognizing him, they shouted, *"AngKungawas TreKickaha!"* They galloped by, their spears stabbing as closely as possible without touching him, the clubs and axes whistling across his face or above his head, and arrows plunging near his feet or even between them.

Wolff was given the same treatment, which he bore without flinching. Like Kickaha, he showed a smile, but he did not think that it was as relaxed.

The Hrowakas wheeled their horses and charged back. This time they pulled their beasts up short, rearing, kicking, and whinnying. Kickaha leaped up and dragged a feather-bonneted youth from his animal. Laughing and panting, the two wrestled on the ground until Kickaha had pinned the Hrowakas. Then Kickaha arose and introduced the loser to Wolff.

"NgashuTangis, one of my brothers-in-law."

Two Amerinds dismounted and greeted Kickaha with much embracing and excited speech. Kickaha waited until they were calmed down and then began to speak long and earnestly. He frequently jabbed his finger toward Wolff. After a fifteen-minute discourse, interrupted now and then by a brief question, he turned smiling to Wolff.

"We're in luck. They're on their way to raid the Tsenakwa, who live fairly close to the Trees of Many Shadows. I explained what we were doing here, though not all of it by any means. They don't know we're bucking the Lord himself, and I'm not about to tell them. But they do know we're on the trail of Chryseis and the gworl and that you're a friend of mine. They also know that Podarge is helping us. They've got a great respect for her and her eagles and would like to do her a favor if they could.

"They've got plenty of spare horses, so take your choice. Only thing I hate about this is that you won't get to visit the lodges of the Bear People and I'll miss seeing my two wives, Giushowei and Angwanat. But you can't have everything."

The warparty rode hard that day and the next, changing horses every half-hour. Wolff became saddle-sore—blanket-sore, rather. By the third morning he was in as good a shape as any of the Bear People and could stay on a horse all day without feeling that he had lockjaw in every muscle of his body and even in some of the bones.

The fourth day, the party was held up for eight hours. A herd of the giant bearded bison marched across their path; the beasts formed a column two miles across and ten miles long, a barrier that no one, man or animal, could cross. Wolff chafed, but the others were not too unhappy, because rider and horse alike needed a rest. Then, at the end of the column, a hundred Shanikotsa hunters rode by, intent on driving their lances and arrows into the bison on the fringes. The Hrowakas wanted to swoop down upon them and slay the entire group and only an impassioned speech by Kickaha kept them back. Afterwards, Kickaha told Wolff that the Bear People thought one of them was equal to ten of any other tribe.

"They're great fighters, but a little bit overconfident and arrogant. If you knew how many times I've had to talk them out of getting into situations where they would have been wiped out!"

They rode on, but were halted at the end of an hour by NgashuTangis, one of the scouts for that day. He charged in yelling and gesturing. Kickaha questioned him, then said to Wolff, "One of Podarge's pets is a couple of miles from here. She landed in a tree and requested NgashuTangis to bring me to her. She can't make it herself; she's been ripped up by a flock of ravens and is in a bad way. Hurry!"

The eagle was sitting on the lowest branch of a lone tree, her talons clutched about the narrow limb, which bent under her weight. Dried red-black blood covered her green feathers, and one eye had been torn out. With the other, she glared at the Bear People, who kept a respectful distance. She spoke in Mycenaean to Kickaha and Wolff.

"I am Aglaia. I know you of old, Kickaha—Kickaha the trickster. And I saw you, O Wolff, when you were a guest of great-winged Podarge, my sister and queen. She it was who sent many of us out to search for the dryad Chryseis and the gworl and the horn of the Lord. But I, I alone, saw them enter the Trees of Many Shadows on the other side of the plain.

"I swooped down on them, hoping to surprise them and seize the horn. But they saw me and formed a wall of knives against which I could only impale myself. So I flew back up, so high they could not see me. But I, far-sighted treader of the skies, could see them."

"They're arrogant, even while dying," Kickaha said softly in English to Wolff. "Rightly so."

The eagle drank water offered by Kickaha, and continued. "When night fell, they camped at the edge of a copse of trees. I landed on the tree below which the dryad slept under a deer-skin robe. It had dried blood on it, I suppose from the man who had been killed by the gworl. They were butchering him, getting ready to cook him over their fires.

"I came down to the ground on the opposite side of the tree. I had hoped to talk to the dryad, perhaps even enable her to escape. But a gworl sitting near her heard the flutter of my wings. He looked around the tree, and that was his mistake, for my claws took him in his eyes. He dropped his knife and tried to tear me loose from his face. And so he did, but much of his face and both eyes came along with my talons. I told the dryad to run then, but she stood up and the robe fell off. I could see then that her hands and her legs were bound.

"I went into the brush, leaving the gworl to wail for his eyes. For his death, too, because his fellows would not be burdened with a blind warrior. I escaped through the woods and back to the plains. There I was able to fly off again. I flew toward the nest of the Bear People to tell you, O Kickaha and O Wolff, beloved of the dryad. I flew all night and on into the day.

"But a hunting pack of the Eyes of the Lord saw me first. They were above and ahead of me, in the glare of the sun. They plummeted down, those play-hawks, and took me by surprise. I fell, driven by their impact and by the weight of a dozen with their talons clamped upon me. I fell, turning over and over and bleeding under the thrusts of flint-sharp beaks.

"Then I, Aglaia, sister to Podarge, righted myself and also gathered my senses. I seized the shrieking ravens and bit their heads off or tore their wings or legs off. I killed the dozen on me, only to be attacked by the rest of the pack. These I fought, and the story was the same. They died, but in their dying they caused my death. Only because they were so many."

There was a silence. She glared at them with her remaining

eye, but the life was swiftly unraveling from it to reveal the blank spool of death. The Bear People had fallen quiet; even the horses had ceased snorting. The wind whispering in from the skies was the loudest noise.

Abruptly, Aglaia spoke in a weak but still arrogantly harsh voice.

"Tell Podarge she need not be ashamed of me. And promise me, O Kickaha—no trickster words to me—promise me that Podarge will be told."

"I promise, O Aglaia," Kickaha said. "Your sisters will come here and carry your body far out from the rims of the tiers, out in the green skies, and you will be launched to float through the abyss, free in death as in life, until you fall into the sun or find your resting place upon the moon."

"I hold you to it, manling," she said.

Her head drooped, and she fell forward. But the iron talons were locked in on the branch so that she swung back and forth, upside down. The wings sagged and spread out, the tips brushing the ends of the grass.

Kickaha exploded into orders. Two men were dispatched to look for eagles to be informed of Aglaia's report and of her death. He said nothing, of course, about the horn, and he had to spend some time in teaching the two a short speech in Mycenaean. After being satisfied that they had memorized it satisfactorily, he sent them on their way. Then the party was delayed further in getting Aglaia's body to a higher position in the tree, where she would be beyond the reach of any carnivore except the puma and the carrion birds.

It was necessary to chop off the limb to which she clung and to hoist the heavy body up to another limb. Here she was tied with rawhide to the trunk and in an upright position.

"There!" Kickaha said when the work was done. "No creature will come near her as long as she seems to be alive. All fear the eagles of Podarge."

The afternoon of the sixth day after Aglaia the party made a long stop at a waterhole. The horses were given a chance to rest and to fill their bellies with the long green grass. Kickaha and Wolff squatted side by side on top of a small hill and chewed on an antelope steak. Wolff was gazing interestedly at a small herd of mastodons only four hundred yards away. Near them, crouched in the grass, was a striped male lion, a 900-pound specimen of Felix Atrox. The lion had some slight hopes of getting a chance at one of the calves.

Kickaha said, "The gworl were damn lucky to make the forest in one piece, especially since they're on foot. Between here and the Trees of Many Shadows are the Tsenakwa and other tribes. And the KhingGatawriT."

"The Half-Horses?" Wolff said. In the few days with the Hrowakas, he had picked up an amazing amount of vocabulary items and was even beginning to grasp some of the complicated syntax.

"The Half-Horses. *Hoi Kentauroi*. Centaurs. The Lord made them, just as he's made the other monsters of this world. There are many tribes of them on the Amerindian plains. Some are Scythian or Sarmatian speakers, since the Lord snatched part of his centaur material from those ancient steppe-dwellers. But others have adopted the tongues of their human neighbors. All have adopted the Plains tribal culture—with some variations."

The warparty came to the Great Trade Path. This was distinguishable from the rest of the plain only by posts driven into the ground at mile-intervals and topped by carved ebony images of the Tishquetmoac god of commerce, Ishquettlammu. Kickaha urged the party into a gallop as they came near it and it did not slow until the Path was far behind.

"If the Great Trade Path ran to the forest, instead of parallel with it," he told Wolff, "we'd have it made. As long as we stayed on it, we'd be undisturbed. The Path is sacrosanct; even the wild Half-Horses respect it. All the tribes get their steel weapons, cloth blankets, jewelry, chocolate, fine tobacco, and so on from the Tishquetmoac, the only civilized people on this tier. I hurried us across the Path because I wouldn't be able to stop the Hrowakas from tarrying for a few days' trade if we came across a merchant caravan. You'll notice our braves have more furs than they need on their horses. That's just in case. But we're okay now."

Six days went by with no sign of enemy tribes except the black-and-red striped tepees of the Irennussoik at a distance. No warriors rode out to challenge them, but Kickaha did not relax until many miles had fallen behind them. The next day the plain began to change: the knee-high and bright green grass was interspersed with a bluish grass only several inches high. Soon the party was riding over a rolling land of blue.

"The stamping ground of the Half-Horse," Kickaha said. He sent the scouts to a greater distance from the main party.

"Don't let yourself be taken alive," he reminded Wolff.

"Especially by the Half-Horse. A human plains tribe might decide to adopt you instead of killing you if you had guts enough to sing merrily and spit in their faces while they roasted you over a low fire. But the Half-Horses don't even have human slaves. They'd keep you alive and screaming for weeks."

On the fourth day after Kickaha's warning, they topped a rise and saw a black band ahead.

"Trees growing along the Winnkaknaw River," Kickaha said. "We're almost halfway to the Trees of Many Shadows. Let's push the horses until we get to the river. I've got a hunch we've eaten up most of our luck."

He fell silent as he and the others saw a flash of sun on white several miles to their right. Then the white horse of Wicked Knife, a scout, disappeared into a shallow between rises. A few seconds later, a dark mass appeared on the rise behind him.

"The Half-Horse!" Kickaha yelled. "Let's go! Make for the river! We can make a stand in the trees along it, if we can get there!"

CHAPTER NINE

With a single lurch, the entire warparty broke into a gallop. Wolff crouched over his horse, a magnificent roan stallion, urging it on although it needed no encouragement. The plain sped by as the roan stretched his heart to drive his legs. Despite his intensity on speed, Wolff kept glancing to his right. Wicked Knife's white mare was visible now and then as she came over a swell of the plain. The scout was directing her at an angle toward his people. Less than a quarter of a mile behind, and gaining, was the horde of Half-Horse. They numbered at least a hundred and fifty, maybe more.

Kickaha brought his stallion, a golden animal with a pale silvery mane and tail, alongside Wolff. "When they catch up with us—which they will—stay by my side! I'm organizing a column of twos, a classic maneuver, tried and true! That way, each man can guard the other's side!"

He dropped back to give orders to the rest. Wolff guided his roan to follow in line behind Wolverine Paws and Sleeps Standing Up. Behind him, White Nose Bear and Big Blanket were trying to maintain an even distance from him. The rest of the party was strung out in a disorder which Kickaha and a councillor, Spider Legs, were trying to break up.

Presently, the forty were arranged in a ragged column. Kickaha rode up beside Wolff and shouted above the pound of hooves and whistling of wind: "They're stupid as porcupines! They wanted to turn and charge the centaurs! But I talked some sense into them!"

Two more scouts, Drunken Bear and Too Many Wives, were riding in from the left to join them. Kickaha gestured at them to fall in at the rear. Instead, the two continued their 90-degree approach and rode on past the tail of the column.

"The fools are going to rescue Wicked Knife—they think!"

The two scouts and Wicked Knife approached toward a converging point. Wicked Knife was only four hundred yards away from the Hrowakas with the Half-Horses several hundred yards behind him. They were lessening the gap with every second, traveling at a speed no horse burdened with a rider could match. As they came closer, they could be seen in enough detail for Wolff to understand just what they were.

They were indeed centaurs, although not quite as the painters of Earth had depicted. This was not surprising. The Lord, when forming them in his biolabs, had had to make certain concessions to reality. The main adjustment had been regulated by the need for oxygen. The large animal part of a centaur had to breathe, a fact ignored by the conventional Terrestrial representations. Air had to be supplied not only to the upper and human torso but to the lower and theriomorphic body. The relatively small lungs of the upper part could not handle the air requirements.

Moreover, the belly of the human trunk would have stopped all supply of nourishment to the large body beneath it. Or, if the small belly was attached to the greater equine digestive organs to transmit the food, diet was still a problem. Human teeth would quickly wear out under the abrasion of grass.

Thus the hybrid beings coming so swiftly and threateningly toward the men did not quite match the mythical creatures that had served as their models. The mouths and necks were proportionately large to allow intake of enough oxygen. In place of the human lungs was a bellows-like organ which drove the air through a throat-like opening and thence into the great lungs of the hippoid body. These lungs were larger than a horse's, for the vertical part increased the oxygen demands. Space for the bigger lungs was made by removal of the larger herbivore digestive organs and substitution of a smaller carnivore stomach. The centaur ate meat, including the flesh of his Amerind victims.

The equine part was about the size of an Indian pony of Earth. The hides were red, black, white, palomino, and pinto. The horsehair covered all but the face. This was almost twice as large as a normal-sized man's and was broad, high-cheekboned, and big-nosed. They were, on a larger scale, the features of the Plains Indians of Earth, the faces of Roman Nose, Sitting Bull, and Crazy Horse. Warpaint streaked their features and feathered bonnets and helmets of buffalo hides with projecting horns were on their heads.

Their weapons were the same as those of the Hrowakas, except for one item. This was the bola: two round stones, each secured to the end of a strip of rawhide. Even as Wolff wondered what he would do if a bola were cast at him, he saw them put into action. Wicked Knife and Drunken Bear and Too Many Wives had met and were racing beside each other about twenty yards ahead of their pursuers. Drunken Bear turned and shot an arrow. The missile plunged into the swelling bellows-organ beneath the human-chest of a Half-Horse. The Half-Horse went down and turned over and over and then lay still. The upper torso was bent at an angle that could result only from a broken spine. This despite the fact that a universal joint of bone and cartilage at the juncture of the human and equine permitted extreme flexibility of the upper torso.

Drunken Bear shouted and waved his bow. He had made the first kill, and his exploit would be sung for many years in the Hrowakas Council House.

If there's anybody left to tell about it, Wolff thought.

A number of bolas, whirled around and around till the stones were barely visible, were released. Rotating like airplane propellors that had spun off from their shafts, the bolas flew through the air. The stone at the end of one struck Drunken Bear on the neck and hurled him from his horse, cutting off his victory chant in the middle. Another bola wrapped itself around the hind leg of his horse to send it crashing into the ground.

Wolff, at the same time as some of the Hrowakas, released an arrow. He could not tell if it went home, for it was difficult to get a good aim and release from a position on a galloping horse. But four arrows did strike, and four Half-Horses fell. Wolff at once drew another arrow from the quiver on his back, noting at the same time that Too Many Wives and his horse were on the ground. Too Many Wives had an arrow sticking from his back.

Now, Wicked Knife was overtaken. Instead of spearing him, the Half-Horses split up to come in on either side of him.

"No!" Wolff cried. "Don't let them do it!"

Wicked knife, however, had not earned his public name for no good reason. If the Half-Horse passed up the chance to kill him so they could take him alive for torture, they would have to pay for their mistake. He flipped his long Tishquetmoac knife through the air into the equine body of the Half-Horse closest to him. The centaur cart-wheeled. Wicked Knife drew another blade from his scabbard and, even as a spear was driven into his horse, he launched himself onto the centaur who had thrust the spear.

Wolff caught a glimpse of him through the massed bodies. He had landed on the back of the centaur, which almost collapsed at the impact of his weight but managed to recover and bear him along. Wicked Knife drove his knife into the back of the human torso. Hooves flashed; the centaur's tail rose into the air above the mob, followed by the rump and the hindlegs.

Wolff thought that Wicked Knife was finished. But no, there he was, miraculously on his feet and then, suddenly, on the horse-barrel of another centaur. This time Wicked Knife held the edge of his blade against his enemy's throat. Apparently he was threatening to cut the jugular vein if the Half-Horse did not carry him out and away from the others.

But a lance, thrust from behind, plunged into Wicked Knife's back. Not, however, before he had carried out his threat and slashed open the neck of the Half-Horse he rode.

"I saw that!" Kickaha shouted. "What a man, that Wicked Knife! After what he did, not even the savage Half-Horse would dare mutilate his body! They honor a foe who gives them a great fight, although they'll eat him, of course."

Now the KhingGatawriT came up closely behind the end of the Hrowakas train. They split up into parts and increased their speed to overtake them on both sides. Kickaha told Wolff that the Half-Horses would not, at first, close in on the Hrowakas in a mass charge. They would try to have some fun with their enemies and would also give their untried young warriors a chance to show their skill and courage.

A black-and-white-spotted Half-Horse, wearing a single hawk's feather in a band around his head, detached himself from the main group on the left. Whirling a bola in his right hand, holding a feathered lance in his left, he charged at an angle toward Kickaha. The stones at the rawhide ends circled to become a blur, then darted from his hand. Their path of flight was downward, toward the legs of his enemy's horse.

Kickaha leaned out and deftly stuck the tip of his lance at the bola. The lancehead was so timed that it met the rawhide in the middle. Kickaha raised the lance, the bola whirled around and around it, and wrapped itself shut. A good part of the energy of the bola was absorbed by the length of the lance. Also, the lance was brought over in an arc to Kickaha's right side nearly striking Wolff, who had to duck. Even so, Kickaha almost lost the lance, for it slid from his hand, carried by the inertia of the bola. But he kept his grip and shook the lance with the bola at its upper end.

The frustrated Half-Horse shook his fist in fury and would have charged Kickaha with his lance. A roar of acclamation and admiration arose from the two columns of centaurs. A chief raced out to forestall the youngster. He spoke a few words to send him in shame back to the main body. The chief was a large roan with a many-feathered bonnet and a number of black chevrons, crossed with a bar, painted on his equine ribs.

"Charging Lion!" Kickaha shouted in English. "He thinks I'm worthy of his attention!"

He yelled something in the chief's language and then whooped with laughter as the dark skin became even darker. Charging Lion shouted back and spurted forward to bring him even with his insulter. The lance in his right hand stabbed at Kickaha, who countered with his own. The two shafts bounced off each other. Kickaha immediately detached his small mammoth-hide shield from his left arm. He blocked another thrust from the centaur's lance with his lance, then spun the shield like a disc. It sailed out and struck Charging Lion's right foreleg.

The centaur slipped and fell on his front legs and skidded upright through the grass. When he attempted to rise, he found that his right front leg was lamed. A yell broke loose from his group; a dozen bonneted chiefs ran with leveled lances at Charging Lion. He bore himself bravely and waited for his death with folded arms as a great, but now defeated and crippled, Half-Horse should.

"Pass the word along to slow down!" Kickaha said. "The horses can't keep this pace up much longer; their lungs are foaming out now. Maybe we can spare them and gain some time if the Half-Horses want to blood some more of their untrieds. If they don't, well, what's the difference?"

"It's been fun," Wolff said. "If we don't make it, we can at least say we weren't bored."

Kickaha rode close enough to clap Wolff on the shoulder. "You're a man after my own heart! I'm happy to have known you. Oh oh! Here comes an unblooded now! But he's going to pick on Wolverine Paws!"

Wolverine Paws, one of Kickaha's fathers-in-law, was at the head of the Hrowakas column and just in front of Wolff. He screamed insults at the Half-Horse charging in with circling bola, and then threw his lance. The Half-Horse, seeing the weapon flying toward him, loosed the bola before he had intended. The lance pierced his shoulder; the bola went true anyway and wrapped itself around Wolverine Paws. Unconscious from a blow by one of the stones, he fell off his horse.

The horses of both Wolff and Kickaha leaped over his body, which was lying before them. Kickaha leaned down to his right and stabbed Wolverine Paws with his lance.

"They won't take delight in torturing you, Wolverine Paws!" Kickaha said. "And you have made them pay for a life with a life."

A period of individual combat followed. Again and again a young untried charged out of the main group to challenge one of the human beings. Sometimes the man won, sometimes the centaur. At the end of a nightmare thirty minutes, the forty Hrowakas had become twenty-eight. Wolff's turn was with a large warrior armed with a club tipped with steel points. He also carried a small round shield with which he tried to duplicate Kickaha's trick. It did not work, for Wolff deflected the shield with the point of his lance. However, his guard was open for a moment, during which the centaur took his advantage. He galloped in so close that Wolff could not turn to draw far back enough to use the lance.

The club was raised high; the sun glittered on the sharp tips of its spike. The huge broad painted face was split with a grin of triumph. Wolff had no time to dodge and if he tried to grab the club he would end with a smashed and mangled hand. Without thinking, he did a thing that surprised both himself and the centaur. Perhaps he was inspired by Wicked Knife's feat. He launched himself from his horse, came in under the club, and grappled the Half-Horse around the neck. His foe squawked with dismay. Then they went down to the ground with a shock that knocked the wind from both.

Wolff leaped up, hoping that Kickaha had grabbed his horse so he could remount. Kickaha was holding it, but he was making no move to bring it back. Indeed, both the Hrowakas and Half-Horse had stopped.

"Rules of war!" Kickaha shouted. "Whoever gets the club first should win!"

Wolff and the centaur, now on his hooves, made a dash for the club, which was about thirty feet behind them. Four-legged speed was too much for two-legged. The centaur reached the club ten feet ahead of him. Without checking his pace, the centaur leaned his human trunk down and scooped up the club. Then he slowed and whirled, so swiftly that he had to rear up on his hind legs.

Wolff had not stopped running. He came in and then up at the Half-Horse even as it reared. A hoof flashed out at him, but he was by it, though the leg brushed against him. He crashed into the upper part, carried it back a little with him, and both fell again.

Despite the impact, Wolff kept his right arm around the centaur's neck. He hung on while the creature struggled to his hooves. The centaur had lost the club and now strove to overcome the human with sheer strength. Again he grinned, for he outweighed Wolff by at least seven hundred pounds. His torso, chest, and arms were also far bulkier than Wolff's.

Wolff braced his feet against the shoving weight of the centaur and would not move back. The grip around the huge neck tightened, and suddenly the Half-Horse could not breathe.

Then the Half-Horse tried to get his knife out, but Wolff grabbed the wrist with his other hand and twisted. The centaur screamed with the pain and dropped the knife.

A roar of surprise came from the watching Half-Horses. They had never seen such power in a mere man before.

Wolff strained, jerked, and brought the struggling warrior to his foreknees. His left fist punched into the heaving bellows beneath the ribs and sank in. The Half-Horse gave a loud whoosh. Wolff released his hold, stepped back, and used his right fist against the thick jaw of the half-unconscious centaur. The head snapped back, and the centaur fell over. Before he could regain consciousness, his skull was smashed by his own club.

Wolff remounted, and the three columns rode on at a canter. For awhile, the Half-Horse made no move against their enemies. Their chiefs seemed to be discussing something. Whatever it was they intended to do, they lost their chance a moment later.

The cavalcades went over a slight rise and down into a broad hollow. This was just deep enough to conceal from them the pride of lions that had been lying there. Apparently the twenty or so of Felis Atrox had fed off a protocamel the night before and had been too drowsy to pay any attention to the noise of the approaching hooves. But now that the intruders were suddenly among them, the great cats sprang into action. Their fury was aggravated even more by their desire to protect the cubs among them.

Wolff and Kickaha were lucky. Although there were huge shapes bounding on every side, none came at them. But Wolff did get close enough to a male to view every awe-inspiring detail, and that was as close as he ever cared to be. The cat was almost as large as a horse and, though he lacked the mane of the African lion, he did not lack for majesty and ferocity. He bounded by Wolff and hurled himself upon the nearest centaur, which went down screaming. The jaws closed on the centaur's throat, and it was dead. Instead of worrying the corpse, as he might normally have done, the male sprang upon another Half-Horse, and this one went down as easily.

All was a chaos of roaring cats and screaming horses, men, and Half-Horse. It was everyone for himself; to hell with the battle that had been going on.

It took only thirty seconds for Wolff and Kickaha and those Hrowakas who had been fortunate enough not to be attacked to ride out of the hollow. They did not need to urge their horses to speed, but they did have trouble keeping them from running themselves to death.

Behind them, but at a distance now, the centaurs who had evaded the lions streamed out of the hollow. Instead of pursuing the Hrowakas at once, they rode to a safe distance from the lions and then paused to evaluate their losses. Actually, they had not suffered more than a dozen casualties, but they had been severely shaken up.

"A break for us!" Kickaha shouted. "However, unless we can get to the woods before they catch up again, we're done for! They aren't going to continue the individual combats anymore. They'll make a concerted charge!"

The woods that they longed for still looked as far off as ever. Wolff did not think that his horse, magnificent beast though it was, could make it. Its coat was dark with sweat, and it was breathing heavily. Yet it pounded on, an engine of finely tempered flesh and spirit that would run until its heart ruptured.

Now the Half-Horse were in full gallop and slowly catching up with them. In a few minutes they were within arrow range. A few shafts came flying by the pursued and plunged into the grass. Thereafter, the centaurs held their fire, for they saw that bows were too inaccurate with the speed and unevenness at which both archer and target were traveling.

Suddenly Kickaha gave a whoop of delight. "Keep going!" he shouted at them all. "May the Spirit of Akjaw-Dimis favor you!"

Wolff did not understand him until he looked at where Kickaha's finger was pointing. Before them, half-hidden by the tall grass, were thousands of little mounds of earth. Before these sat creatures that looked like striped prairie dogs.

The next moment, the Hrowakas had ridden into the colony with the Half-Horse immediately behind them. Shouts and screams arose as horses and centaurs, stepping into holes, went crashing down. The beasts and the Half-Horses that had fallen down, kicked and screamed with the pain of broken legs. The centaurs just behind the first wave reared to halt themselves, and those following rammed into them. For a minute, a pile of tangled and kicking four-legged bodies was spread across the border of the prairie-dog field. The Half-Horses lucky enough to be far enough behind halted and watched their stricken comrades. Then they trotted cautiously, intent on where they placed their hooves. They cut the throats of those with broken legs and arms.

The Hrowakas, though aware of what was taking place behind them, had not stayed to watch. They pushed on but at a reduced pace. Now, they had ten horses and twelve men; Hums Like A Bee and Tall Grass were riding double with two whose horses had not broken their legs.

Kickaha, looking at them, shook his head. Wolff knew what he was thinking. He would have to order Hums Like A Bee and Tall Grass to get off and go on foot. Otherwise, not only they but the men who had picked them up would inevitably be overtaken. Then Kickaha, saying, "To hell with it, I won't abandon them!" dropped back. He spoke briefly to the tandem riders and brought his horse back up alongside Wolff. "If they go, we all go," he said. "But you don't have to stay with us, Bob. Your loyalty lies elsewhere. No reason for you to sacrifice yourself for us and lose Chryseis and the horn."

"I'll stay," Wolff said.

Kickaha grinned and slapped him on the shoulder. "I'd hoped we could get to the woods, but we won't make it. Almost but not quite. By the time we get to that big hill just half a mile ahead, we'll be caught up with. Too bad. The woods are only another half-mile away."

The prairie-dog colony was as suddenly behind them as it had been before them. The Hrowakas urged their beasts to a gallop. A minute later, the centaurs had passed safely through the field, and they, too, were at full speed. Up the hill went the pursued and at the top they halted to form a circle.

Wolff pointed down the side of the hill and across the plain at a small river. There were woods along it, but it was not that which caused his excitement. At the river's edge, partially blocked by the trees, white tepees shone.

Kickaha looked long before saying, "The Tsenakwa. The mortal enemy of the Bear People, as who isn't?"

"Here they come," Wolff said. "They must have been notified by sentinels."

He gestured at a disorganized body of horsemen riding out of the woods, the sun striking off white horses, white shields, and white feathers and sparking the tips of lance.

One of the Hrowakas, seeing them, began a high-pitched wailing song. Kickaha shouted at him, and Wolff understood enough to know that Kickaha was telling him to shut up. Now was no time for a death-song; they would cheat the Half-Horse and the Tsenakwa yet.

"I was going to order our last stand here," Kickaha said. "But not now. We'll ride toward the Tsenakwa, then cut away from them and toward the woods along the river. How we come out depends on whether or not both our enemies decide to fight. If one refuses, the other will get us. If not . . . Let's go!"

Haiyeeing, they pounded their heels against the ribs of their beasts. Down the hill, straight toward the Tsenakwa, they rode. Wolff glanced back over his shoulder and saw that the Half-Horse were speeding down the side of the hill after them. Kickaha yelled, "I didn't think they'd pass this up. There'll be a lot of women wailing in the lodges tonight, but it won't be only among the Bear People!"

Now the Hrowakas were close enough to discern the devices on the shields of the Tsenakwa. These were black swastikas, a symbol Wolff was not surprised to see. The crooked cross was ancient and widespread on Earth; it was known by the Trojans, Cretans, Romans, Celts, Norse, Indian Buddhists and Brahmans, the Chinese, and throughout pre-Columbian North America. Nor was he surprised to see that the oncoming Indians were red-haired. Kickaha had told him that the Tsenakwa dyed their black locks.

Still in an unordered mass but now bunched more closely together, the Tsenakwa leveled their lances and gave their charge-cry, an imitation of the scream of a hawk. Kickaha, in the lead, raised his hand, held it for a moment, then chopped it downward. His horse veered to the left and away, the line of the Bear people following him, he the head and the others the body of the snake.

Kickaha had cut it close, but he had used correct and exact timing. As the Half-Horse and Tsenakwa plunged with a crash and flurry into each other and were embroiled in a melee, the Hrowakas pulled away. They gained the woods, slowed to go through the trees and underbrush, and then were crossing the river. Even so, Kickaha had to argue with several of the braves. These wanted to sneak back across the river and raid the tepees of the Tsenakwa while their warriors were occupied with the Half-Horse.

"Makes sense to me," Wolff said, "if we stay there only long enough to pick up some horses. Hums Like A Bee and Tall Grass can't keep on riding double."

Kickaha shrugged and gave the order. The raid took five minutes. The Hrowakas recrossed the river and burst from the trees and among the tepees with wild shouts. The women and children screamed and took refuge in the trees or lodges. Some of the Hrowakas wanted not only the horses but loot. Kickaha said that he would kill the first man he caught stealing anything besides bows and arrows. But he did reach down off his horse and give a pretty but battling woman a long kiss.

"Tell your men I would have taken you to bed and made you forever after dissatisfied with the puny ones of your tribe!" Kickaha said to her. "But we have more important things to do!" Laughing, he released the woman, who ran into her lodge. He did pause long enough to make water into the big cooking pot in the middle of the camp, a deadly insult, and then he ordered the party to ride off.

CHAPTER TEN

They rode on for two weeks and then were at the edge of the Trees of Many Shadows. Here Kickaha took a long farewell of the Hrowakas. These also each came to Wolff and, laying their hands upon his shoulders, made a farewell speech. He was one of them now. When he returned, he should take a house and wife among them and ride out on hunts and war with them. He was *KwashingDa,* the Strong One; he had made his kill side by side with them; he had outwrestled a Half-Horse; he would be given a bear cub to raise as his own; he would be blessed by the Lord and have sons and daughters, and so forth and so on.

Gravely, Wolff replied that he could think of no greater honor than to be accepted by the Bear People. He meant it.

Many days later, they had passed through the Many Shadows. They lost both horses one night to something that left footprints ten times as large as a man's, and four-toed. Wolff was both saddened and enraged, for he had a great affection for his animal. He wanted to pursue the WaGanassit and take vengeance. Kickaha threw his hands up in horror at the suggestion.

"Be happy you weren't carried off, too!" he said. "The WaGanassit is covered with scales that are half-silicon. Your arrows would bounce off. Forget about the horses. We can come back someday and hunt it down. They can be trapped and then roasted in a fire, which I'd like to do, but we have to be practical. Let's go."

On the other side of the Many Shadows, they built a canoe and went down a broad river that passed through many large and small lakes. The country was hilly here, with steep cliffs at many places. It reminded Wolff of the dells of Wisconsin.

"Beautiful land, but the Chacopewachi and the Enwaddit live here."

Thirteen days later, during which they had had to paddle furiously three times to escape pursuing canoes of warriors, they left the canoe. Having crossed a broad and high range of hills, mostly at night, they came to a great lake. Again they built a canoe and set out across the waters. Five days of paddling brought them to the base of the monolith, Abharhploonta. They began their slow ascent, as dangerous as that up the first monolith. By the time they reached the top, they had expended their supply of arrows and were suffering several nasty wounds.

"You can see why traffic between the tiers is limited," Kickaha said. "In the first place, the Lord has forbidden it. However, that doesn't keep the irreverent and adventurous, nor the trader, from attempting it.

"Between the rim and Dracheland is several thousand miles of jungle with large plateaus interspersed here and there. The Guzirit River is only a hundred miles away. We'll go there and look for passage on a riverboat."

They prepared flint tips and shafts for arrows. Wolff killed a tapirlike animal. Its flesh was a little rank, but it filled their bellies with strength. He wanted then to push on, finding Kickaha's reluctance aggravating.

Kickaha looked up into the green sky and said, "I was hoping one of Podarge's pets would find us and have news for us. After all, we don't know which direction the gworl are taking. They have to go toward the mountain, but they could take two paths. They could go all the way through the jungle, a route not recommended for safety. Or they could take a boat down the Guzirit. That has its dangers, too, especially for rather outstanding creatures like the gworl. And Chryseis would bring a high price in the slave market."

"We can't wait forever for an eagle," Wolff said.

"No, nor will we have to," Kickaha said. He pointed up, and Wolff, following the direction of his fingertip, saw a flash of yellow. It disappeared, only to come into view a moment later. The eagle was dropping swiftly, wings folded. Shortly, it checked its drop and glided in.

Phthie introduced herself and immediately thereafter said that she carried good news. She had spotted the gworl and the woman, Chryseis, only four hundred miles ahead of them. They had taken passage on a merchant boat and were traveling down the Guzirit toward the Land of Armored Men.

"Did you see the horn?" Kickaha asked.

"No," Phthie replied. "But they doubtless have it concealed in one of the skin bags they are carrying. I snatched one of the bags away from a gworl on the chance it might contain the horn. For my troubles, I got a bag full of junk and almost received an arrow through my wing."

"The gworl have bows?" Wolff asked, surprised.

"No. The rivermen shot at me."

Wolff, asking about the ravens, was told that there were many. Apparently the Lord must have ordered a number to keep watch on the gworl.

"That's bad," Kickaha said. "If they spot us, we're in real trouble."

"They don't know what you look like," Phthie said. "I've eavesdropped on the ravens when they were talking, hiding when I longed to seize them and tear them apart. But I have orders from my mistress, and I obey. The gworl have tried to describe you to the Eyes of the Lord. The ravens are looking for two traveling together, both tall, one black-haired, the other bronze-haired. But that is all they know, and many men conform to that description. The ravens, however, will be watching for two men on the trail of the gworl."

"I'll dye my beard, and we'll get Khamshem clothes," Kickaha said.

Phthie said that she must be getting on. She had been on her way to report to Podarge, having left another sister to continue the surveillance of the gworl, when she had spied the two. Kickaha thanked her and made sure that she would carry his regards to Podarge. After the giant bird had launched herself from the rim of the monolith, the men went into the jungle.

"Walk softly, speak quietly," Kickaha said. "Here be tigers. In fact, the jungle's lousy with them. Here also be the great axebeak. It's a wingless bird so big and fierce even one of Podarge's pets would skedaddle away from it. I saw no tigers and an axebeak tangle once, and the tigers didn't hang around long before they caught on it'd be a good idea to take off fast."

Despite Kickaha's warnings, they saw very little life except for a vast number of manycolored birds, monkeys, and mouse-sized antlered beetles. For the beetles, Kickaha had one word: "poisonous". Thereafter, Wolff took care before bedding down that none were about.

Before reaching their immediate destination, Kickaha looked for a plant, the *ghubharash*. Locating a group after a half-day's search, he pounded the fibers, cooked them, and extracted a blackish liquid. With this he stained his hair, beard, and his skin from top to bottom.

"I'll explain my green eyes with a tale of having a slave-mother from Teutonia," he said. "Here. Use some yourself. You could stand being a little darker."

They came to a half-ruined city of stone and wide-mouthed squatting idols. The citizens were a short, thin, and dark people who dressed in maroon capes, and black loincloths. Men and women wore their hair long and plastered with butter, which they derived from the milk of piebald goats that leaped from ruin to ruin and fed on the grasses between the cracks in the stone. These people, the Kaidushang, kept cobras in little cages and often took their pets out to fondle. They chewed dhiz, a plant which turned their teeth black and gave their eyes a smoldering look and their motions a slowness.

Kickaha, using H'vaizhum, the pidgin rivertalk, bartered

with the elders. He traded a leg of a hippopotamus-like beast he and Wolff had killed for Khamshem garments. The two donned the red and green turbans adorned with *kigglibash* feathers, sleeveless white shirts, baggy pantaloons of purple, sashes that wound around and around their waists many times, and the black, curling toed slippers.

Despite their dhiz-stupored minds, the elders were shrewd in their trading. Not until Kickaha brought a very small sapphire from his bag—one of the jewels given him by Podarge—would they sell the pearl-encrusted scabbards and the scimitars in their hidden stock.

"I hope a boat comes along soon," Kickaha said. "Now that they know I have stones, they might try to slit our throats. Sorry, Bob, but we're going to have to keep watch at night. They also like to send in their snakes to do their dirty work for them."

That very day, a merchantman sailed around the bend of the river. At sight of the two standing on the rotting pier and waving long white handkerchiefs, the captain ordered the anchor dropped and sails lowered.

Wolff and Kickaha got into the small boat lowered for them and were rowed out to the *Khrillquz*. This was about forty feet long, low amidships but with towering decks fore and aft, and one fore-and-aft sail and jib. The sailors were mainly of that branch of Khamshem folk called the Shibacub. They spoke a tongue the phonology and structure of which had been described by Kickaha to Wolff. He was sure that it was an archaic form of Semitic influenced by the aboriginal tongues.

The captain, Arkhyurel, greeted them politely on the poopdeck. He sat cross-legged on a pile of cushions and rich rugs and sipped on a tiny cup of thick wine.

Kickaha, calling himself Ishnaqrubel, gave his carefully prepared story. He and his companion, a man under a vow not to speak again until he returned to his wife in the far off land of Shiashtu, had been in the jungle for several years. They had been searching for the fabled lost city of Ziqooant.

The captain's black and tangled eyebrows rose, and he stroked the dark-brown beard that fell to his waist. He asked them to sit down and to accept a cup of the Akhashtum wine while they told their tale. Kickaha's eyes shone and he grinned as he plunged into his narration. Wolff did not understand him, yet he was sure that his friend was in raptures with his long, richly detailed, and adventurous lies. He only hoped Kickaha would not get too carried away and arouse the captain's incredulity.

The hours passed while the caravel sailed down the river. A

sailor clad only in a scarlet loincloth, bangs hanging down below his eyes, played softly on a flute on the foredeck. Food was carried to them on silver and gold platters: roasted monkey, stuffed bird, a black hard bread, and a tart jelly. Wolff found the meat too highly spiced, but he ate.

The sun neared its nightly turn around the mountain, and the captain arose. He led them to a little shrine behind the wheel; here was an idol of green jade, Tartartar. The captain chanted a prayer, the prime prayer to the Lord. Then Arkhyurel got down on his knees before the minor god of his own nation and made obeisance. A sailor sprinkled a little incense on the tiny fire glowing in the hollow in Tartartar's lap. While the fumes spread over the ship, those of the captain's faith prayed also. Later, the mariners of other gods made their private devotions.

That night, the two lay on the mid-deck on a pile of furs which the captain had furnished them.

"I don't know about this guy Arkhyurel," Kickaha said. "I told him we failed to locate the city of Ziqooant but that we did find a small treasure cache. Nothing to brag about but enough to let us live modestly without worry when we return to Shiashtu. He didn't ask to see the jewels, even though I said I'd give him a big ruby for our passage. These people take their time in their dealings; it's an insult to rush business. But his greed may overrule his sense of hospitality and business ethics if he thinks he can get a big haul just by cutting our throats and dumping our bodies into the river."

He stopped for a moment. Cries of many birds came from the branches along the river; now and then a great saurian bellowed from the bank or from the river itself.

"If he's going to do anything dishonorable, he'll do it in the next thousand miles. This is a lonely stretch of river; after that, the towns and cities begin to get more numerous."

The next afternoon, sitting under a canopy erected for their comfort, Kickaha presented the captain with the ruby, enormous and beautifully cut. With it, Kickaha could have purchased the boat itself and the crew from the captain. He hoped that Arkhyurel would be more than satisfied with it; the captain himself could retire on its sale if he wished. Kickaha then did what he had wanted to avoid but knew that he could not. He brought out the rest of the jewels: diamonds, sapphires, rubies, garnets, tourmalines and topazes. Arkhyurel smiled and licked his lips and fondled the stones for three hours. Finally he forced himself to give them back.

That night, while lying on their beds on the deck, Kickaha brought out a parchment map which he had borrowed from the captain. He indicated a great bend of the river and tapped a circle marked with the curlicue syllabary symbols of Khamshem writing.

"The city of Khotsiqsh. Abandoned by the people who built it, like the one from which we boarded this boat, and inhabited by a half-savage tribe, the Weezwart. We'll quietly leave ship the night we drop anchor there and cut across the thin neck of land to the river. We may be able to pick up enough time to intercept the boat that's carrying the gworl. If we don't, we'll still be way ahead of this boat. We'll take another merchant. Or, if none is available, we'll hire a Weezwart dugout and crew."

Twelve days later the Khrillquz tied up alongside a massive but cracked pier. The Weezwart crowded the stone tongue and shouted at the sailors and showed them jars of dhiz, and of laburnum, singing birds in wooden cages, monkeys and servals on the end of leashes, artifacts from hidden and ruined cities in the jungle, bags and purses made from the pebbly hides of the river saurians, and cloaks from tigers and leopards. They even had a baby axeback, which they knew the captain would pay a good price for and would sell to the Bashishub, the king, of Shibacub. Their main wares, however, were their women. These, clad from head to foot in cheap cotton robes of scarlet and green, paraded back and forth on the pier. They would flash open their robes and then quickly close them, all the while screaming the price of a night's rent to the women-starved sailors. The men, wearing only white turbans and fantastic codpieces, stood to one side, chewed dhiz, and grinned. All carried six-foot long blow-guns and long, thin, crooked knives stuck into the tangled knots of hair on top of their heads.

During the trading between the captain and Weezwart, Kickaha and Wolff prowled through the cyclopean stands and falls of the city. Abruptly, Wolff said, "You have the jewels with you. Why don't we get a Weezwart guide and take off now? Why wait until nightfall?"

"I like your style, friend," Kickaha said. "Okay. Let's go."

They found a tall thin man, Wiwhin, who eagerly accepted their offer when Kickaha showed him a topaz. At their insistence, he did not tell his wife where he was going but straightway led them into the jungle. He knew the paths well and, as promised, delivered them to the city of Qirruqshak within two days. Here he demanded another jewel, saying that he would not tell anybody at all about them if he was given a bonus.

"I did not promise you a bonus," Kickaha said. "But I like the fine spirit of free enterprise you show, my friend. So here's another. But if you try for a third, I shall kill you."

Wiwhin smiled and bowed and took the second topaz and

trotted off into the jungle. Kickaha, staring after him, said, "Maybe I should've killed him anyway. The Weezwart don't even have the word *honor* in their vocabulary."

They walked into the ruins. After a half-hour of climbing and threading their way between collapsed buildings and piles of dirt, they found themselves on the river-side of the city. Here were gathered the Dholinz, a folk of the same language family as the Weezwart. But the men had long, drooping moustaches and the women painted their upper lips black and wore nose-rings. With them was a group of merchants from the land which had given all the Khamshem-speakers their name. There was no river-caravel by the pier. Kickaha, seeing this, halted and started to turn back into the ruins. He was too late, for the Khamshem saw him and called out to them.

"Might as well brave it out," Kickaha muttered to Wolff. "If I holler, run like hell! Those birds are slave-dealers."

There were about thirty of the Khamshem, all armed with scimitars and daggers. In addition, they had about fifty soldiers, tall broad-shouldered men, lighter than the Khamshem, with swirling patterns tattooed on their faces and shoulders. These, Kickaha said, were the Sholkin mercenaries often used by the Khamshem. They were famous spearmen, mountain people, herders of goats, scorners of women as good for nothing but housework, fieldwork, and bearers of children.

"Don't let them take you alive," was Kickaha's final warning before he smiled and greeted the leader of the Khamshem. This was a very tall and thickly muscled man named Abiru. He had a face that would have been handsome if his nose had not been a little too large and curved like a scimitar. He answered Kickaha politely enough, but his large black eyes weighed them as if they were so many pounds of merchandisable flesh.

Kickaha gave him the story he had told Arkhyurel but shortened it considerably and left out the jewels. He said that they would wait until a merchant boat came along and would take it back to Shiashtu. And how was the great Abiru doing?

(By now, Wolff's quickness at picking up languages enabled him to understand the Khamshem tongue when it was on a simple conversational basis.)

Abiru replied that, thanks to the Lord and Tartartar, this business venture had been very rewarding. Besides the usual type of slave-material picked up, he had captured a group of very strange creatures. Also, a woman of surpassing beauty, the like of which had never been seen before. Not, at least, on this tier.

Wolff's heart began to beat hard. Was it possible?

Abiru asked if they would care to take a peek at his captives.

Kickaha flicked a look of warning at Wolff but replied that he would very much like to see both the curious beings and the fabulously beautiful woman. Abiru beckoned to the captain of the mercenaries and ordered him and ten of his men to come along. Then Wolff scented the danger of which Kickaha had been aware from the beginning. He knew that they should run, though this was not likely to be successful. The Sholkin seemed accustomed to bringing down fugitives with their spears. But he wanted desperately to see Chryseis again. Since Kickaha made no move, Wolff decided not to do so on his own. Kickaha, having more experience, presumably knew how best to act.

Abiru, chatting pleasantly of the attractions of the capital city of Khamshem, led them down the underbrush-grown street and to a great stepped building with broken statues on the levels. He halted before an entrance by which stood ten more Sholkin. Even before they went in, Wolff knew that the gworl were there. Riding over the stink of unwashed human bodies was the rotten-fruit odor of the bumpy people.

The chamber within was huge and cool and twilighty. Against the far wall, squatting on the dirt piled on the stone floor, was a line of about a hundred men and women and thirty gworl. All were connected by long, thin iron chains around iron collars about their necks.

Wolff looked for Chryseis. She was not there.

Abiru, answering the unspoken question, said, "I keep the cat-eyed one apart. She has a woman attendant and a special guard. She gets all the attention and care that a precious jewel should."

Wolff could not restrain himself. He said, "I would like to see her."

Abiru stared and said, "You have a strange accent. Didn't companion say you were from the land of Shiashtu, also?"

He waved a hand at the soldiers, who moved forward, their spears leveled. "Never mind. If you see the woman, you will see her from the end of a chain."

Kickaha sputtered indignantly. "We are subjects of the king of Khamshem and free men! You cannot do this to us! It will cost you your head, after certain legal tortures, of course!"

Abiru smiled. "I do not intend to take you back to Khamshem, friend. We are going to Teutonia, where you will bring a good price, being a strong man, albeit too talkative. However, we can take care of that by slicing off your tongue."

The scimitars of the two were removed along with the bag.

Herded by the spears, they moved to the end of the line, immediately behind the gworl, and were secured with iron collars. Abiru, dumping the contents of the bag on the floor, swore as he saw the pile of jewels.

"So, you did find something in the lost cities? How fortunate for us. I'm almost—but not quite—tempted to release you for having enriched me so."

"How corny can you get?" Kickaha muttered in English. "He talks like a grade-B movie villain. Damn him! If I get the chance, I'll cut out more than his tongue."

Abiru, happy with his riches, left. Wolff examined the chain attached to the collar. It was made of small links. He might be able to break it if the iron was not too high a quality. On Earth, he had amused himself, secretly of course, by snapping just such chains. But he could not try until nightfall.

Behind Wolff, Kickaha whispered, "The gworl won't recognize us in this getup, so let's leave it that way."

"What about the horn?" Wolff said.

Kickaha, speaking the early Middle High German form of Teutonic, tried to engage the gworl in conversation. After narrowly missing getting hit in the face with a gob of saliva, he quit. He did manage to talk to one of the Sholkin soldiers and some of the human slaves. From them he gleaned much information.

The gworl had been passengers on the *Qaqiirzhub*, captained by one Rakhhamen. Putting in at this city, the captain had met Abiru and invited him aboard for a cup of wine. That night—in fact, the night before Wolff had entered the city—Abiru and his men had seized the boat. During the struggle, the captain and several of his sailors had been slain. The rest were now in the chain-line. The boat had been sent on down the river and up a tributary with a crew to be sold to a river-pirate of whom Abiru had heard.

As for the horn, none of the crew of the *Qaqiirzhub* had heard of it. Nor would the soldier supply any news. Kickaha told Wolff that he did not think that Abiru was likely to let anybody else learn about it. He must recognize it, for everybody had heard of the horn of the Lord. It was part of the universal religion and described in the various sacred literatures.

Night came. Soldiers entered with torches and food for the slaves. After meal time, two Sholkin remained within the chamber and an unknown number stood guard outside. The sanitary arrangements were abominable; the odor became stifling. Apparently Abiru did not care about observing the proprieties as laid down by the Lord. However, some of the more religious Sholkin must have complained, for several Dholinz entered and cleaned up. Water in buckets was dashed over each slave, and several buckets were left for drinking. The gworl howled when the water struck them and complained and cursed for a long time afterwards. Kickaha added to Wolff's store of information by telling him that the gworl, like the kangaroo rat and other desert animals of Earth, did not have to drink water. They had a biological device, similar to the arid-dwellers, which oxidized their fat into the hydrogen oxide required.

The moon came up. The slaves lay on the floor or leaned against the wall and slept. Kickaha and Wolff pretended to do likewise. When the moon had come around into position so that it could be seen through the doorway, Wolff said, "I'm going to try to break the chains. If I don't have time to break yours, we'll have to do a Siamese twin act."

"Let's go," Kickaha whispered back.

The length of the chain between each collar was about six feet. Wolff slowly inched his way toward the nearest gworl to give himself enough slack. Kickaha crept along with him. The journey took about fifteen minutes, for they did not want the two sentinels in the chamber to become aware of their progress. Then Wolff, his back turned to the guards, took the chain in his two hands. He pulled and felt the links hold fast. Slow tension would not do the job. So, a quick jerk. The links broke with a noise.

The two Sholkin, who had been talking loudly and laughing to keep each other awake, stopped. Wolff did not dare to turn over to look at them. He waited while the Sholkin discussed the possible origin of the sound. Apparently it did not occur to them that it could be the chain parting. They spent some time holding the torches high and peering up toward the ceiling. One made a joke, the other laughed, and they resumed their conversation.

"Want to try for two?" Kickaha said.

"I hate to, but we'll be handicapped if I don't," Wolff said.

He had to wait awhile, for the gworl to whom he had been attached had been awakened by the breaking. He lifted his head and muttered something in his file-against-steel speech. Wolff began sweating even more heavily. If the gworl sat up or tried to stand up, his motion would reveal the damage.

After a heart-piercing minute, the gworl settled back down and soon was snoring again. Wolff relaxed a little. He even grinned tightly, for the gworl's actions had given him an idea.

"Crawl up toward me as if you wanted to warm yourself against me," Wolff said softly.

"You kidding?" Kickaha whispered back. "I feel as if I'm in a steam bath. But okay. Here goes."

He inched forward until his head was opposite Wolff's knees.

"When I snap the chain, don't go into action," Wolff said.

"I have an idea for bringing the guards over here without alarming those outside."

"I hope they don't change guards just as we're starting to operate," Kickaha said.

"Pray to the Lord," Wolff replied. "Earth's."

"He helps him who helps himself," Kickaha said.

Wolff jerked with all his strength; the links parted with a noise. This time, the guards stopped talking and the gworl rose up abruptly. Wolff bit down hard on the toe of the gworl. The creature did not cry out but grunted and started to rise. One of the guards ordered him to remain seated, and both started toward him. The gworl did not understand the language. He did understand the tone of voice, and the spear waved at him. He lifted his foot and began to rub it, meanwhile grating curses at Wolff.

The torches became brighter as the feet of the guards scraped against the stone exposed beneath the loose dirt. Wolff said, "Now!"

He and Kickaha arose simultaneously, whirled, and were facing the surprised Sholkin. A spearhead was within Wolff's reach. His hand slid along it, grasped the shaft just behind the point, and jerked. The guard opened his mouth to yell, but it snapped shut as the lifted butt of the spear cracked against his jaw.

Kickaha had not been so fortunate. The Sholkin stepped back and raised his spear to throw it. Kickaha went at him as a tackler after the man with the ball; he came in low, rolled, and the spear clanged against the wall.

By then, the silence was gone. One guard started to yell. The gworl picked up the weapon that had fallen by his side and threw it. The head drove into the exposed neck of the guard, and the point came out through the back of the neck.

Kickaha jerked the spearhead loose, drew the dead guard's knife from his scabbard, and flipped it. The first Sholkin to enter from outside received it to the hilt in his solar plexus. Seeing him go down, others who had been so eager to follow him withdrew. Wolff took the knife from the other corpse, shoved it into his sash, and said, "Where do we go from here?"

Kickaha slid the knife from the solar plexus and wiped it on the corpse's hair. "Not through that door. Too many."

Wolff pointed at a doorway at the far end and started to run toward it. On the way, he scooped up the torch dropped by the guard. Kickaha did the same. The doorway was partly choked up by dirt, forcing them to get down on their hands and knees and crawl through. Presently they were at the place through which the dirt had dropped. The moon revealed an empty place in the stone slabs of the ceiling.

"They must know about this," Wolff said. "They can't be that careless. We'd better go further back in."

They had scarcely moved past the point below the break in the roof when torches flared above. The two scuttled ahead as fast as they could while Sholkin voices came excitedly through the opening. A second later, a spear slammed into the dirt, narrowly missing Wolff's leg.

"They'll be coming in after us, now that they know we've left the main chamber," Kickaha said.

They went on, taking branches which seemed to offer access to the rear. Suddenly the floor sank beneath Kickaha. He tried to scramble on across before the stone on which he was would drop, but he did not make it. One side of a large slab came up, and that side which had dropped propelled Kickaha into a hole. Kickaha yelled, at the same time releasing the hold on his torch. Both fell.

Wolff was left staring at the tipped slab and the gape beside it. No light came from the hole, so the torch had either gone out or the hole was so deep that the flare was out of sight. Moaning in his anxiety, he crawled forward and held the torch over the edge while he looked below. The shaft was at least ten feet wide and fifty deep. It had been dug out of the dirt and at various places down it large pieces had fallen off. The bottom was a heap of dirt. But there was no Kickaha nor even a depression to indicate where he had landed.

Wolff called his name, at the same time hearing the shouts of the Sholkin as they crawled through the corridors in pursuit.

Receiving no answer, he extended his body as far as he dared over the lip of the shaft and examined the depth more closely. All his waving about of the torch to illuminate the dark places showed nothing but the fallen extinguished torch.

Some of the edges of the bottom remained black as if there were holes in the sides. He could only conclude that Kickaha had gone into one of these.

Now the sound of voices became louder and the first flickerings of a torch came from around the corner at the end of the hall. He could do nothing but continue. He rose as far as possible, threw his torch ahead of him to the other side, and leaped with all the strength of his legs. He shot in an almost horizontal position, hit the lip, which was wet soft earth, and slid forward on his face. He was safe, although his legs were sticking out over the edge.

Picking up the torch, which was still burning, he crawled on. At the end of the corridor he found one branch completely blocked by fallen earth. The other was partially stopped up by a great slab of smoothly cut stone lying at a forty-five degree angle to horizontal. By the sacrifice of some skin on his chest and back, he squeezed through between the earth and the stone. Beyond was an enormous chamber, even larger than the one in which the slaves had been kept.

There was a series of rough terraces formed by slippage of stone at the opposite end. He made his way up these toward the corner of the ceiling and the wall. A patch of moonlight shone through this, his only means of exit. He put his torch out. If the Sholkin were roaming around the top of the building, they would see the light from it coming through the small hole. At the cavity, he crouched for awhile on the narrow ledge beneath it and listened carefully. If his torch had been seen, he would be caught as he slid out of the hole, helpless to defend himself. Finally, hearing only distant shouts, and knowing that he must use this only exit, he pulled himself through it.

He was near the top of the mound of dirt which covered the rear part of the building. Below him were torches. Abiru was standing in their light, shaking his fist at a soldier and yelling.

Wolff looked down at the earth beneath his feet, imagined the stone and the hollows they contained, and the shaft down which Kickaha had hurtled to his death.

He raised his spear and murmured, "Ave atque vale, Kickaha!"

He wished he could take some more Sholkin lives—especially that of Abiru—in payment for Kickaha's. But he had to be practical. There was Chryseis, and there was the horn. But he felt empty and weak, as if part of his soul had left him.

CHAPTER ELEVEN

That night he hid in the branches of a tall tree some distance from the city. His plan was to follow the slavers and rescue Chryseis and the horn at the first chance. The slavers would have to take the trail near which he waited; it was the only one leading inward to Teutonia. Dawn came while he waited, hungry and thirsty. By noon he became impatient. Surely they would not still be looking for him. At evening, he decided that he had to have at least a drink of water. He climbed down and headed for a nearby stream. A growl sent him up another tree. Presently a family of leopards slipped through the bush and lapped at the water. By the time they were through and had slid back into the bush, the sun was close to the corner of the monolith.

He returned to the trail, confident that he had been too close to it for a large train of human beings to walk by unheard. Yet no one came. That night he sneaked into the ruins and close to the building from which he had escaped. No one was in evidence. Sure now that they had left, he prowled through the bush-grown lanes and streets until he came upon a man sitting against a tree. The man was half-conscious from dhiz, but Wolff woke him by slapping him hard against his cheeks. Holding his knife against his throat, he questioned him. Despite his limited Khamshem and the Dholinz's even lesser mastery, they managed to communicate. Abiru and his party had left that morning on three large war-canoes with hired Dholinz paddlers.

Wolff knocked the man unconscious and went down to the pier. It was deserted, thus giving him a choice of any craft there he wanted. He took a narrow light boat with a sail and set off down the river.

Two thousand miles later, he was on the borders of Teutonia and the civilized Khamshem. The trail had led him down the Guzirit River for three hundred miles, then across country. Although he should have caught up with the slow-moving train long before, he had lost them three times and been detained at other times by tigers and axebeaks.

Gradually the land sloped upward. Suddenly a plateau rose from the jungle. A climb of a mere six thousand feet was nothing to a man who had twice scaled thirty thousand. Once over the rim, he found himself in a different country. Though the air was no cooler, it bred oak, sycamore, yew, box, elder, walnut, cottonwood and linden. However, the animals differed. He had walked no more than two miles through the twilight of an oak forest before he was forced to hide.

A dragon slowly paced by him, looked at him once, hissed, and went on. It resembled the conventional Western representations, was about forty feet long, ten feet high, and was covered with large scaly plates. It did not breathe fire. In fact, it stopped a hundred feet from Wolff's tree-branch refuge and began to eat upon a tall patch of grass. So, Wolff thought, there was more than one type of dragon. Wondering how he would be able to tell the carnivorous type from the herbivorous without first assuring a safe observation post, Wolff climbed down from the tree. The dragon continued to munch while its belly, or bellies, emitted a weak thunder of digestion.

More cautiously than before, Wolff passed beneath the giant limbs of the trees and the moss, cataracts of green, that hung from the limbs. Dawn of the next day found him leaving the edge of the forest. Before him the land dipped gently. He could see for many miles. To his right, at the bottom of a valley, was a river. On the opposite side, topping a column of shaggy rock, was a tiny castle. At the foot of the rock was a minute village. Smoke rose from the chimneys to bring a lump in his throat. It seemed to him that he would like nothing better than to sit down at a breakfast table over a cup of coffee with friends, after a good night's sleep in a soft bed, and chatter away about nothing in particular. God! How he missed the faces and the voices of genuine human beings, of a place where every hand was not against him!

A few tears trickled down his cheek. He dried them and went on his way. He had made his choice and must take the bad with the good, just as he would have in the Earth he had renounced. And this world, at this moment, anyway, was not so bad. It was fresh and green with no telephone lines, billboards, paper and cans strewn along the countryside, no smog or threat of bomb. There was much to be said for it, no matter how bad his present situation might be. And he had that for which many men would have sold their souls: youth combined with the experience of age.

Only an hour later, he wondered if he would be able to retain the gift. He had come to a narrow dirt road and was striding along it when a knight rode around the bend in the road, followed by two men-at-arms. His horse was huge and black and accoutered partly in armor. The knight was clad in black plate-and-mail armor which, to Wolff, looked like the type worn in Germany of the thirteenth century. His visor was up, revealing a grim hawk's face with bright blue eyes.

The knight reined in his horse. He called to Wolff in the Middle High German speech with which Wolff had become acquainted through Kickaha and also through his studies on Earth. The language had, of course, changed somewhat and was loaded with Khamshem and aboriginal loanwords. But Wolff could make out most of what his accoster said.

"Stand still, oaf!" the man cried. "What are you doing with a bow?"

"May it please your august self," Wolff replied sarcastically, "I am a hunter and so bear the king's license to carry a bow."

"You are a liar! I know every lawful hunter for miles hereabouts. You look like a Saracen to me or even a Yidshe, you are so dark. Throw down your bow and surrender, or I will cut you down like the swine you are!"

"Come and take it," Wolff said, his rage swelling.

The knight couched his lance, and his steed broke into a gallop.

Wolff resisted the impulse to hurl himself to either side or back from the glittering tip of the lance. At what he hoped was the exact split-second, he threw himself forward. The lance dipped to run him through, slid less than an inch over him, and then drove into the ground. Like a pole-vaulter, the knight rose from the saddle and, still clutching the lance, described an arc. His helmet struck the ground first at the end of the arc, the impact of which must have knocked him out or broken his neck or back, for he did not move.

Wolff did not waste his time. He removed the scabbarded sword of the knight and placed the belt around his waist. The dead man's horse, a magnificent roan, had come back to stand by his ex-master. Wolff mounted him and rode off.

Teutonia was so named because of its conquest by a group of The Teutonic Order or Teutonic Knights of St Mary's Hospital at Jerusalem. This order originated during the Third Crusade but later deviated from its original purpose. In 1229 *der Deutsche Orden* began the conquest of Prussia to convert the Baltic pagans and to prepare for colonization by Germans. A group had entered the Lord's planet on this tier, either through accident, which did not seem likely, or because the Lord had deliberately opened a gate for them or forcibly caused them to enter.

Whatever the cause, the Ritters of the Teutonic Knights had conquered the aborigines and established a society based on that which they had left on Earth. This, of course, had changed both because of natural evolution and the Lord's desire to model it to his own wishes. The original single kingdom or Grand Marshalry had degenerated into a number of independent kingdoms. These, in turn, consisted of loosely bound baronetcies and a host of outlaw or robber baronetcies.

Another aspect of the plateau was the state of Yidshe. The founders of this had entered through a gate coevally with the Teutonic Knights. Again, whether they had entered accidentally or through design of the Lord was unknown. But a number of Yiddish-speaking Germans had established themselves at the eastern end of the plateau. Though originally merchants, they had become masters of the native population. Also, they had adopted the feudal-chivalry setup of the Teutonic Order—probably had had to do so to survive. It was this state that the first knight had referred to when he had accused Wolff of being a Yidshe.

Thinking of this, Wolff had to chuckle. Again, it might have been accident that the Germans had entered into a level where the archaic-Semitic Khamshem already existed and where their contemporaries were the despised Jews. But Wolff thought he could see the ironic face of the Lord smiling behind the situation.

Actually, there were not any Christians or Jews in Dracheland. Although the two faiths still used their original titles, both had become perverted. The Lord had taken the place of Yahweh and Gott, but he was addressed by these names. Other changes in theology had followed: ceremonies, rituals, sacraments, and the literature had subtly become twisted. The parent faiths of both would have rejected their descendants in this world as heretics.

Wolff made his way toward von Elgers'. He could not do so as swiftly as he wished, because he had to avoid the roads and the villages along the way. After being forced to kill the knight, he did not even dare cut through the baronetcy of von Laurentius, as he had at first planned. The entire country would be searching for him; men and dogs would be everywhere. The rough hills marking the boundary were his most immediate form of passage, which he took.

Two days later, he came to a point where he could descend without being within the suzerainty of von Laurentius. As he was clambering down a steep but not especially difficult hill, he came around a corner. Below him was a broad meadow by a riverlet. Two camps were pitched at opposite ends. Around the brave flag-and-pennon draped pavilions in the center of each were a number of smaller tents, cooking fires, and horses. Most of the men were in two groups. They were watching their champion and his antagonist, who were charging each other with couched lances. Even as Wolff saw them, they met together in the middle of the field with a fearful clang. One knight went sailing backward with the lance of the other jammed into his shield. The other, however, lost his balance and fell with a clang several seconds later.

Wolff studied the tableau. It was no ordinary jousting tourney. The peasants and the townspeople who should have thronged the sides and the jerrybuilt stadium with its flowerbed of brilliantly dressed nobility and ladies were absent. This was a lonely place beside the road where champions had pitched their tents and were taking on all qualified passersby.

Wolff worked his way down the hill. Although exposed to the sight of those below, he did not think that they would take much interest in a lone traveler at this time. He was right. No one hastened from either camp to question him. He was able to walk up to the edge of the meadow and make a leisurely inspection.

The flag above the pavilion to his left bore a yellow field with a Solomon's seal. By this he knew that a Yidshe champion had pitched his tent here. Below the national flag was a green banner with a silver fish and hawk. The other camp had several state and personal pennons. One of them leaped out into Wolff's gaze and caused him to cry out with surprise. On a white field was a red ass's head with a hand below it, all fingers clenched but the middle. Kickaha had once told him of it, and Wolff had gotten a big laugh out of it. It was just like Kickaha to pick such a coat of arms.

Wolff sobered then, knowing that, more likely, it was borne by the man who took care of Kickaha's territory while he was gone.

He changed his decision to pass on by the field. He had to determine for himself that the man using that banner was not Kickaha, even though he knew that his friend's bones must be rotting under a pile of dirt at the bottom of a shaft in a ruined city of the jungle.

Unchallenged, he made his way across the field and into the camp at the western end. Men-at-arms and retainers stared, only to turn away from his glare. Somebody muttered, "Yidshe dog!" but none owned to the comment when he turned. He went on around a line of horses tethered to a post and up to the knight who was his goal. This one was clad in shining red armor, visor down, and held a huge lance upright while he waited his turn. The lance bore near its tip a pennon on which were the red ass's head and human hand.

Wolff placed himself near the prancing horse, making it even more nervous. He cried out in German, "Baron von Horstmann?"

There was a muffled exclamation, a pause, and the knight's hand raised his visor. Wolff almost wept with joy. The merry long-lipped face of Finnegan-Kickaha-von Horstmann was inside the helmet.

"Don't say anything," Kickaha cautioned. "I don't know how in hell you found me, but I'm sure happy about it. I'll see you in a moment. That is, if I come back alive. This funem Laksfalk is one tough hombre."

CHAPTER TWELVE

Trumpets fared, Kickaha rode out to a spot indicated by the marshals. A shaven-headed, long-robed priest blessed him while, at the other end of the field, a rabbi was saying something to Baron funem Laksfalk. The Yidshe champion was a large man in a silver armor, his helmet shaped like a fish's head. His steed was a huge powerful black. The trumpets blew again. The two contenders dipped their lances in salute. Kickaha briefly gripped his lance with his left hand while he crossed himself with his right. (He was a stickler for observing the religious rules of the people among whom he happened to be at the moment.)

Another blast of long-shafted, big-mouthed trumpets was followed by the thunder of the hooves of the knights' horses and the cheers of the onlookers. The two met exactly in the middle of the field, as did the lance of each in the middle of the other's shield. Both fell with a clangor that startled the birds from the nearby trees, as they had been startled many times that day. The horses rolled on the ground.

The men of each knight ran out onto the field to pick up their chief and to drag away the horses, both of which had broken their necks. For a moment, Wolff thought that the Yidshe and Kickaha were also dead, for neither stirred. After being carried back, however, Kickaha came to. He grinned feebly and said, "You ought to see the other guy."

"He's okay," Wolff said after a glance at the other camp.

"Too bad," Kickaha replied. "I was hoping he wouldn't give us any more trouble. He's held me up too long as it is."

Kickaha ordered all but Wolff to leave the tent. His men seemed reluctant to leave him but they obeyed, though not without warning looks at Wolff. Kickaha said, "I was on my way from my castle to von Elgers' when I passed funem Laksfalk's pavilion. If I'd been alone, I would have thumbed my nose at his challenge and ridden on. But there were also Teutoniacs there, and I had my own men to consider. I couldn't afford to get a reputation of cowardice; my own men would've pelted me with rotten cabbage and I'd have had to fight every knight in the land to prove my courage. I figured that it wouldn't take me long to straighten out the Yidshe on who the best man was, and then I could take off.

"It didn't work out that way. The marshals had me listed in the Number Three position. That meant I had to joust with three men for three days before I'd get to the big time. I protested; no use. So I swore to myself and sweated it out. You saw my second encounter with funem Laksfalk. We both knocked each other off the saddle the first time, too. Even so, that's more than the others have done. They're burned up because a Yidshe has defeated every Teuton except me. Besides, he's killed two already and crippled another for life."

While listening to Kickaha, Wolff had been taking the armor off. Kickaha sat up suddenly, groaning and wincing, and said, "Hey, how in hell did you get here?"

"I walked mostly. But I thought you were dead."

"The report wasn't too grossly exaggerated. When I fell down that shaft I landed halfway up on a ledge of dirt. It broke off and started a little cave-in that buried me after I landed on the bottom. But I wasn't knocked out long, and the dirt only lightly covered my face, so I wasn't asphyxiated. I lay quiet for a while because the Sholkin were looking down the hole then. They even threw a spear down, but it missed me by a mole's hair.

"After a couple of hours, I dug myself out. I had a time getting out, I can tell you. The dirt kept breaking off, and I kept falling back. It must've taken me ten hours, but I was lucky at that. Now, how did *you* get here, you big lunk?"

Wolff told him. Kickaha frowned and said, "So I was right in figuring that Abiru would come to von Elgers' on his way. Listen, we got to get out of here and fast. How would you like to take a swing at the big Yid?"

Wolff protested that he knew nothing of the fine points of jousting, that it took a lifetime to learn. Kickaha said, "If you were going to break a lance with him, you'd be right. But we'll challenge him to a contest with swords, no shields. Broad-swording isn't exactly duelling with a rapier or saber; it's main strength and that's what you've got!"

"I'm not a knight. The others saw me enter as a common vagrant."

"Nonsense! You think these chevaliers don't go around in disguise all the time? I'll tell them you're a Saracen, a pagan Khamshem, but you're a real good friend of mine, I rescued you from a dragon or some cock-and-bull story like that. They'll eat it up. I got it! You're the Saracen Wolf—there's a famous knight by that name. You've been journeying in disguise, hoping to find me and pay me back for saving you from the dragon. I'm too hurt to break another lance with funem Laksfalk—that's no lie; I'm so stiff and sore I can hardly move—and you're taking up the gauntlet for me."

Wolff asked what excuse he would give for not using the lance.

Kickaha said, "I'll give them some story. Say a thieving knight stole your lance and you've sworn never to use one until you get the stolen one back. They'll accept that. They're always making some goofy vow or other. They act just like a bunch of knights from King Arthur's Round Table. No such knights ever existed on Earth, but it must have pleased the Lord to make these act as if they just rode out of Camelot. He was a romantic, whatever else you can say about him."

Wolff said he was reluctant, but if it would help speed them to von Elgers', he would do anything. Kickaha's own armor was not large enough for Wolff, so the armor of a Yid-she knight Kickaha had killed the day before was brought in. The retainers clad him in blue plates and chain-mail and then led him out to his horse. This was a beautiful palomino mare that had also belonged to the knight Kickaha had slain, the Ritter oyf Roytfeldz. With only a little difficulty, Wolff mounted the charger. He had expected that the armor would be so heavy a crane would have to lift him upon the saddle. Kickaha told him that that might have once been true here, but the knights had long since gone back to lighter plates and more chain-mail.

The Yidshe go-between came to announce that funem Laksfalk had accepted the challenge despite the Saracen Wolf's lack of credentials. If the valiant and honorable robber Baron Horst von Horstmann vouched for the Wolf, that was good enough for funem Laksfalk. The speech was a formality. The Yidshe champion would not for one moment have thought of turning down a challenge.

"Face is the big thing here," Kickaha said to Wolff. Having managed to limp out of his tent, he was giving his friend last-minute instructions. "Man, am I glad you came along. I couldn't have taken one more fall, and I didn't dare back out."

Again, the trumpets flourished. The palomino and the black broke into a headlong gallop. They passed each other going at full speed, during which time both men swung their swords. They clanged together; a paralyzing shock ran down Wolff's hand and arm. However, when he turned his charger, he saw that his antagonist's sword was on the ground. The Yidshe was dismounting swiftly to get to the blade before Wolff. He was in such a hurry he slipped and fell headlong onto the ground.

Wolff rode his horse up slowly and took his time dismounting to allow the other to recover. At this chivalrous move, both camps broke into cheers. By the rules, Wolff could have stayed in the saddle and cut funem Laksfalk down without permitting him to pick up his weapon.

On the ground, they faced each other. The Yidshe knight raised his visor, revealing a handsome face. He had a thick moustache and pale blue eyes. He said, "I pray you let me see your face, noble one. You are a true knight for not striking me down while helpless."

Wolff lifted his visor for a few seconds. Both then advanced and brought their blades together again. Once more, Wolff's stroke was so powerful that it tore the blade of the other from his grip.

Funem Laksfalk raised his visor, this time with his left arm. He said, "I cannot use my right arm. If you will permit me to use my left?"

Wolff saluted and stepped back. His opponent gripped the long hilt of his sword and, stepping close, brought it around from the side with all his force. Once more, the shock of Wolff's stroke broke the Yidshe's grasp.

Funem Laksfalk lifted his visor for the third time. "You are such a champion as I have never met. I am loath to admit it, but you have defeated me. And that is something I have never said nor thought to say. You have the strength of the Lord himself."

"You may keep your life, your honor, and your armor and horse," Wolff replied. "I want only that my friend von Horstmann and I be allowed to go on without further challenges. We have an appointment."

The Yidshe answered that it would be so. Wolff returned to his camp, there to be greeted joyously, even by those who had thought of him as a Khamshem dog.

Chortling, Kickaha ordered camp struck. Wolff asked him if he did not think they could make far better time unencumbered with a train.

"Sure, but it's not done very often," Kickaha replied. "Oh, well, you're right. I'll send them on home. And we'll get these damn locomotive plates off."

They had not ridden far before they heard the drum of hooves. Coming up the road behind them was funem Laksfalk, also minus his armor. They halted until he had overtaken them.

"Noble knights," he said, smiling, "I know that you are on a quest. Would it be too much for me to ask to join? I would feel honored. I also feel that only by assisting you can I redeem my defeat."

Kickaha looked at Wolff and said, "It's up to you. But I like his style."

"Would you bind yourself to aid us in whatever we do? As long as it is not dishonorable, of course. You may release yourself from your oath at any time, but you must swear by all that's holy that you will never aid our enemies."

"By God's blood and the beard of Moses, I swear."

That night, while they made camp in a brake alongside a brook, Kickaha said, "There's one problem that having funem Laksfalk along might complicate. We have to get the stain off your skin, and that beard has to go, too. Otherwise, if we run into Abiru, he might identify you."

"One lie always leads to another," Wolff said. "Well, tell him that I'm the younger son of a baron who kicked me out because my jealous brother falsely accused me. I've been traveling around since then, disguised as a Saracen. But I intend to return to my father's castle—he's dead now—and challenge my brother to a duel."

"Fabulous! You're a second Kickaha! But what about when he learns of Chryseis and the horn?"

"We'll think of something. Maybe the truth. He can always back out when he finds he's bucking the Lord."

The next morning they rode until they came to the village of

Etzelbrand. Here Kickaha purchased some chemicals from the local white-wizard and made a preparation to remove the stain. Once past the village, they stopped off at the brook. Funem Laksfalk watched with interest, then amazement, then suspicion as the beard came off, followed by the stain.

"God's eyes! You were a Khamshem, now you could be a Yidshe!"

Kickaha thereupon launched into a three-hour, much-detailed story in which Wolff was the bastard son of a Yidshe maiden lady and a Teutoniac knight on a quest. The knight, a Robert von Wolfram, had stayed at a Yidshe castle after covering himself with glory during a tournament. He and the maiden had fallen in love, too much so. When the knight had ridden out, vowing to return after completing his quest, he had left Rivke pregnant. But von Wolfram had been killed and the girl had had to bear young Robert in shame. Her father had kicked her out and sent her to a little village in Khamshem to live there forever. The girl had died when giving birth to Robert, but a faithful old servant had revealed the secret of his birth to Robert. The young bastard had sworn that when he gained manhood, he would go to the castle of his father's people and claim his rightful inheritance. Rivke's father was dead now but his brother, a wicked old man, held the castle. Robert intended to wrest the baronetcy from him if he would not give it up.

Funem Laksfalk had tears in his eyes at the end of the story. He said, "I will ride with you, Robert, and help you against your wicked uncle. Thus may I redeem my defeat."

Later, Wolff reproached Kickaha for making up such a fantastic story, so detailed that he might easily be tripped up. Moreover, he did not like to deceive such a man as the Yidshe knight.

"Nonsense! You couldn't tell him the whole truth, and it's easier to make up a whole lie than a half-truth! Besides, look at how much he enjoyed his little cry! And, I am Kickaha, the *kickaha*, the tricky one, the maker of fantasies and of realities. I am the man whom boundaries cannot hold. I slip from one to another, in-again-out-again Finnegan. I seem to be killed, yet I pop up again, alive, grinning, and kicking! I am quicker than men who are stronger than me, and stronger than those who are quicker! I have few loyalties, but those are unshakable! I am the ladies' darling wherever I go, and many are the tears shed after I slip through the night like a red-headed ghost! But tears cannot hold me any more than chains! Off I go, and where I will appear or what my name will be, few know! I am the Lord's gadfly; he cannot sleep at nights because I elude his Eyes, the ravens, and his hunters, the gworl!"

Kickaha stopped and began laughing uproariously. Wolff had to grin back. Kickaha's manner made it plain that he was poking fun at himself. However, he did half-believe it, and why should he not? What he said was not actually exaggeration.

This thought opened the way to a train of speculation that brought a frown to Wolff. Was it possible that Kickaha was the Lord himself in disguise? He could be amusing himself by running with hare and hound both. What better entertainment for a Lord, a man who had to look far and deep for something new with which to stave off ennui? There were many unexplained things about him.

Wolff, searching Kickaha's face for some clue to the mystery, felt his doubts evaporate. Surely that merry face was not the mask for a hideously cold being who toyed with lives. And then there was Kickaha's undeniably Hoosier accent and idioms. Could a Lord master these?

Well, why not? Kickaha had evidently mastered other languages and dialects as well.

So it went in Wolff's mind that long afternoon as they rode. But dinner and drink and good fellowship dispelled them so that, at bedtime, he had forgotten his doubts. The three had stopped at a tavern in the village of Gnazelschist and eaten heartily. Wolff and Kickaha devoured a roast suckling pig between them. Funem Laksfalk, although he shaved and had other liberal views of his religion, refused the taboo pork. He ate beef—although he knew it had not been slaughtered à la kosher. All three downed many steins of the excellent local dark beer, and during the drink-conversation Wolff told funem Laksfalk a somewhat edited story about their search for Chryseis—a noble quest indeed, they agreed, and then they all staggered off to bed.

In the morning, they took a shortcut through the hills which would save them three days' time—if they got through. The road was rarely traveled, and with good reason, for outlaws and dragons frequented the area. They made good speed, saw no men-of-the-woods and only one dragon. The scaly monster scrambled up from a ditch a hundred yards ahead of them. It snorted and disappeared into the trees on the other side of the road, as eager as they to avoid a fight.

Coming down out of the hills to the main highway, Wolff said, "A raven's following us."

"Yeah, I know it, but don't get your neck hot. They're all over the place. I doubt that it knows who we are. I sincerely hope it doesn't."

At noon of the following day, they entered the territory of the Komtur of Tregyln. More than twenty-four hours later, they arrived within sight of the castle of Tregyln, the Baron von Elgers' seat of power. This was the largest castle Wolff had so far seen. It was built of black stone and was situated on top of a high hill a mile from the town of Tregyln.

In full armor, pennoned lances held upright, the three rode boldly to the moat that surrounded the castle. A warder came out of a small blockhouse by the moat and politely inquired of them their business.

"Take word to the noble lord that three knights of good fame would be his guests," Kickaha said. "The Barons von Horstmann and von Wolfram and the far-famed Yidshe baron, funem Laksfalk. We look for a noble to hire us for fighting or to send us on a quest."

The sergeant shouted at a corporal, who ran off across the drawbridge. A few minutes afterwards, one of von Elgers' sons, a youth splendidly dressed, rode out to welcome them. Inside the huge courtyard, Wolff saw something that disturbed him. Several Khamshem and Sholkin were lounging around or playing dice.

"They won't recognize either one of us," Kickaha said. "Cheer up. If they're here, then so are Chryseis and the horn."

After making sure that their horses were well taken care of, the three went to the quarters given them. They bathed and put on the brilliantly colored new clothes sent up to them by von Elgers. Wolff observed that these differed little from the garments worn during the thirteenth century. The only innovations, Kickaha said, were traceable to aboriginal influence.

By the time they entered the vast dining-hall, the supper was in full blast. Blast was the right word, for the uproar was deafening. Half the guests were reeling, and the others did not move much because they had passed the reeling stage. Von Elgers managed to rise to greet his guests. Graciously, he apologized for being found in such a condition at such an early hour.

"We have been entertaining our Khamshem guest for several days. He has brought unexpected wealth to us, and we've been spending a little of it on a celebration."

He turned to introduce Abiru, did so too swiftly, and almost fell. Abiru rose to return their bow. His black eyes flickered like a sword point over them; his smile was broad but mechanical. Unlike the others, he appeared sober. The three took their seats, which were close to the Khamshem because the previous occupants had passed out under the table. Abiru seemed eager to talk to them.

"If you are looking for service, you have found your man. I am paying the baron to conduct me to the hinterland, but I can always use more swords. The road to my destination is long and hard and beset with many perils."

"And where is your destination?" Kickaha asked. No one looking at him would have thought him any more than idly interested in Abiru for he was hotly scanning the blonde beauty across the table from him.

"There is no secret about that," Abiru said. "The lord of Kranzelkracht is said to be a very strange man, but it is also said that he has more wealth even than the Grand Marshal of Teutonia."

"I know that for a fact," Kickaha replied. "I have been there, and I have seen his treasures. Many years ago, so it is said, he dared the displeasure of the Lord and climbed the great mountain to the tier of Atlantis. He robbed the treasure house of the Rhadamanthus himself and got away with a bagful of jewels. Since then, von Kranzelkracht has increased his wealth by conquering the states around his. It is said that the Grand Marshal is worried by this and is thinking of organizing a crusade against him. The Marshal claims that the man is a heretic. But if he were, would not the Lord have blasted him with lightning long ago?"

Abiru bowed his head and touched his forehead with his fingertips.

"The Lord works in mysterious ways. Besides, who but the Lord knows the truth? In any event, I am taking my slaves and certain possessions to Kranzelkracht. I expect to make an enormous profit from my venture, and those knights bold enough to share it will gain much gold—not to mention fame."

Abiru paused to drink from a glass of wine. Kickaha, aside to Wolff, said, "The man's as big a liar as I am. He intends to use us to get him as far as Kranzelkracht, which is near the foot of the monolith. Then he will take Chryseis and the horn up to Atlantis, where he should be paid with a houseful of jewels and gold for the two.

"That is, unless his game is even deeper than I think at this moment."

He lifted his stein and drank for a long time, or appeared to. Setting the stein down with a crash, he said, "I'll be damned if there isn't something familiar about Abiru! I had a funny feeling the first time I saw him, but I was too busy thereafter to think much about it. Now, I know I've seen him before."

Wolff replied that that was not amazing. How many faces had he seen during his twenty-year wanderings?

"Maybe you're right," Kickaha muttered. "But I don't think it was any slight acquaintance I had with him. I'd sure like to scrape off his beard."

Abiru arose and excused himself, saying that it was the hour of prayer to the Lord and his personal deity, Tartartar. He would be back after his devotions. At this, von Elgers beckoned to two men-at-arms and ordered them to accompany him to his quarters and make sure that he was safe. Abiru bowed and thanked him for his consideration. Wolff did not miss the intent behind the baron's polite words. He did not trust the Khamshem, and Abiru knew it. Von Elgers, despite his drunkenness, was aware of what was going on and would detect anything out of the way.

"Yeah, you're right about him," Kickaha said. "He didn't get to where he is by turning his back on his enemies. And try to conceal your impatience, Bob. We've got a long wait ahead of us. Act drunk, make a few passes at the ladies—they'll think you're queer if you don't. But don't go off with any. We got to keep each other in sight so we can take off together when the right time comes."

CHAPTER THIRTEEN

Wolff drank enough to loosen the wires that seemed to be wound around him. He even began to talk with the Lady Alison, wife of the baron of the Wenzelbricht March. A dark-haired and blue-eyed woman of statuesque beauty, she wore a clinging white samite gown. It was so low cut that she should have been satisfied with its exhilarating effect on the men, but she kept dropping her fan and picking it up herself. At any time other than this, Wolff would have been happy to break his woman-fast with her. It was obvious he would have no trouble doing so, for she was flattered that the great von Wolfram was interested in her. She had heard of his victory over von Laksberg. But he could think only of Chryseis, who must be somewhere in the castle. Nobody had mentioned her, and he dared not. Yet he was aching to do so and several times found that he had to bite the question off the tip of his tongue.

Presently, and just at the right time for him—since he could not any longer refuse the Lady Alison's bold hints without offending her—Kickaha was at his side. Kickaha had brought Alison's husband along to give Wolff a reasonable excuse for leaving. Later, Kickaha revealed that he had dragged von Wenzelbricht away from another woman on the pretext that his wife demanded he come to her. Both Kickaha and Wolff walked away, leaving the beer-stupored baron to explain just what he wanted of her. Since neither he nor his wife knew, they must have had an interesting, if mystifying, conversation.

Wolff gestured at funem Laksfalk to join them. Together, the three pretended to stagger off to the toilet. Once out of sight of those in the dining-hall, they hurried down a hall away from their supposed destination. Unhindered, they climbed four flights of steps. They were armed only with daggers, for it would have been an insult to wear armor or swords to dinner. Wolff, however, had managed to untie a long cord from the draperies in his apartment. He wore this coiled around his waist under his shirt.

The Yidshe knight said, "I overheard Abiru talk with his lieutenant, Rhamnish. They spoke in the trade language of H'vaizhum, little knowing that I have traveled on the Guzirit River in the jungle area. Abiru asked Rhamnish if he had found out yet where von Elgers had taken Chryseis. Rhamnish said that he had spent some gold and time in talking to servants and guards. All he could find out was that she is on the east side of the castle. The gworl, by the way, are in the dungeon."

"Why should von Elgers keep Chryseis from Abiru?" Wolff said. "Isn't she Abiru's property?"

"Maybe the baron has some designs on her," Kickaha said. "If she's as extraordinary and beautiful as you say . . ."

"We've got to find her!"

"Don't get your neck hot. We will. Oh, oh, there's a guard at the end of the hall. Keep walking toward him—stagger a little more."

The guard raised his spear as they reeled in front of him. In a polite but firm voice, he told them they must go back. The baron had forbidden anybody, under pain of death, to proceed further.

"All right," Wolff said, slurring the words. He started to turn, then suddenly leaped and grabbed the spear. Before the startled sentry could loose the yell from his open mouth, he was slammed against the door and the shaft of the spear was brought up hard against his throat. Wolff continued to press it. The sentry's eyes goggled, his face became red, then blue. A minute later, he slumped forward, dead.

The Yidshe dragged the body down the hall and into a side-room. When he returned, he reported that he had hidden the corpse behind a large chest.

"Too bad," Kickaha said cheerfully. "He may have been a nice kid. But if we have to fight our way out, we'll have one less in our way."

However, the dead man had had no key to unlock the door.

"Von Elgers is probably the only man who has one, and we'd play hell getting it off him," Kickaha said. "Okay. We'll go around."

He led them back down the hall to another room. They climbed through its tall pointed window. Beyond its ledge was a series of projections, stones carved in the shape of dragon heads, fiends, boars. The adornments had not been spaced to provide for easy climbing, but a brave or desperate man could ascend them. Fifty feet below them, the surface of the moat glittered dully in the light of torches on the drawbridge. Fortunately, thick black clouds covered the moon and would prevent those below from seeing the climbers.

Kickaha looked down at Wolff, who was clinging to a stone gargoyle, one foot on a snake-head. "Hey, did I forget to tell you that the baron keeps the moat stocked with water-dragons? They're not very big, only about twenty feet long, and they don't have any legs. But they're usually underfed."

"There are times when I find your humor in bad taste," Wolff said fiercely. "Get going."

Kickaha gave a low laugh and continued climbing. Wolff followed, after glancing down to make sure that the Yidshe was doing all right. Kickaha stopped and said. "There's a window here, but it's barred. I don't think there's anyone inside. It's dark."

Kickaha continued climbing. Wolff paused to look inside the window. It was black as the inside of a cave fish's eye. He reached through the bars and groped around until his fingers closed on a candle. Lifting it carefully so that it would come out of its holder, he passed it through the bars. With one arm hooked around a steel rod, he hung while he fished a match from the little bag on his belt with the other hand.

From above, Kickaha said, "What are you doing?"

Wolff told him, and Kickaha said, "I spoke Chryseis' name a couple of times. There's no one in there. Quit wasting time."

"I want to make sure."

"You're too thorough; you pay too much attention to detail. You got to take big cuts if you want to chop down a tree. Come on."

Not bothering to reply, Wolff struck the match. It flared up and almost went out in the breeze, but he managed to stick it inside the window quickly enough. The flare of light showed a bedroom with no occupant.

"You satisfied?" Kickaha's voice came, weaker because he was climbing upward. "We got one more chance, the bartizan. If there's no one . . . Anyway, I don't know how—*ugh!*"

Afterwards, Wolff was thankful that he had been so reluctant to give up his hopes that Chryseis would be in the room. He had let the match burn out until it threatened his fingers and only then let go of it. Immediately after that and Kickaha's muffled exclamation, he was struck by a falling body. The impact felt as if it had almost torn his arm loose from its socket. He gave a grunt that echoed the one from above and hung on with one arm. Kickaha clung to him for several seconds, shivered, then breathed deeply and resumed his climb. Neither said a word about it, but both knew that if it had not been for Wolff's stubbornness, Kickaha's fall would also have knocked Wolff from a precarious hold on a gargoyle. Possibly funem Laksfalk would have been dislodged also, for he was directly below Wolff.

The bartizan was a large one. It was about one third of the way up the wall, projected far outward from the wall, and a light fell from its cross-shaped window. The wall a little distance above it was bare of decoration.

An uproar broke loose below and a fainter one within the castle. Wolff stopped to look down toward the drawbridge, thinking that they must have been seen. However, although there were a number of men-at-arms and guests on the drawbridge and the grounds outside, many with torches, not a single one was looking up toward the climbers. They seemed to be searching for someone in the bushes and trees.

He thought that their absence and the body of the guard had been noted. They would have to fight their way out. But let them find Chryseis first and get her loose; then would be time to think of battle.

Kickaha, ahead of him, said, "Come on, Bob!" His voice was so excited that Wolff knew he must have located Chryseis. He climbed swiftly, more swiftly than good sense permitted. It was necessary to climb to one side of the projection, for its underside angled outward. Kickaha was lying on the flat top of the bartizan and just in the act of pulling himself back from its edge. "You have to hang upside down to look in the window, Bob. She's there, and she's alone. But the window's too narrow for either of you to go through."

Wolff slid out over the edge of the projection while Kickaha grabbed his legs. He went out and over, the black moat below, and bent down until he would have fallen if his legs had not been held. The slit in the stone showed him the face of Chryseis, inverted. She was smiling but tears were rolling down her cheeks.

Afterward, he did not exactly remember what they said to each other, for he was in a fever of exaltation, succeeded by a chill of frustration and despair, then followed by another fever. He felt as if he could talk forever, and he reached his hand out to touch hers. She strained against the opening in the rock in vain to reach him.

"Never mind, Chryseis," he said. "You know we're here. We're not going to leave until we take you away, I swear it."

"Ask her where the horn is!" Kickaha said.

Hearing him, Chryseis said, "I do not know, but I think that von Elgers has it."

"Has he bothered you?" Wolff asked savagely.

"Not so far, but I do not know how long it will be before he takes me to bed," she replied. "He's restrained himself only because he does not want to lower the price he'll get for me. He says he's never seen a woman like me."

Wolff swore, then laughed. It was like her to talk thus frankly, for in the Garden world self-admiration was an accepted attitude.

"Cut out the unnecessary chatter," Kickaha said. "There'll be time for that if we get her out."

Chryseis answered Wolff's questions as concisely and clearly as possible. She described the route to this room. She did not know how many guards were stationed outside her door or on the way up.

"I do know one thing that the baron does not," she said. "He thinks that Abiru is taking me to von Kranzelkracht. I know better. Abiru means to ascend the Doozvillnava to Atlantis. There he will sell me to the Rhadamanthus."

"He won't sell you to anybody, because I'm going to kill him," Wolff said. "I have to go now, Chryseis, but I'll be back as soon as possible. And I won't be coming this way. Until then, I love you."

Chryseis cried, "I have not heard a man tell me that for a thousand years! Oh, Robert Wolff, I love you! But I am afraid! I . . ."

"You don't have to be afraid of anything," he said. "Not while I am alive, and I don't intend to die."

He gave the word for Kickaha to drag him back onto the rooftop of the bartizan. He rose and almost fell over from dizziness, for his head was gorged with blood.

"The Yidshe has already started down," Kickaha said. "I sent him to find out if we can get back the way we came and also to see what's causing the uproar."

"Us?"

"I don't think so. The first thing they'd do, they'd check on Chryseis. Which they haven't done."

The descent was even slower and more dangerous than the climb up, but they made it without mishap. Funem Laksfalk was waiting for them by the window which had given them access to the outside.

"They've found the guard you killed," he said. "But they don't think we had anything to do with it. The gworl broke loose from the dungeon and killed a number of men. They also seized their own weapons. Some got outside, but not all."

The three left the room and merged quickly with the searchers. They had no chance to go up the flight of steps at the end of which was the room where Chryseis was imprisoned. Without a doubt, Von Elgers would have made sure that the guards were increased.

They wandered around the castle for several hours, acquainting themselves with its layout. They noted that, though the shock of the gworl's escape had sobered the Teutons somewhat, they were still very drunk. Wolff suggested that they go to their room, and talk about possible plans. Perhaps they could think of something reasonably workable.

Their room was on the fifth story and by a window at an angle below the window of Chryseis' bartizan. To get to it, they had to pass many men and women, all stinking of beer and wine, reeling, babbling away, and accomplishing very little. Their room could not have been entered and searched, for only they and the chief warder had the keys. He had been too busy elsewhere to get to their room. Besides, how could the gworl enter through a locked door?

The moment Wolff stepped into his room, he knew that they had somehow entered. The musty rotten-fruit stench hit him in the nostrils. He pulled the other two inside and swiftly shut and locked the door behind them. Then he turned with his dagger in his hand. Kickaha also, his nostrils dilating and his eyes stabbing, had his blade out. Only funem Laksfalk was unaware that anything was wrong except for an unpleasant odor.

Wolff whispered to him; the Yidshe walked toward the wall to get their swords, then stopped. The racks were empty.

Silently and slowly, Wolff went into the other room. Kickaha, behind him, held a torch. The flame flickered and cast humped shadows that made Wolff start. He had been sure that they were the gworl.

The light advanced; the shadows fled or changed into harmless shapes.

"They're here," Wolff said softly. "Or they've just left. But where could they go?"

Kickaha pointed at the high drapes that were drawn over the window. Wolff strode up to them and began thrusting through the red-purple velvet cloth. His blade met only air and the stone of the wall. Kickaha pulled the drapes back to reveal what the dagger had told him. There were no gworl.

"They came in through the window," the Yidshe said. "But why?"

Wolff lifted his eyes at that moment, and he swore. He stepped back to warn his friends, but they were already looking upward. There, hanging upside down by their knees from the heavy iron drapery rod, were two gworl. Both had long, bloody knives in their hands. One, in addition, clutched the silver horn.

The two creatures stiffened their legs the second they realized they were discovered. Both managed to flip over and come down heads-up. The one to the right kicked out with his feet. Wolff rolled and then was up, but Kickaha had missed with his knife and the gworl had not. It slid from his palm through a short distance into Kickaha's arm.

The other threw his knife at funem Laksfalk. It struck the Yidshe in the solar plexus with a force that made him bend over and stagger back. A few seconds later, he straightened up to reveal why the knife had failed to enter his flesh. Through the tear in his shirt gleamed the steel of light chain-mail.

By then, the gworl with the horn had gone through the window. The others could not rush to the window because the gworl left behind was putting up a savage battle. He knocked down Wolff again, but with his fist this time. He threw himself like a whirlwind at Kickaha, his fists flailing, and drove him back. The Yidshe, his knife in hand, jumped at him and thrust for his belly, only to have his wrist seized and turned until he cried out with pain and the knife fell from his fist.

Kickaha, lying on the floor, raised one leg and then drove the heel of his foot against the gworl's ankle. He fell, although he did not hit the floor because Wolff seized him. Around and around, their arms locked around each other, they circled. Each was trying to break the other's back and also trying to trip the other. Wolff succeeded in throwing him over. They toppled against the wall with the gworl receiving the most damage when the back of his head struck the wall.

For a flicker of an eyelid he was stunned. This gave Wolff enough time to pull the stinking, hairy, bumpy creature hard against him and pull with all his strength against the gworl's spine. Too heavily muscled and too heavily boned, the gworl resisted the spine-snapping. By then, the other two men were upon him with their knives. They thrust several times and would have continued to try for a fatal spot in the tough cartilage-roughened hide had Wolff not told them to stop.

Stepping back, he released the gworl, who fell bleeding and glaze-eyed to the floor. Wolff ignored him for a moment to look out the window after the gworl who had escaped with the horn. A party of horsemen, holding torches, was thundering over the drawbridge and out into the country. The light showed only the smooth black waters of the moat; there was no gworl climbing down the wall. Wolff turned back to the gworl who had remained behind.

"His name is Diskibibol, and the other is Smeel," Kickaha said.

"Smeel must have drowned," Wolff said. "Even if he could

swim, the water-dragons might have gotten him. But he can't swim."

Wolff thought of the horn lying in the muck at the bottom of the moat. "Apparently no one saw Smeel fall. So the horn's safe there, for the time being."

The gworl spoke. Although he used German, he could not master the sounds accurately. His words grated deep in the back of his throat. "You will die, humans. The Lord will win; Arwoor is the Lord; he cannot be defeated by filth such as you. But before you die, you will suffer the most . . . the . . . the most . . ."

He began coughing, threw up blood, and continued to do so until he was dead.

"We'd better get rid of his body," Wolff said. "We might have a hard time explaining what he was doing here. And von Elgers might connect the missing horn with their presence here."

A look out of the window showed him that the search party was far down the trail road leading to the town. For the moment, at least, no one was on the bridge. He lifted the heavy corpse up and shoved it out the window. After Kickaha's wound was bandaged, Wolff and the Yidshe wiped up the evidences of the struggle.

Only after they were through did funem Laksfalk speak. His face was pale and grim. "That was the horn of the Lord. I insist that you tell me how it got here and what your part is in this . . . this seeming blasphemy."

"Now's the time for the whole truth," Kickaha said. "You tell him, Bob. For once, I don't feel like hogging the conversation."

Wolff was concerned for Kickaha, for his face, too, was pale, and the blood was oozing out through the thick bandages. Nevertheless, he told the Yidshe what he could as swiftly as possible.

The knight listened well, although he could not help interjecting questions frequently or swearing when Wolff told him something particularly amazing.

"By God," he said when Wolff seemed to be finished, "this tale of another world would make me call you a liar if the rabbis had not already told me that my ancestors, and those of the Teutons, had come from just such a place. Then there is the Book of the Second Exodus, which says the same thing and also claims that the Lord came from a different world.

"Still, I had always thought these tales the stuff that holy men, who are a trifle mad, dream up. I would never have dreamed of saying so aloud, of course, for I did not want to be stoned for heresy. Also, there's always the doubt that these could be true. And the Lord punishes those who deny him; there's no doubt of that.

"Now, you put me in a situation no man could envy. I know you two for the most redoubtable knights it has ever been my fortune to encounter. You are such men as would not lie; I would stake my life on that. And your story rings true as the armor of the great dragon-slayer, fun Zilberbergl. Yet, I do not know."

He shook his head. "To seek to enter the citadel of the Lord himself, to strike again the Lord! That frightens me. For the first time in my life, I, Leyb fumen Laksfalk, admit that I am afraid."

Wolff said, "You gave your oath to us. We release you but ask that you do as you swore. That is, you tell no one of us or our quest."

Angrily, the Yidshe said, "I did not say I would quit you! I will not, at least not yet. There is this that makes me think you might be telling the truth. The Lord is omnipotent, yet his holy horn has been in your hands and those of the gworl, and the Lord has done nothing. Perhaps ..."

Wolff replied that he did not have time to wait for him to make up his mind. The horn must be recovered now, while there was the opportunity. And Chryseis must be freed at the first chance. He led them from the room and into another, unoccupied at the moment. There they took three swords to replace theirs, which the gworl must have cast out of the window into the moat. Within a few minutes, they were outside the castle and pretending to search through the woods for the gworl.

By then most of the Teutons outside had returned to the castle. The three waited until the stragglers decided that no gworl were around. When the last of these had gone across the drawbridge, Wolff and his friends put out their torches. Two sentries remained at the guardhouse by the end of the bridge. These, however, were a hundred yards distant and could not see into the shadows where the three crouched. Moreover, they were too busy discussing the events of the night and looking into the darkness of the woods. They were not the original sentries, for these had been killed by the gworl when they had made their dash for freedom across the bridge.

"The point just below our window should be where the horn is," Wolff said. "Only ..."

"The water-dragons," Kickaha said. "They'll have dragged off Smeel and Diskibibol's bodies to their lairs, wherever those are. But there might be some others cruising around. I'd go, but this wound of mine would draw them at once."

"I was just talking to myself," Wolff said. He began to take off his clothes. "How deep's the moat?"

"You'll find out," Kickaha said.

Wolff saw something gleam redly in the reflected light from the distant bridge torches. An animal's eyes, he thought. The next moment, he and the others were caught within something sticky and binding. The stuff, whatever it was, covered his eyes and blinded him.

He fought savagely but silently. Though he did not know who his assailants were, he did not intend to arouse the castle people. However the struggle came out, the issue did not concern them; he knew that.

The more he thrashed, the tighter the webs clung to him and bound him. Eventually, raging, breathing hard, he was helpless. Only then did a voice speak, low and rasping. A knife cut the web to leave his face exposed. In the dim light of the distant torches, he could see two other figures wrapped in the stuff and a dozen crooked shapes. The rotten-fruit stench was powerful.

"I am Ghaghrill, the Zdrrikh'agh of Abbkmung. You are Robert Wolff and our great enemy Kickaha, and the third one I do not know."

"The Baron funem Laksfalk!" the Yidshe said. "Release me, and you will soon find out whether I am a good man to know or not, you stinking swine!"

"Quiet! We know you have somehow slain two of my best killers, Smeel and Diskibibol, though they could not have been so fierce if they allowed themselves to be defeated by such as you. We saw Diskibibol fall from where we hid in the woods. And we saw Smeel jump with the horn."

Ghagrill paused, then said, "You, Wolff, will go after the horn into the waters and bring it back to us. If you do, I swear by the honor of the Lord that we will release all three of you. The Lord wants Kickaha, too, but not as badly as the horn, and he said that we were not to kill him, even if we had to let him go to keep from killing him. We obey the Lord, for he is the greatest killer of all."

"And if I refuse?" Wolff said. "It is almost certain death for me with the water-dragons in the moat."

"It will be certain death for you if you don't."

Wolff considered. He was the logical choice, he had to admit. The quality and relationship of the Yidshe was unknown to the gworl, so they could not let him go after the horn; he might fail to return. Kickaha was a prize second only to the horn. Besides, he was wounded, and the blood from the wound would attract the water-monsters. Wolff, if he cared for Kickaha, would return. They could not, of course, be sure of the depth of his feelings for Kickaha. That was a chance they would have to take.

One thing was certain. No gworl was about to venture into such deep water if he had someone else to do it for him.

"Very well," Wolff said. "Let me loose, and I will go after the horn. But at least give me a knife to defend myself against the dragons."

"No," Ghaghrill said.

Wolff shrugged. After he was cut loose of the web-net, he removed all of his clothes except his shirt. This covered the cord wound around his waist.

"Don't do it, Bob," Kickaha said. "You can't trust a gworl any more than his master. They will take the horn from you and then do to us what they wish. And laugh at us for being their tools."

"I don't have any choice," Wolff said. "If I find the horn, I'll be back. If I don't return, you'll know I died trying."

"You'll die anyway," Kickaha replied. There was a smack of a fist against flesh. Kickaha cursed but did so softly.

"Speak any more, Kickaha," Ghaghrill said, "and I will cut out your tongue. The Lord did not forbid that."

CHAPTER FOURTEEN

Wolff looked up at the window, from which a torch-light still shone. He walked into the water, which was chilly but not cold. His feet sank into thick gluey mud which evoked images of the many corpses whose rotting flesh must form part of this mud. And he could not keep from thinking of the saurians swimming out there. If he was lucky, they would not be in the immediate neighbourhood. If they had dragged off the bodies of Smeel and Diskibibol . . . Better quit dwelling on them and start swimming.

The moat was at least two hundred yards wide at this point. He even stopped at the midway point to tread water and turn around to look at the shore. From this distance he could see nothing of the group.

On the other hand, they could not see him either. And Ghaghrill had given him no time limit to return. However, he knew that if he were not back before dawn, he would not find them there.

At a spot immediately below the light from the window, he dived. Down he went, the water becoming colder almost with every stroke. His ears began to ache, then to hurt intensely. He blew some bubbles of air out to relieve the pressure, but he was not helped much by this. Just as it seemed that he could go no deeper without his ears bursting, his hand plunged into soft mud. Restraining the desire to turn at once and swim upwards for the blessed relief from pressure and the absolutely needed air, he groped around on the floor of the moat. He found nothing but mud and, once, a bone. He drove himself until he knew he had to have air.

Twice he rose to the surface and then dived again. By now, he knew that even if the horn were lying on the bottom, he might not ever find it. Blind in the murky waters, he could pass within an inch of the horn and never know it. Moreover, it was possible that Smeel had thrown the horn far away from him when he had fallen. Or a water-dragon could have carried it off with Smeel's corpse, even swallowed the horn.

The third time, he swam a few strokes to the right from his previous dives before plunging under. He dived down at what he hoped was a ninety-degree angle from the bottom. In the blackness, he had no way of determining direction. His hand plowed into the mud; he settled close to it to feel around, and his fingers closed upon cold metal. A quick slide of them along the object passed over seven little buttons.

When he reached the surface, he trod water and gasped for wind. Now to make the trip back, which he hoped he could do. The water-dragons could still show up.

Then he forgot the dragons, for he could see nothing. The torchlight from the drawbridge, the feeble moonglow through the clouds, the light from the window overhead, all these were gone.

Wolff forced himself to keep on treading water while he thought his situation through. For one thing, there was no breeze. The air was stale. Thus, he could only be in one place, and it was his fortune that such a place happened to be just where he had dived. Also, it was his luck that he had come up from the bottom at an oblique angle.

Still, he could not see which way was shoreward and which way castleward. To find out took only a few strokes. His hand contacted stone—stone bricks. He groped along it until it began to curve inward. Following the curve, he finally came to that which he had hoped for. It was a flight of stone steps that rose out of the water and led upward.

He climbed up it, slowly, his hand out for a sudden obstacle. His feet slid over each step, ready to pause if an opening appeared or a step seemed loose. After twenty steps upward, he came to their end. He was in a corridor cut out of stone.

Von Elgers, or whoever had built the castle, had constructed a means for secret entrance and exit. An opening below water level in the walls led to a chamber, a little port, and from thence into the castle. Now, Wolff had the horn and a way to get unnoticed into the castle. But he did not know what to do.

Should he return the horn to the gworl first? Afterward, he and the two others could return this way and search for Chryseis.

He doubted that Ghaghrill would keep his word. However, even if the gworl were to release their captives, if they swam to this place, Kickaha's wound would draw the saurians and all three would be lost. Chryseis would have no chance of getting free. Kickaha could not be left behind while the other two went back to the castle. He would be exposed as soon as dawn came. He could hide in the woods, but the chances were that another hunting party would be searching that area then. Especially after it was discovered that the three stranger knights were gone.

He decided to go on down the hall. This was too good a chance to pass up. He would do his best before daylight. If he failed, then he would go back with the horn.

The horn! No use taking that with him. Should he be captured without it, his knowledge of its location might help him.

He returned to where the steps came to an end below the water. He dived down to a depth of about ten feet and left the horn on the mud.

Back in the corridor, he shuffled until he came to more steps at its end. The flight led upward on a tight spiraling course. A count of steps led him to think that he had ascended at least five stories. At every estimated story he felt around the narrow walls for doors or releases to open doors. He found none.

At what could have been the seventh story, he saw a tiny beam of light from a hole in the wall. Bending down, he peered through it. By the far end of the room, seated at a table, a bottle of wine before him, was Baron von Elgers. The man seated across the table from the baron was Abiru.

The baron's face was flushed by more than drink. He snarled at Abiru, "That's all I intend to say, Khamshem! You will get the horn back from the gworl, or I'll have your head! Only first you'll be taken to the dungeon! I have some curious iron devices there that you will be interested in!"

Abiru rose. His face was as pale beneath its dark pigment as the baron's was crimson.

"Believe me, sire, if the horn has been taken by the gworl, it will be recovered. They can't have gone far with it—if they have it—and they can easily be tracked down. They can't pass themselves off as human beings, you know. Besides, they're stupid."

The baron roared, stood up, and crashed his fist against the top of the table.

"Stupid! They were clever enough to break out of my dungeon, and I would have sworn that no one could do that! And they found my room and took the horn! You call that stupid!"

"At least," Abiru said, "they didn't steal the girl, too. I'll get something out of this. She should fetch a fabulous price."

"She'll fetch nothing for you! She is mine!"

Abiru glared and said, "She is my property. I obtained her at great peril and brought her all this way at much expense. I am entitled to her. What are you, a man of honor or a thief?"

Von Elgers struck him and knocked him down. Abiru, rubbing his cheek, got to his feet at once. Looking steadily at the baron, his voice tight, he said, "And what about my jewels?"

"They are in my castle!" the baron shouted. "And what is in my castle is the von Elgers'!"

He strode away out of Wolff's sight but apparently opened a door. He bellowed for the guard, and when they had come they took Abiru away between them.

"You are fortunate I do not kill you!" the baron raged. "I am allowing you to keep your life, you miserable dog! You should get down on your knees and thank me for that! Now get out of the castle at once. If I hear that you are not making all possible speed to another state, I will have you hung on the nearest tree!"

Abiru did not reply. The door closed. The baron paced back and forth for awhile, then abruptly came toward the wall behind which Wolff was crouched. Wolff left the peephole and retreated far down the steps. He hoped he had chosen the right direction in which to go. If the baron came down the staircase, he could force Wolff into the water and perhaps back out into the moat. But he did not think the baron intended to come that way.

For a second the light was cut off. A section of wall swung out with the baron's finger thrust through the hole. The torch held by von Elgers lit the well. Wolff crouched down behind the shadow cast by a turn of the corkscrew case. Presently, the light became weaker as the baron carried it up the steps. Wolff followed.

He could not keep his eyes on von Elgers all the time, for he had to dodge down behind various turns to keep from being detected if the baron should look downward. So it was that he did not see von Elgers leave the stairs nor know it until the light suddenly went out.

He went swiftly after the baron, although he did pause by the peephole. He stuck his finger in it and lifted upward. A small section gave way, a click sounded, and a door swung open for him. The inner side of the door formed part of the wall of the baron's quarters. Wolff stepped into the room, chose a thin eight-inch dagger from a rack in the wall, and went back out to the stairs. After shutting the door, he climbed upward.

This time he had no light from a hole to guide him. Nor was he even sure that he had stopped at the same place as the baron. He had made a rough estimate of the height from himself to the baron when the baron had disappeared. There was nothing else to do but feel around for the device which the baron must have used to open another door. When he placed his ear against the wall to listen for voices, he heard nothing.

His fingers slid over bricks and moisture-crumbled mortar until they met wood. That was all he could find: stone and a wooden frame in which a broad and high panel of wood was smoothly inset. There was nothing to indicate an open-sesame.

He climbed a few steps more and continued to probe. The bricks were innocent of any trigger or catch. He returned to the spot opposite the door and felt the wall there. Nothing.

Now he was frantic. He was sure that von Elgers had gone to Chryseis' room, and not just to talk. He went back down the steps and fingered the walls. Still nothing.

Again he tried the area around the door with no success. He pushed on one side of the door, only to find it would not budge. For a moment he thought of hammering on the wood and attracting von Elgers. If the baron were to come through to investigate, he would be helpless for a moment to an attack from above.

He rejected the idea. The baron was too canny to fall for such a trick. While he was unlikely to go for help, because he would not want to reveal the passageway to others, he could leave Chryseis' room through the regular door. The guard posted outside it might wonder where he came from, although he would probably think that the baron had been inside before the watch had been changed. In any case, the baron could permanently shut the mouth of a suspicious guard. Wolff pushed in on the other side of the door, and it swung inward. It had not been locked; all it needed was pressure on the correct side.

He groaned softly at missing the obvious so long and stepped through. It was dark beyond the door; he was in a small room, almost a closet. This was composed of mortared bricks, except at one side. Here a metal rod poked from the wooden wall. Before working it, Wolff placed his ear against the wall. Muffled voices came through, too faint for him to recognize.

The metal rod had to be pulled out to activate the release on the door. Dagger in hand, Wolff stepped through it. He was in a large chamber of great stone blocks. There was a large bed with four ornately carved posters of glossy black wood and a bright-pink tasseled canopy. Beyond it was the narrow cross-shaped window through which he had looked earlier that night.

Von Elgers' back was to him. The baron had Chryseis in his arms and was forcing her toward the bed. Her eyes were closed, and her head was turned away to avoid von Elgers' kisses. Both of them were still fully clothed.

Wolff bounded across the room, seized the baron by the shoulder, and pulled him backward. The baron let loose of Chryseis to reach for the dagger in his scabbard, then remembered that he had brought none. Apparently he had not intended to give Chryseis a chance to stab him.

His face, so flaming before, was gray now. His mouth worked, the cry for help to the guards outside the door frozen by surprise and fear.

Wolff gave him no chance to summon help. He dropped the dagger to strike the baron on the chin with his fist. Von Elgers, unconscious, slumped. Wolff did not want to waste any time, so he brushed by Chryseis, huge-eyed and pale. He cut off two strips of cloth from the bedsheets. The smaller he placed inside the baron's mouth, the larger he used as a gag. Then he removed a piece of the cord around his waist and tied von Elgers' hands in front of him. Hoisting the limp body over his shoulder, he said to Chryseis, "Come on. We can talk later."

He did pause to give instructions to Chryseis to close the wall-door behind them. There was no sense in letting others find the passageway when they finally came to investigate the baron's long absence. Chryseis held the torch behind him as they went down the steps. When they had come to the water, Wolff told her what they must do to escape. First, he had to retrieve the horn. Having done so, he scooped up water with his hands and threw it on the baron's face. When he saw his eyes open, he informed him of what he must do.

Von Elgers shook his head no. Wolff said, "Either you go with us as hostage and take your chances with the water-dragons or you die right now. So which is it?"

The baron nodded. Wolff cut his bonds but attached the end of the cord to his ankle. All three went into the water. Immediately, von Elgers swam out to the wall and dived. The others followed under the wall, which only went about four feet below the surface. Coming up on the other side, Wolff saw that the clouds were beginning to break. The moon would soon be bearing down in all her green brightness.

As directed, the baron and Chryseis swam at an angle toward the other side of the moat. Wolff followed with the end of the cord in one hand. With its burden, they could not go swiftly. In fifteen minutes the moon would be rounding the monolith, with the sun not far behind it at the other corner. There was not much time for Wolff to carry out his plan, but it was impossible to keep control of the baron unless they took their time.

Their point of arrival at the bank of the moat was a hundred yards beyond where the gworl and their captives waited. Within a few minutes they were around the curve of the castle and out of sight of the gworl and the guards on the bridge even if the moon became unclouded. This path was a necessary evil—evil because every second in the water meant more chance for the dragons to discover them.

When they were within twenty yards of their goal, Wolff felt rather than saw the roil of water. He turned to see the surface lift a little and a small wave coming toward him. He drew up his feet and kicked. They struck something hard and solid enough to allow him to spring away. He shot backward, dropping the end of the cord at the same time. The bulk passed between him and Chryseis, struck von Elgers, and was gone.

So was Wolff's hostage.

They abandoned any attempt to keep from making splashing noises. They swam as hard as they could. Only when they reached the bank and scrambled up onto it and ran to a tree did they stop. Sobbing for breath, they clung to the trunk.

Wolff did not wait until he had fully regained his breath. The sun would be around Doozvillnavava within a few minutes. He told Chryseis to wait for him. If he did not return shortly after sunaround, he would not be coming for a long time—if ever. She would have to leave and hide in the woods and then do whatever she could.

She begged him not to go, for she could not stand the idea of being all alone here.

"I have to," he said, handing her an extra dagger which he had stuck through his shirt and secured by knotting the shirttail about it.

"I will use it on myself if you are killed," she said.

He was in agony at the thought of her being so helpless, but there was nothing he could do about it.

"Kill me now before you leave me," she said. "I've gone through too much; I can't stand any more."

He kissed her lightly on the lips and said, "Sure you can. You're tougher than you used to be and always were tougher than you thought. Look at you now. You can say *kill* and *death* without so much as flinching."

He was gone, running crouched over toward the spot where he had left his friends and the gworl. When he estimated he was about twenty yards from them, he stopped to listen. He heard nothing except the cry of a nightbird and a muffled shout from somewhere in the castle. On his hands and knees, the dagger in his teeth, he crawled toward the place opposite the light from the window of his quarters. At any moment he expected to smell the musty odor and to see a clump of blackness against the lesser dark.

But there was nobody there. Only the glimmer-gray remnants of the web-nets remained to show that the gworl had actually been there.

He prowled around the area. When it became evident that there was no clue and that the sun would shortly expose him to the bridge guards, he returned to Chryseis. She clung to him and cried a little.

"See! I'm here after all," he said. "But we have to get out of here now."

"We're going back to Okeanos?"

"No, we're going after my friends."

They trotted away, past the castle and toward the monolith. The absence of the baron would soon be noticed. For miles around, no ordinary hiding place would be safe. And the gworl, knowing this, must also be making speed toward Doozvillnavava. No matter how badly they wanted the horn, they could not hang around now. Moreover, they must think that Wolff had drowned or been taken by a dragon. To them, the horn might be out of reach just now, but they could return when it was safe to do so.

Wolff pushed hard. Except for brief rests, they did not stop until they had reached the thick forest of the Rauhwald. There they crawled beneath the tangled thorns and through the intertwined bushes until their knees bled and their joints ached. Chryseis collapsed. Wolff gathered many of the plentiful berries for them to feed upon. They slept all night, and in the morning resumed their all-fours progress. By the time they had reached the other side of the Rauhwald, they were covered with thorn-wounds. There was no one waiting for them on the other side, as he had feared there would be.

This and another thing made him happy. He had come across evidence that the gworl had also passed this way. There were bits of coarse gworl hair on thorns and pieces of cloth. No doubt Kickaha had managed to drop these to mark the way if Wolff should be following.

CHAPTER FIFTEEN

After a month, they finally arrived at the foot of the monolith, Doozvillnavava. They knew they were on the right trail, since they had heard rumors of the gworl and even talked with those who had sighted them from a distance.

"I don't know why they've gone so far from the horn," he said. "Perhaps they mean to hole up in a cave in the face of the mountain and will come back down after the cry for them has died out."

"Or it could be," Chryseis said, "that they have orders from the Lord to bring Kickaha back first. He has been like an insect on the Lord's eardrum so long that the Lord must be crazed even by the thought of him. Maybe he wants to make sure that Kickaha is out of the way before he sends the gworl again for the horn."

Wolff agreed that she could be right. It was even possible that the Lord was going to come down from the palace via the same cords by which he had lowered the gworl. That did not seem likely, however, for the Lord would not want to be stranded. Could he trust the gworl to hoist him back up?

Wolff looked at the eye-staggering heights of the continent-broad tower of Doozvillnavava. It was, according to Kickaha, at least twice as high as the monolith of Abharhploonta, which supported the tier of Dracheland. It soared 60,000 feet or more, and the creatures that lived on the ledges and recesses and in the caves were fully as dreadful and hungry as those on the other monoliths. Doozvillnavava was gnarled and scoured and slashed and bristly; its ravaged face had an enormous recession that gave it a dark and gaping mouth; the giant seemed ready to eat all who dared to annoy it.

Chryseis, also examining the savage cliffs and their incredible height, shivered. But she said nothing; she had quit voicing her fears some time ago.

It could be that she was no longer concerned with herself, Wolff thought, but was intent upon the life within her. She was sure that she was pregnant.

He put his arm around her, kissed her, and said, "I'd like to start at once, but we'll have to make preparations for several days. We can't attack that monster without resting or without enough food."

Three days later, dressed in tough buckskin garments and carrying ropes, weapons, climbing tools, and bags of food and water, they began the ascent. Wolff bore the horn in a soft leather bag tied to his back.

Ninety-one days later, they were at an estimated halfway point. And at least every other step had been a battle against smooth verticality, rotten and treacherous rock, or against the predators. These included the many-footed snake he had encountered on Thayaphayawoed, wolves with great rock-gripping paws, the boulder ape, ostrich-sized axebeaks, and the small but deadly downdropper.

When the two climbed over the edge of the top of Doozvillnavava, they had been 186 days on the journey. Neither was the same, physically or mentally, as at the start. Wolff weighed less but he had far more endurance and wiriness to his strength. He bore the scars of downdroppers, boulder apes, and axebeaks on his face and body. His hatred for the Lord was even more intense, for Chryseis had lost the foetus before they had gotten 10,000 feet up. Such was to be expected, but he could not forget that they would not have had to make the climb if it had not been for the Lord.

Chryseis had been toughened in body and spirit by her experiences before she had started up Doozvillnavava. Yet the things and situations on this monolith had been far worse than anything previously, and she might have broken. That she did not vindicated Wolff's original feeling that she was basically of strong fiber. The effects of the millenia of sapping life in the Garden had been sloughed off. The Chryseis who conquered this monolith was much like the woman who had been abducted from the savage and demanding life of the ancient Aegean. Only she was far wiser.

Wolff waited for several days to rest and hunt and repair the bows and make new arrows. He also kept a watch for an eagle. He had not been in contact with any since he had talked to Phthie in the ruined city by the river of Guzirit. No green-bodied yellow-headed bird appeared, so he reluctantly decided to enter the jungle. As on Dracheland, a thousand-mile thick belt of jungle circled the entire rim. Within the belt was the land of Atlantis. This, exclusive of the monolith in its center, covered an area the size of France and Germany combined.

Wolff had looked for the pillar on top of which was the Lord's palace, since Kickaha had said that it could be seen from the rim even though it was much more slender than any of the other monoliths. He could see only a vast and dark continent of clouds, jagged and coiled with lightning. Idaquizzoorhruz was hidden. Now, whenever Wolff ascended a high hill or climbed a tall tree, could he see it. A week later, the stormclouds continued to shroud the pillar of stone. This worried him, for he had not seen such a storm in the three and a half years that he had been on this planet.

Fifteen days passed. On the sixteenth, they found on the narrow green-fraught path a headless corpse. A yard away in the bush was the turbaned head of a Khamshem.

"Abiru could be trailing the gworl, too," he said. "Maybe the gworl took his jewels when they left von Elgers' castle. Or, more likely, he thinks they have the horn."

A mile and a half further on, they came across another Khamshem, his stomach ripped open and his entrails hanging out. Wolff tried to get information out of him until he found that the man was too far gone. Wolff put him out of his pain, noting that Chryseis did not even look away while he did so. Afterward, he put his knife in his belt and held the Khamshem's scimitar in his right hand. He felt that he would soon need it.

A half-hour later, he heard shouts and whoops down the trail. He and Chryseis concealed themselves in the foliage beside the path. Abiru and two Khamshem came running with death loping after them in the form of three squat Negroids with painted faces and long kinky scarlet-dyed beards. One threw his spear; it sailed through the air to end in the back of a Khamshem. He plunged forward without a sound and slid on the soft damp earth like a sailboat launched into eternity, the spear as the mast. The other two Khamshem turned to make a stand.

Wolff had to admire Abiru, who fought with great skill and courage. Although his companion went down with a spear in his solar plexus, Abiru continued to slash with his scimitar. Presently two of the savages were dead, and the third turned tail. After the Negroid had disappeared, Wolff came up silently behind Abiru. He struck with the edge of his palm to paralyze the man's arm and cause the scimitar to drop.

Abiru was so startled and scared he could not talk. On seeing Chryseis step out from the bushes, his eyes bulged even more. Wolff asked him what the situation was. After a struggle, Abiru regained his tongue and began to talk. As Wolff had guessed, he had pursued the gworl with his men and a number of Sholkin. Some miles from here, he had caught up with them. Rather, they had caught him. The ambush had been half-successful, for it had slain or incapacitated a good third of the Khamshem. All this had been done without loss to the gworl, who had cast knives from trees or from the bushes.

The Khamshem had broken away and fled, hoping to make a stand in a better place down the trail—if they could find one. Then both hunted and hunter had run into a horde of black savages.

"And there'll be more of them soon looking for you," Wolff said. "What about Kickaha and funem Laksfalk?"

"I do not know about Kickaha. He was not with the gworl. But the Yidshe knight was."

For a moment, Wolff thought of killing Abiru. However, he disliked doing it in cold blood and he also wanted to ask him more questions. He believed that there was more to him than he pretended to be. Shoving Abiru on ahead with the point of the scimitar, he went down the trail. Abiru protested that they would be killed; Wolff told him to shut up. In a few minutes they heard the shouts and screams of men in battle. They crossed a shallow stream and were at the bottom of a steep, high hill.

This was so rocky that comparatively little vegetation covered it. Along a line up the hill was the wake of the fight—dead and wounded gworl, Khamshem, Sholkin, and savages. Near the top of the hill, their backs against a V-shaped wall and under an overhang formed by two huge boulders, three held off the blacks. These were a gworl, a Khamshem, and the Yidshe baron. Even as Wolff and Chryseis started to go up, the Khamshem fell, pierced by several of the shovel-sized spearheads. Wolff told Chryseis to go back. For answer, she fitted an arrow to her bow and shot. A savage in the rear of the mob fell backward, the shaft sticking from his back.

Wolff smiled grimly and began to work his own bow. He and Chryseis chose only those at the extreme rear, hoping to shoot down a number before those at the front noticed. They were successful until the twelfth fell. A savage happened to glance back and see the man behind him crumple. He yelled and pulled at the arms of those nearest him. These immediately brandished their spears and began running down the hill toward the two, leaving most of their party to attack the gworl and the Yidshe. Before they had reached the bottom half of the hill, four more were down.

Three more tumbled headlong and rolled down with shafts in them. The remaining six lost their zeal to come at close quarters. Halting, they threw their spears, which were launched at such a distance that the archers had no trouble dodging them. Wolff and Chryseis, operating coolly and skilfully from much practice and experience, then shot four more. The two survivors, screaming, ran back up to their fellows. Neither made it, although one was only wounded in the leg.

By then, the gworl had fallen. Funem Laksfalk was left alone against forty. He did have a slight advantage, which was that they could get to him only two at a time. The walls of the boulders and the barricade of corpses prevented the others from swarming over him. Funem Laksfalk, his scimitar bloody and swinging, sang loudly some Yiddish fighting song.

Wolff and Chryseis took partial cover behind two boulders and renewed their rear attack. Five more fell, but the quivers of both were then empty. Wolff said, "Pull some from the corpses and use them again. I'm going to help him."

He picked up a spear and ran at an angle across and up the hill, hoping that the savages would be too occupied to see him. When he had come around the hill, he saw two savages crouched on top of the boulder. These were kept from jumping down upon the Yidshe's rear by the overhang of the roughly shaped boulders. But they were waiting for a moment when he would venture too far out from its protection.

Wolff hurled his spear and caught one in the buttocks. The savage cried out and pitched forward from the rock and, presumably, on his fellows below. The other stood up and whirled around in time to get Wolff's knife in his belly. He fell backward off the rock.

Wolff lifted a small boulder and heaved it on top of one of the great boulders and climbed up after it. Then he lifted the small boulder again, raised it above his head, and walked to the front of the great boulder. He yelled and threw it down into the crowd. They looked up in time to see the rock descending on them. It smashed at least three and rolled down the hill. At that, the survivors fled in a panic. Perhaps they thought that there must be others than Wolff. Or, because they were undisciplined savages, they had been unnerved by too many losses already. The sight of so many of their dead shot down behind them must also have added to their panic.

Wolff hoped they would not return. To add fuel to their fright, he leaped down and picked up the boulder again and sent it crashing down the hill after them. It leaped and bounded as if it were a wolf after a rabbit and actually struck one more before it reached bottom.

Chryseis, from behind her boulder, put two more arrows into the savages.

He turned to the baron and found him lying on the ground. His face was gray, and blood was welling from around the spearhead driven into his chest.

"You!" he said faintly. "The man from the other world. You saw me fight?"

Wolff stepped down by him to examine the wound. "I saw. You fought like one of Joshua's warriors, my friend. You fought as I have never seen any fight. You must have slain at least twenty."

Funem Laksfalk managed to smile a trifle. "It was twenty-five. I counted them."

Then he smiled broadly and said, "We are both stretching the truth a trifle, as our friend Kickaha would say. But not too much. It was a great fight. I only regret that I had to fight unfriended and unarmored and in a lonely place where none will ever know that a funem Laksfalk added honor to the name. Even if it was against a bunch of howling and naked savages."

"They will know," Wolff said. "I will tell them some day."

He did not give false words of comfort. He and the Yidshe both knew that death was around the corner, sniffing eagerly at the end of the track.

"Do you know what happened to Kickaha?" he said.

"Ah, that trickster! He slipped his chains one night. He tried to loosen mine, too, but he could not. Then he left, with the promise that he would return to free me. And so he will, but he will be too late."

Wolff looked down the hill. Chryseis was climbing toward him with several arrows which she had recovered from corpses. The blacks had regrouped at the foot and were talking animatedly among themselves. Others came out of the jungle to join them. The fresh ones swelled the number to forty. These were led by a man garbed in feathers and wearing a hideous wooden mask. He whirled a bull-roarer, leaped up and down, and seemed to be haranguing them.

The Yidshe asked Wolff what was happening. Wolff told him. The Yidshe spoke so weakly that Wolff had to put his ear close to the knight's mouth.

"It was my fondest dream, Baron Wolff, that I would some day fight by your side. Ah, what a noble pair of knights we would have made, in armor and swinging our . . . *S'iz kalt*."

The lips became silent and blue. Wolff rose to look down the hill again. The savages were moving up and also spreading out to prevent flight. Wolff set to work dragging bodies and piling them to form a rampart. The only hope, a weak one, was to permit passage for only one or two to attack at a time. If they lost enough men, they might get discouraged and leave. He did not really think so, for these savages showed a remarkable persistence despite what must be to them staggering losses. Also, they could always retreat just far enough to wait for Wolff and Chryseis to be driven from their refuge by thirst and hunger.

The savages stopped halfway up to give those who had gone around the hill time to establish their stations. Then, at a cry from the man in the wooden mask, they climbed up as swiftly as possible. The two defenders made no move until the thrown spears rattled against the sides of the boulders or plunged into the barricade of dead. Wolff shot twice, Chryseis three times. Not one arrow missed.

Wolff loosed his final shaft. It struck the mask of the leader and knocked him back down the hill. A moment later he threw off the mask. Although his face was bleeding, he led the second charge.

A weird ululation arose from the jungle. The savages stopped, spun, and became silent as they stared at the green around the hill. Again, the swelling-falling cry came from somewhere in the trees.

Abruptly, a bronze-haired man clad only in a leopard loincloth raced from the jungle. He carried a spear in one hand and a long knife in the other. Coiled around his shoulder was a lariat, and a quiver and bow were hung from a belt over the other shoulder. Behind him, a mass of hulking long-armed, mound-chested, and long-fanged apes poured from the trees.

At sight of these, the savages cried out aloud and tried to run around the hill. Other apes appeared from the other side; like hairy jaws, the two columns closed on the blacks.

There was a brief fight. Some apes fell with spears in their bellies, but most of the blacks threw down their weapons and tried to run or else crouched trembling and paralyzed. Only twelve escaped.

Wolff, smiling and laughing in his relief, said to the man in the leopard-skin, "And how are you named on this tier?"

Kickaha grinned back. "I'll give you one guess."

His smile died when he saw the baron. "Damn it! It took me too much time to find the apes and then to find you! He was a good man, the Yidshe; I liked his style. Damn it! Anyway, I promised him that if he died I'd take his bones back to his ancestral castle, and that's one promise I'll keep. Not just now, though. We have some business to attend to."

Kickaha called some of the apes to be introduced. "As you'll notice," he said to Wolff, "they're built more like your friend Ipsewas than true apes. Their legs are too long and their arms too short. Like Ipsewas and unlike the great apes of my favorite childhood author, they have the brains of men. They hate the Lord for what he has done to them; they not only want revenge, they want a chance to walk around in human bodies again."

Not until then did Wolff remember Abiru. He was nowhere to be seen. Apparently he had slipped off when Wolff had gone to funem Laksfalk's aid.

That night, around a fire and eating roast deer, Wolff and Chryseis heard about the cataclysm taking place in Atlantis. It had started with the new temple that the Rhadamanthus of Atlantis had started to build. Ostensibly the tower was for the greater glory of the Lord. It was to reach higher than any building ever known on the planet. The Rhadamanthus recruited his entire state to erect the temple. He kept on adding story to story until it looked as if he wanted to reach the sky itself.

Men asked each other when there would be an end to the work. All were slaves with but one purpose in mind: build. Yet they dared not speak openly, for the soldiers of the Rhadamanthus killed all who objected or who failed to labor. Then it became obvious that the Rhadamanthus had something else besides a temple in his crazed mind. The Rhadamanthus intended to erect a means to storm the heavens themselves, the palace of the Lord.

"A thirty-thousand-foot building?" said Wolff.

"Yeah. It couldn't be done, of course, not with the technology available in Atlantis. But the Rhadamanthus was mad; he really thought he could do it. Maybe he was encouraged because the Lord hadn't appeared for so many years, and he thought that maybe the rumors were true that the Lord was gone. Of course, the ravens must have told him different, but he could have figured they were lying to protect themselves."

Kickaha said that the devastating phenomena now destroying Atlantis were proof of more than that the Lord was revenging himself against the hubris of Rhadamanthus. The Lord must have finally unlocked the secrets of how to operate some of the devices in the palace.

"The Lord who disappeared would have taken precautions against a new occupant manipulating his powers. But the new Lord has at last succeeded in learning where the controls of the storm-makers are."

Proof: the gigantic hurricanes, tornados, and continual rain sweeping the land. The Lord must be out to rid this tier of all life.

Before reaching the edge of the jungle, they met the tidal wave of refugees. These had stories of houses and great buildings blown down, of men picked up and carried off and smashed by the winds, of the floods that were stripping the earth of trees and all life and even washing away the hills.

By then, Kickaha's party had to lean to walk against the wind. The clouds closed around them; rain struck them; lightning blinded and crashed on all sides.

Even so, there were periods when the rain and lightning ceased. The energies loosed by Arwoor had to spend themselves, and new forces had to be built up before being released again. In these comparative lulls, the party made progress, although slowly. They crossed swollen rivers bearing the wreck of a civilization: houses, trees, furniture, chariots, the corpses of men, women, children, dogs, horses, birds and wild animals. The forests were uprooted or smashed by the strokes of electrical bolts. Every valley was running with water; every depression was filled. And a choking stench filled the air.

When their journey was little more than half-completed, the clouds began to thin away. They were in the sunshine again, but in a land silent with death. Only the roar of water or the cry of a bird that had somehow survived broke the stone of quiet. Sometimes the howl of a demented human being sent chills through them, but these were few.

The last cloud was carried off. And the white monolith of Idaquizzoorhruz shone before them, three hundred miles away on the horizonless plain. The city of Atlantis—or what was left of it—was a hundred miles distant. It took them twenty days to reach its outskirts through flood and debris.

"Can the Lord see us now?" Wolff asked.

Kickaha said, "I suppose he could with some sort of telescope. I'm glad you asked, though, because we'd better start traveling by night. Even so, we'll be spotted by them."

He pointed at a raven flying over.

Passing through the ruins of the capital city, they came near the imperial zoo of Rhadamanthus. There were some strong cages left standing, and one of these contained an eagle. On the muddy bottom were a number of bones, feathers, and beaks. The caged eagles had evaded starvation by eating each other. The lone survivor sat emaciated, weak and miserable on the highest perch.

Wolff opened the cage, and he and Kickaha talked to the eagle, Armonide. At first, Armonide wanted nothing but to attack them, enfeebled though she was. Wolff threw her several pieces of meat, then the two men continued their story. Armonide said that they were liars and had some human, and therefore evil, purpose in mind. When she had heard Wolff's story through and his pointing out that they did not have to release her, she began to believe. When Wolff explained that he had a plan in mind to gain revenge upon the Lord, the dullness in her eyes was replaced by a sharp light. The idea of actually assaulting the Lord, perhaps successfully, was more food than meat itself. She stayed with them for three days, eating, gaining strength, and memorizing exactly what she was to tell Podarge.

"You will see the Lord's death yet, and new and youthful and lovely maiden bodies will be yours," Wolff said. "But only if Podarge does as I ask her."

Armonide launched herself from a cliff, swooped down, flapped her spreading wings, and began to climb. Presently the green feathers of her body were absorbed by the green sky. Her red head became a black dot, and then it too was gone.

Wolff and his party remained in the tangle of fallen trees until night before going on. By now, through some subtle process, Wolff had become the nominal leader. Before, Kickaha had had the reins in his hands with the approval of all. Something had happened to give Wolff the power of decision-making. He did not know what, for Kickaha was as boisterous and vigorous as before. And the passing of captainship had not been caused by a deliberate effort on Wolff's part. It was as if Kickaha had been waiting until Wolff had learned all he could from him. Then Kickaha had handed over the baton.

They traveled strictly within the night-hours, during which time they saw very few ravens. Apparently there was no need for them in this area since it was under the close surveillance of the Lord himself. Besides, who would dare intrude here after the anger of the Lord had been so catastrophically wrought?

On arriving at the great tumbled mass of Rhadamanthus' tower, they took refuge within the ruins. There was more than enough metal for Wolff's plan. Their only two problems were getting enough food and trying to conceal the noise of their sawing and hammering and the glare of their little smithies. The first was solved when they discovered a storehouse of grain and dried meat. Much of the supplies had been destroyed by fire and then by water, but there was enough left to see them through several weeks. The second was dealt with by working deep within the underground chambers. The tunneling took five days, a period which did not concern Wolff because he knew that it would be some time before Armonide would reach Podarge—if she got to her destination at all. Many things could happen to her on the way, especially an attack by the ravens.

"What if she doesn't make it?" Chryseis asked.

"Then we'll have to think of something else," Wolff replied. He fondled the horn and pressed its seven buttons. "Kickaha knows the gate through which he came when he left the palace. We could go back through it. But it would be folly. The present Lord would not be so stupid as not to leave a heavy guard there."

Three weeks passed. The supply of food was so low that hunters would have to be sent out. This was dangerous even at night, for there was no telling when a raven might be around. Moreover, for all Wolff knew the Lord could have devices for seeing as easily at night as at day.

At the end of the fourth week, Wolff had to give up his dependence on Podarge. Either Armonide had not reached her or Podarge had refused to listen.

That very night, as he sat under cover of a huge plate of bent steel and stared at the moon, he heard the rustle of wings. He peered into the darkness. Suddenly, moonlight shone on something black and pale, and Podarge was before him. Behind her were many winged shapes and the gleam of moon on yellow beaks and redly shining eyes.

Wolff led them down through the tunnels and into a large chamber. By the small fires, he looked again into the tragically beautiful face of the harpy. But now that she thought she could strike back at the Lord, she actually looked happy. Her flock had carried food along, so, while all ate, Wolff explained his plan to her. Even as they were discussing the details, one of the apes, a guard, brought in a man he had caught skulking about the ruins. He was Abiru the Khamshem.

"This is unfortunate for you and a sorry thing for me," Wolff said. "I can't just tie you up and leave you here. If you escaped and contacted a raven, the Lord would be forewarned. So, you must die. Unless you can convince me otherwise."

Abiru looked about him and saw only death.

"Very well," he said. "I had not wanted to speak nor will I speak before everyone, if I can avoid it. Believe me, I must talk to you alone. It is as much for your life as for mine."

"There is nothing you can say that could not be said before all," Wolff replied. "Speak up."

Kickaha placed his mouth close to Wolff's ear and whispered, "Better do as he says."

Wolff was astonished. The doubts about Kickaha's true identity came back to him. Both requests were so strange and unexpected that he had a momentary feeling of disassociation. He seemed to be floating away from them all.

"If no one objects, I will hear him alone," he said. Podarge frowned and opened her mouth, but before she could say anything she was interrupted by Kickaha. "Great One, now is the time for trust. You must believe in us, have confidence. Would you lose your only chance for revenge and for getting your human body back? You must go along with us on this. If you interfere, all is lost."

Podarge said, "I do not know what this is all about, and I feel that I am somehow being betrayed. But I will do as you say, Kickaha, for I know of you and know that you are a bitter enemy of the Lord. But do not try my patience too far."

Then Kickaha whispered an even stranger thing to Wolff. "Now I recognize Abiru. That beard and the stain on his skin fooled me, plus not having heard his voice for twenty years."

Wolff's heart beat fast with an undefined apprehension. He took his scimitar and conducted Abiru, whose hands were bound behind him, into a small room. And here he listened.

CHAPTER SIXTEEN

An hour later, he returned to the others. He looked stunned.

"Abiru will go with us," he said. "He could be very valuable. We need every hand we can get and every man with knowledge."

"Would you care to explain that?" Podarge said. She was narrow-eyed, the mask of madness forming over her face.

"No, I will not and cannot," he replied. "But I feel more strongly than ever that we have a good chance for victory. Now, Podarge how strong are your eagles? Have they flown so far tonight that we must wait until tomorrow night for them to rest?"

Podarge answered that they were ready for the task ahead of them. She wanted to delay no longer.

Wolff gave his orders, which were relayed by Kickaha to the apes, since they obeyed only him. They carried out the large crossbars and the ropes to the outside, and the others followed them.

In the bright light of the moon, they lifted the thin but strong cross-bars. The human beings and the fifty apes then fitted themselves into the weblike cradles beneath the cross-bars and tied straps to secure themselves. Eagles gripped the ropes attached to each of the four ends of the bars and another gripped the rope tied to the center of the cross. Wolff gave the signal. Though there had been no chance to train, each bird jumped simultaneously into the air, flapped her wings and slowly rose upward. The ropes were paid out to over fifty feet to give the eagles a chance to gain altitude before the cross-bars and the human attached to each had to be lifted.

Wolff felt a sudden jerk, and he uncoiled his bent legs to give an extra push upward. The bar tilted to one side, almost swinging him over against one of the bars. Podarge, flying over the others, gave an order. The eagles pulled up more rope or released more length to adjust for balance. In a few seconds, the cross-bars were at the correct level.

On Earth this plan would not have been workable. A bird the size of the eagle probably could not have gotten into the air without launching herself from a high cliff. Even then, her flight would have been very slow, maybe too slow to keep from stalling or sinking back to Earth. However, the Lord had given the eagles muscles with strength to match their weight.

They rose up and up. The pale sides of the monolith, a mile away, glimmered in the moonlight. Wolff clutched the straps of his cradle and looked at the others. Chryseis and Kickaha waved back. Abiru was motionless. The shattered and prone wreck of Rhadamanthus' tower became smaller. No ravens flew by to be startled and to wing upward to warn the Lord. Those eagles not serving as carriers spread wide to forestall such a possibility. The air was filled with an armada; the beat of their wings drummed loudly in Wolff's ears, so loudly that he could not imagine the noise not traveling for miles.

The time came when this side of ravaged Atlantis was spread out in the moonlight for him to scan in one sweep of the eye. Then the rim appeared, and part of the tier below it. Dracheland became visible as a great half-disc of darkness. The hours crept by. The mass of Amerindia appeared, grew and was suddenly chopped off at the rim. The garden of Okeanos, so far below Amerindia and so narrow, could not be seen.

Both the moon and the sun were visible now because of the comparative slenderness of this monolith. Nevertheless, the eagles and their burdens were still in darkness, in the shadow of Idaquizzoorhruz. It would not last for long. Soon this side would be under the full glare of the daytime luminary. Any ravens would be able to see them from miles away. The party had, however, drifted close to the monolith, so that anyone on top would have to be on the edge to detect them.

At last, after over four hours, just as the sun touched them, they were level with the top. Beside them was the garden of the Lord, a place of flaming beauty. Beyond rose the towers and minarets and flying buttresses and spiderweb architectures of the palace of the Lord. It soared up for two hundred feet and covered, according to Kickaha, more than three hundred acres.

They did not have time to appreciate its wonder, for the ravens in the garden were screaming. Already the hundreds of Podarge's pets had swooped down upon them and were killing them. Others were winging toward the many windows to enter and seek out the Lord.

Wolff saw a number get inside before the traps of the Lord could be activated. Shortly thereafter, those attempting to climb in through the openings disappeared in a clap of thunder and a flash of lightning. Charred to the bone, they fell off the ledges and onto the ground below or on the rooftops or buttresses.

The human beings and the apes settled to the ground just outside a diamond-shaped door of rose stone set with rubies. The eagles released the ropes and gathered by Pordarge to wait for her orders.

Wolff untied the ropes from the metal rings on the cross-bars. Then he lifted the bars above his head. After running to a point just a few feet from the diamond-shaped doorway, he cast the steel cross into it. One bar went through the entrance; the two at right angles to it jammed against the sides of the door.

Flame exploded again and again. Thunder deafened him. Tongues of searing voltage leaped out at him. Suddenly, smoke poured from within the palace, and the lightning ceased. The ravaging device had either burned out from the load or was temporarily discharged.

Wolff took one glance around him. Other entrances were also spurting bursts of flame or else their defenses had burned out. Eagles had taken many of the cross-bars and were dropping them at an angle into the windows above. He leaped over the white-hot liquid of his cross-bar and through the door. Chryseis and Kickaha joined him from another entrance. Behind Kickaha came the horde of giant apes. Each carried a sword or battleaxe in his hand.

Kickaha asked, "Is it coming back to you?"

Wolff nodded. "Not all, but enough, I hope. Where's Abiru?"

"Podarge and a couple of the apes are keeping on eye on him. He could try something for his own purposes."

Wolff in the lead, they walked down a hall the walls of which were painted with murals that would have delighted and awed the most critical of Terrestrials. At the far end was a low gate of delicate and intricate tracery and of a shimmering bluish metal. They proceeded toward it but stopped as a raven, fleeing for its life, sped over them. Behind it came an eagle.

The raven passed over the gate, and as it did so it flew headlong into an invisible screen. Abruptly, the raven was a scatter of thin slices of flesh, bones and feathers. The pursuing eagle screamed as it saw this and tried to check her flight, but too late. She too was cut into strips.

Wolff pulled the left section of the gate toward him instead of pushing in on it as he would naturally have done. He said, "It should be okay now. But I'm glad the raven triggered the screen first. I hadn't remembered it."

Still, he stuck his sword forward to test, then it came back to him that only living matter activated the trap. There was nothing to do but to trust that he could remember correctly. He walked forward without feeling anything but the air, and the others followed.

"The Lord will be holed up in the center of the palace,

where the defense control room is," he said. "Some of the defenses are automatic, but there are others he can operate himself. That is, if he's found out how to operate them, and he's certainly had enough time to learn."

They padded through a mile of corridors and rooms, each one of which could have detained anyone with a sense of beauty for days. Every now and then a boom or a scream announced a trap set off somewhere in the palace.

A dozen times, they were halted by Wolff. He stood frowning for awhile until he suddenly smiled. Then he would move a picture at an angle or touch a spot on the murals: the eye of a painted man, the horn of a buffalo in a scene of the Amerindian plains, the hilt of a sword in the scabbard of a knight in a Teutoniac tableau. Then he would walk forward.

Finally, he summoned an eagle. "Go bring Podarge and the others," he said. "There is no use their sacrificing themselves any more. I will show the way."

He said to Kickaha, "The sense of *déjà vu* is getting stronger every minute. But I don't remember all. Just certain details."

"As long as they're the significant details, that's all that matters at this moment," Kickaha said. His grin was broad, and his face was lit with the delight of conflict. "Now you can see why I didn't dare to try re-entry by myself. I got the guts but I lack the knowledge."

Chryseis said, "I don't understand."

Wolff pulled her to him and squeezed her. "You will soon. That is, if we make it. I've much to tell you, and you have much to forgive."

A door ahead of them slid into the wall, and a man in armor clanked toward them. He held a huge axe in one hand, swinging it as if it were a feather.

"It's no man," Wolff said. "It's one of the Lord's taloses."

"A robot!" Kickaha said.

Wolff thought, *Not quite in the sense Kickaha means.* It was not all steel and plastic and electrical wires. Half of it was protein, formed in the biobanks of the Lord. It had a will for survival that no machine of all-inanimate parts could have. This was a strength and also a weakness.

He spoke to Kickaha, who ordered the apes behind him to obey Wolff. A dozen stepped forward, side by side, and hurled their axes simultaneously. The talos dodged but could not evade all. It was struck with a force and precision that would have chopped it apart if it had not been armor-plated. It fell backward and rolled, then rose to its feet. While it was down, Wolff ran at it. He struck at it with his scimitar at the juncture of shoulder and neck. The blade broke without cutting into the metal. However, the force of the blow did knock the talos down again.

Wolff dropped his weapons, seized the talos around its waist, and lifted it. Silently, for it had no voice-chords, the armored thing kicked and reached down to grip Wolff. He hurled it against the wall, and it crashed down on the floor. As it began to get to its feet once more, Wolff drew his dagger and drove it into one of the eye-holes. There was a crack as the plastic over the eye gave way and was dislodged. The tip of the knife broke off, and Wolff was hurled back by a blow from the mailed fist. He came back quickly, grabbed the extended fist again, turned, and flopped it over his back. Before it could arise, it found itself gripped and hoisted high again. Wolff ran to the window and threw it headlong out.

It turned over and over and smashed against the ground four stories below. For a moment it lay as if broken, then it began to rise again. Wolff shouted at some eagles outside on a buttress. They launched themselves, soared down, and a pair grabbed the talos' arms. Up they rose, found it too heavy, and sank back. But they were able to keep it aloft a few inches from the ground. Over the surface, between buttresses and curiously carved columns, they flew. Their destination was the edge of the monolith, from which they would drop the talos. Not even its armor could withstand the force at the end of the 30,000-foot fall.

Wherever the Lord was hidden, he must have seen the fate of the single talos he had released. Now, a panel in the wall slid back, and twenty taloses came out, each with an axe in his hand. Wolff spoke to the apes. These hurled their axes again, knocking down many of the things. The gorilla-sized anthropoids charged in and several seized each talos. Although the mechanical strength of each android was more than that of a single ape, the talos was outmatched by two. While one ape wrestled with an android, the other gripped the helmet-head and twisted. Metal creaked under the strain; suddenly, neck-mechanisms broke with a snap. Helmets rolled on the floor with an ichorish liquid flowing out. Other taloses were lifted up and passed from hand to hand and dumped out of the window. Eagles carried each one off to the rim.

Even so, seven apes died, cut down by axes or with their own heads twisted off. The quick-to-learn protein brains of the semiautomatons imitated the actions of their antagonists, if it was to their advantage.

A little further on in the hall, thick sheets of metal slid down before and behind them to block off advance or retreat.

Wolff had forgotten this until just a second before the plates were lowered. They descended swiftly but not so swiftly that he did not have time to topple a marble stone pedestal with a statue on it. The end of the fallen column lay under the plate and prevented its complete closure. The forces driving the plate were, however, so strong that the edge of the plate began to drive through the stone. The party slid on their backs through the decreasing space. At the same time, water flooded into the area. If it had not been for the delay in closing the plate, they would have been drowned.

Sloshing ankle deep in the water, they went down the hall and up another flight of steps. Wolff stopped them by a window, through which he cast an axe. No thunder and lightning resulted, to he leaned out and called Podarge and her eagles in to him. Having been blocked off by the plates, they had gone outside to find another route.

"We are close to the heart of the palace, to the room in which the Lord must be," he said. "Every corridor from here on in has walls which hold dozens of laser beam-projectors. The beams can form a network through which no one could penetrate alive."

He paused, then said, "The Lord could sit in there forever. The fuel for his projectors will not give out, and he has food and drink enough to last for any siege. But there's an old military axiom which states that any defense, no matter how formidable, can be broken if the right offense is found."

He said to Kickaha, "When you took the gate through the Atlantean tier, you left the crescent behind you. Do you remember where?"

Kickaha grinned and said, "Yeah! I stuck it behind a statue in a room near the swimming pool. But what if it was found by the gworl?"

"Then I'll have to think of something else. Let's see if we can find the crescent."

"What's the idea?" Kickaha said in a low voice.

Wolff explained that Arwoor must have an escape route from the control room. As Wolff remembered it, there was a crescent set in the floor and several loose ones available. Each of these, when placed in contact with the immobile crescent, would open a gate to the universe for which the loose one had a resonance. None of them gave access to other levels of the planet in this universe. Only the horn could affect a gate between tiers.

"Sure," Kickaha said. "But what good will the crescent do us even if we find it? It has to be matched up against another, and where's the other? Anyway, anyone using it would only be taken through to Earth."

Wolff pointed over his back to indicate the long leather box slung there by a strap. "I have the horn."

They started down a corridor. Podarge strode after them. "What are you up to?" she asked fiercely.

Wolff answered that they were looking for means to get within the control room. Podarge should stay behind to handle any emergency. She refused, saying that she wanted them in her sight now that they were so close to the Lord. Besides, if they could get through to the Lord, they would have to take her along. She reminded Wolff of his promise that the Lord would be hers to do with as she wished. He shrugged and walked on.

They located the room in which was the statue behind which Kickaha had concealed the crescent. But it had been overturned in the struggle between apes and gworl. Their bodies lay sprawled around the room. Wolff stopped in surprise. He had seen no gworl since entering the palace and had taken it for granted that all had perished during the fight with the savages. The Lord had not sent all of them after Kickaha.

Kickaha cried, "The crescent's gone!"

"Either it was found some time ago or someone just found it after the statue was knocked over," Wolff said. "I have an idea of who did take it. Have you seen Abiru?"

Neither of the others had seen him since shortly after the invasion of the palace had started. The harpy, who was supposed to keep an eye on him, had lost him.

Wolff ran toward the labs with Kickaha and Podarge, wings half-opened, behind him. By the time he had covered the 3000 feet to it, Wolff was winded. Breathing hard, he stopped at the entrance.

"Vannax may be gone already and within the control room," he said. "But if he's still in there working on the crescent, we'd better enter quietly and hope to surprise him."

"Vannax?" Podarge said.

Wolff swore mentally. He and Kickaha had not wanted to reveal the identity of Abiru until later. Podarge hated any Lord so much that she would have killed him at once. Wolff wanted to keep him alive because Vannax, if he did not try to betray them, could be valuable in the taking of the palace. Wolff had promised Vannax that he could go into another world to try his luck there if he helped them against Arwoor. And Vannax had explained how he had managed to get back to this universe. After Kickaha (born Finnegan) had accidentally come here, taking a crescent with him, Vannax had continued his search for another. He had been successful in, of all places, a pawn shop in Peoria, Illinois. How it had gotten there and what Lord had lost it on Earth would never be known. Doubtless there were other crescents in obscure places on Earth. However, the crescent he had found had passed him through a gate located on the Amerindian tier. Vannax had climbed Thayaphayawoed to Khamshem, where he had been lucky enough to capture the gworl, Chryseis, and the horn. Thereafter, he had made his way toward the palace hoping to get within.

Wolff muttered, "The old saying goes that you can't trust a Lord."

"What did you say?" Podarge asked. "And I repeat, who is Vannax?"

Wolff was relieved that she did not know the name. He answered that Abiru had sometimes disguised himself under that name. Not wanting to reply to any more questions, and feeling that time was vital, he entered the laboratory. It was a room broad enough and high-ceilinged enough to house a dozen jet airliners. Cabinets and consoles and various apparatuses, however, gave it a crowded appearance. A hundred yards away, Vannax was bent over a huge console, working with the buttons and levers.

Silently, the three advanced on him. They were soon close enough to see that two crescents were locked down on the console. On the broad screen above Vannax was the ghostly image of a third semicircle. Wavy lines of light ran across it.

Vannax suddenly gave an *ah!* of delight as another crescent appeared by the first on the screen. He manipulated several dials to make the two images move toward each other and then merge into a single one again.

Wolff knew that the machine was sending out a frequency-tracer and had located that of the crescent set into the floor of the control room. Next, Vannax would subject the crescents clamped to the console to a treatment which would change their resonance to match that of the control room. Where Vannax had gotten the two semicircles was a mystery until Wolff thought of that crescent which must have accompanied him when he passed through the gate to the Amerindian tier. Somehow, during the time between his capture and the flight, he had gotten hold of this crescent. He must have hidden it in the ruins before the ape had captured him.

Vannax looked up from his work, saw the three, glanced at the screen, and snatched the two crescents from the spring-type clamps on the console. The three ran toward him as he placed one crescent on the floor and then the other. He laughed, made an obscene gesture, and stepped into the circle, a dagger in his hand.

Wolff gave a cry of despair, for they were too far away to stop him. Then he stopped and threw a hand over his eyes, but too late to shut out the dazzling flash. He heard Kickaha and Podarge, also blinded, shouting. He heard Vannax's scream and smelled the burned flesh and clothes.

Sightlessly, he advanced until his feet touched the hot corpse.

"What the hell happened?" Kickaha said. "God, I hope we're not permanently blinded!"

"Vannax thought he was slipping in through Arwoor's gate in the control room," Wolff said. "But Arwoor had set a trap. He could have been satisfied with wrecking the matcher, but it must have amused him to kill the man who would try it."

He stood and waited, knowing that time was getting short and that he was not serving his cause or anyone else's by his patience with his blindness. But there was nothing else he could do. And, after what seemed like an unbearably long time, sight began to come back.

Vannax was lying on his back, charred and unrecognizable. The two crescents were still on the floor and undamaged. These were separated a moment later by Wolff with a scribe from a console.

"He was a traitor," Wolff said in a low voice to Kickaha. "But he did us a service. I meant to try the same trick, only I was going to use the horn to activate the crescent you hid after I'd changed its resonance."

Pretending to inspect other consoles for booby-traps, he managed to get Kickaha and himself out of ear-range of Podarge.

"I didn't want to do it," he whispered. "But I'm going to have to. The horn must be used if we're to drive Arwoor out of the control room or get him before he can use his crescents to escape."

"I don't get you," Kickaha said.

"When I had the palace built, I incorporated a thermitic substance in the plastic shell of the control room. It can be triggered only by a certain sequence of notes from the horn, combined with another little trick. I don't want to set the stuff off because the control room will then also be lost. And this place will be indefensible later against any other Lords."

"You better do it," Kickaha said. "Only thing is, what's to keep Arwoor from getting away through the crescents?"

Wolff smiled and pointed at the console. "Arwoor should have destroyed that instead of indulging his sadistic imagination. Like all weapons, it's two-edged."

He activated the controls, and, again, an image of the crescent shone on the screen. Curving lines of light ran across the plate. Wolff went to another console and opened a little door on the top to reveal a panel with unmarked controls. After flipping two, he pressed a button. The screen went blank.

"The resonance of his crescent has been changed," Wolff said. "When he goes to use it with any of the others he has, he'll get a hell of a shock. Not the kind Vannax got. He just won't have a gate through which to escape."

"You Lords are a mean, crafty, sneaky bunch," Kickaha said. "But I like your style, anyway."

He left the room. A moment later, his shouts came down the corridor. Podarge started to leave the room, then stopped to glare suspiciously at Wolff. He broke into a run. Podarge, satisfied he was coming, raced ahead. Wolff stopped and removed the horn from the case. He reached a finger into its mouth, hooked it through the only opening in the weblike structure therein large enough to accept his finger. A pull drew the web out. He turned it around and inserted it with its front now toward the inside of the horn. Then he put the horn back into the case and ran after the harpy.

She was with Kickaha, who was explaining that he thought he had seen a gworl but it was just a prowling eagle. Wolff said they must go back to the others. He did not explain that it was necessary that the horn be within a certain distance of the control room walls. When they had returned to the hall outside the control room, Wolff opened the case. Kickaha stood behind Podarge, ready to knock her unconscious if she started any trouble. What they could do with the eagles, besides sicking the apes on them, was another matter.

Podarge exclaimed when she saw the horn but made no hostile move. Wolff lifted the horn to his lips and hoped he could remember the correct sequence of notes. Much had come back to him since he had talked with Vannax; much was yet lost.

He had just placed the mouthpiece to his lips when a voice roared out. It seemed to come from ceiling and walls and floor, from everywhere. It spoke in the language of the Lords, for which Wolff was glad. Podarge would not know the tongue.

"Jadawin! I did not recognize you until I saw you with the horn! I thought you looked familiar—I should have known. But it's been such a long time! How long?"

"It's been many centuries, or millenia, depending upon the time scale. So, we two old enemies face each other again. But this time you have no way out. You will die as Vannax died."

"How so?" roared Arwoor's voice.

"I will cause the walls of your seemingly impregnable fortress to melt. You will either stay inside and roast or come out and die another way. I don't think you'll stay in."

Suddenly he was seized with a concern and a sense of injustice. If Podarge should kill Arwoor, she would not be killing the man who was responsible for her present state. It did not matter that Arwoor would have done the same thing if he had been the Lord of this world at that time.

On the other hand, he, Wolff, was not to blame, either. He was not the lord Jadawin who had constructed this universe and then manipulated it so foully for so many of its creatures and abducted Terrestrials. The attack of amnesia had been complete; it had wiped all of Jadawin from him and made him a blank page. Out of the blankness had emerged a new man, Wolff, one incapable of acting like Jadawin or any of the other lords.

And he was still Wolff, except that he remembered what he had been. The thought made him sick and contrite and eager to make amends as best he could. Was this the way to start, by allowing Arwoor to die horribly for a crime he had not commited?

"Jadawin!" boomed Arwoor. "You may think you have won this move! But I have topped you again! I have one more coin to put on the table, and its value is far more than what your horn will do to me!"

"And what is that?" Wolff asked. He had a black feeling that Arwoor was not bluffing.

"I've planted one of the bombs I brought with me when I was dispossessed of Chiffaenir. It's under the palace, and when I so desire, it will go off and blow the whole top of this monolith off. It's true I'll die, too, but I'll take my old enemy with me! And your woman and your friends will die, too! Think of them!"

Wolff was thinking of them. He was in an agony.

"What are your terms?" he asked. "I know that you don't want to die. You're so miserable you *should* want to die, but you've clung to your worthless life for ten thousand years."

"Enough of insults! Will you or won't you? My finger is an inch above the button." Arwoor chuckled and continued, "Even if I'm bluffing, which I'm not, you can't afford to take the chance."

Wolff spoke to the others, who had been listening without understanding but knew that something drastic had happened. He explained as much as he dared, omitting any connection of himself with the Lords.

Podarge, her face a study in combined frustration and madness, said, "Ask him what his terms are."

She added, "After this is all over, you have much to explain to me, O Wolff."

Arwoor replied, "You must give me the silver horn, the all-precious and unique work of the master, Ilmarwolkin. I will use it to open the gate in the pool and pass through to the Atlantean tier. That is all I want, except your promise that none will come after me until the gate is closed."

Wolff considered for a few seconds. Then he said, "Very well. You may come out now. I swear to you on my honor as Wolff and by the Hand of Detiuw that I will give you the horn and I will send no one after you until the gate is closed."

Arwoor laughed and said, "I'm coming out."

Wolff waited until the door at the end of the hall was swinging out. Knowing that he could not be overheard by Arwoor then, he said to Podarge, "Arwoor thinks he has us, and he may well be confident. He will emerge through the gate at a place forty miles from here, near Ikwekwa, a suburb of the city of Atlantis. He would still be at the mercy of you and your eagles if there were not another resonant point only ten miles from there. This point will open when the horn is blown and admit him to another universe. I will show you where it is after Arwoor goes through the pool."

Arwoor advanced confidently. He was a tall, broad-shouldered and good-looking man with wavy blond hair and blue eyes. He took the horn from Wolff, bowed ironically, and walked on down the hall. Podarge stared at him so madly that Wolff was afraid that she would leap upon him. But he had told her that he must keep his promises: the one to her and the one to Arwoor.

Arwoor strode past the silent and menacing files as if they were no more than statues of marble. Wolff did not wait for him to get to the pool, but went at once into the control room. A quick examination showed him that Arwoor had left a device which would depress the button to set off the bomb. Doubtless he had given himself plenty of time to get away. Nevertheless, Wolff sweated until he had removed the device. By then, Kickaha had returned from watching Arwoor go through the gate in the pool.

"He got away, all right," he said, "but it wasn't as easy as he had thought. The place of emergence was under water, caused by the flood he himself had created. He had to drop into the water and swim for it. He was still swimming when the gate closed."

Wolff took Podarge into a huge map room, and indicated the town near which the gate was. Then, in the visual-room, he showed her the gate at close range on a screen. Podarge studied the map and the screen for a minute. She gave an order to her eagles, and they trooped out after her. Even the apes were awed by the glare of death in their eyes.

Arwoor was forty miles from the monolith, but he had ten miles to travel. Moreover, Podarge and her pets were launching themselves from a point 30,000 feet up. They would descend at such an angle and for such a distance that they could build up great speed. It would be a close race between Podarge and her quarry.

While he waited before the screen, Wolff had time to do much thinking. Eventually, he would tell Chryseis who he was and how he had come to be Wolff. She would know that he had been to another universe to visit one of the rare friendly lords. The Vaernirn became lonely, despite their great powers, and wanted to socialize now and then with their peers. On his return to this universe, he had fallen into a trap set by Vannax, another dispossessed Lord. Jadawin had been hurled into the universe of Earth, but he had taken the surprised Vannax with him. Vannax had escaped with a crescent after the savage tussle on the hill slope. What had happened to the other crescent, Wolff did not know. But Vannax had not had it, that was sure.

Amnesia had struck then, and Jadawin had lost all memory —had become, in effect, a baby, a *tabula rasa*. Then the Wolffs had taken him in, and his education as an Earthman had begun.

Wolff did not know the reason for the amnesia. It might have been caused by a blow on the head during his struggle with Vannax. Or it might have resulted from the terror of being marooned and helpless on an alien planet. Lords had depended upon their inherited science so long that, stripped of them, they became less than men.

Or his loss of memory might have come from the long struggle with his conscience. For years before being thrust willynilly into another world, he had been dissatisfied with himself, disgusted with his ways and saddened by his loneliness and insecurity. No being was more powerful than a Lord, yet none was lonelier or more conscious that any minute might be his last. Other Lords were plotting against him; all had to be on guard every minute.

Whatever the reason, he had become Wolff. But, as Kickaha pointed out, there was an affinity between him and the horn and the points of resonance. It had been no accident that he had happened to be in the basement of that house in Arizona when Kickaha had blown the horn. Kickaha had had his suspicions that Wolff was a dispossessed Lord deprived of his memory.

Wolff knew now why he had learned the languages here so extraordinarily quickly. He was remembering them. And he had had such a swift and powerful attraction to Chryseis because she had been his favorite of all the women of his domain. He had even been thinking of bringing her to the palace and making her his Lady.

She did not know who he was on meeting him as Wolff because she had never seen his face. That cheap trick of the dazzling radiance had concealed his features. As for his voice, he had used a device to magnify and distort it, merely to further awe his worshippers. Nor was his great strength natural, for he had used the bioprocesses to equip himself with superior muscles.

He would make such amends as he could for the cruelty and arrogance of Jadawin, a being now so little a part of him. He would make new human bodies in the biocylinders and insert in them the brains of Podarge and her sisters, Kickaha's apes, Ipsewas, and any others who so desired. He would allow the people of Atlantis to rebuild, and he would not be a tyrant. He was not going to interfere in the affairs of the world of tiers unless it was absolutely necessary.

Kickaha called him to the screen. Arwoor had somehow found a horse in that land of dead and was riding him furiously.

"The luck of the devil!" Kickaha said, and he groaned.

"I think the devil's after him," Wolff said. Arwoor had looked behind and above him and then begun to beat his horse with a stick.

"He's going to make it!" Kickaha said. "There's a Temple of the Lord only a half-mile ahead!"

Wolff looked at the great white stone structure on top of a high hill. Within it was the secret chamber which he himself had used when he had been Jadawin.

He shook his head and said, "No!"

Podarge swooped within the field of vision. She was coming at great speed, her wings flapping, her face thrust forward, white against the green sky. Behind her came her eagles.

Arwoor rode the horse as far up the hill as he could. Then the mare's legs gave out, and she collapsed. Arwoor hit the ground running. Podarge dived at him. Arwoor dodged like a rabbit fleeing from a hawk. The harpy followed him in his zigzags, guessed which way he would go during one of his sideleaps, and was on him. Her claws struck his back. He threw his hands in the air and his mouth became an O through which soared a scream, voiceless to the watchers of the screen.

Arwoor fell with Podarge upon him. The other eagles landed and gathered to watch.

In a future world of strangers,
the hunter and the hunted are one . . .

EYE OF CAT

ROGER ZELAZNY

Winner of 3 Nebula and 3 Hugo Awards

William Blackhorse Singer, the last Navajo tracker on a future earth, has stocked the Interstellar Life Institute with its most exotic creatures. But one of Singer's prizes preys upon his mind: a metamorph. The one-eyed shapeshifter Cat, whose home planet has been destroyed. Singer offers Cat freedom to help him defend Earth against a terrible predator, and Cat accepts. The price: permission to hunt the hunter. And the deadly game begins. In a fierce, global hunt, Singer flees his extra-sentient killer. And suddenly, he is pursuing not life, but the mysteries of his people, and the blinding vision of his own primeval spirit . . .

'Zelazny's best book since *Lord of Light.*' *Joe Haldeman.*
'The interweaving of old tales and futuristic adventures is genuinely moving . . .'
New York Times Book Review.
'The melting together of perceptions of the future and the past are brilliant, effective and moving.'
Vonda McIntyre.

SCIENCE FICTION 0 7221 9442 0 £1.95

Also available by Roger Zelazny in Sphere Science Fiction:

THE HAND OF OBERON
MY NAME IS LEGION
SIGN OF THE UNICORN
DAMNATION ALLEY
NINE PRINCES IN AMBER
THE GUNS OF AVALON
THE COURTS OF CHAOS

From one of Science Fiction's most acclaimed writers comes an outstanding new edition to the popular DORSAI series

LOST DORSAI

Gordon R. Dickson

WINNER OF THE NEBULA AWARD FOR THE BEST NOVELLA OF 1981

Revolution gripped the mighty kingdom of El Conde . .

As the gap between rich and poor yawned cavernously wider, the massed ranks of the Naharese exploded into bitter rebellion. Men who had been trained by the galaxy's most famous warriors, the Dorsai, now took up arms against them. And into this chaos were flung a handful of noble Dorsai warriors, whose innate honour bound them to secure El Conde from the rebels. Their might was pitted against the most impossible odds: but one of their number faced battle first of another kind entirely, forced to grapple with a sudden, terrifying loss of conviction in the ways of warriorhood central to his whole existence . . .

SCIENCE FICTION 0 7221 30201 £1.95

TERROR FROM BEYOND THE STARS

THE QUEEN OF THE LEGION

Jack Williamson

From the innermost core of the Nebula they swarm forth in their nightmarish hordes . . . Beware the shadowflashers: terrible parasites who will ruthlessly enslave your mind and body. They have already captured AKKA, the great secret weapon. They have killed the Keeper of the Peace . . . and they will stop at nothing. Who now can stand between the human race and ultimate destruction . . . ?

Jil Gyrel, courageous daughter of a lost Legion pilot, has inherited her father's prescience and his uncanny navigational gifts. She is the first to sense the inhuman danger . . . but can the strength of this valiant girl alone save the future of Mankind?

QUEEN OF THE LEGION is the fourth novel in the classic LEGION OF SPACE series – a thrilling tale of a battle against the most monstrous evil ever to emerge from the treacherous regions of outer space.

SCIENCE FICTION 0 7221 9196 0 £1.95

MILLENNIUM

JOHN VARLEY

JUST WHEN YOU THOUGHT IT WAS SAFE TO GO BACK INTO THE FUTURE . . .

Someone fouls up and leaves a twonky behind. A twonky's the kind of thing that, for the surreptitious time-traveller, can really spell disaster. In this case, it was Pinky's stunner – a 99th-century weapon mislaid on a 20th-century airliner.

And what were Pinky and the snatch squad doing there anyway? Believe it or not, rescuing the victims of an about-to-be-fatal accident, transporting them safely into the future and putting dummies in their place. Because there's no point in tinkering with the timestream, and people will expect to find bodies in a plane crash.

But not twonkies. So someone had to stay there and look for the damn thing, because if anyone ever found out, the whole future could be finished long before it ever begun . . .

'Brilliant, inventive and satisfying.'

New York Times Book Review

GENERAL FICTION 0 7221 8839 0 £1.99